THE
Death Watch

Other Piatkus Books by Daoma Winston:

FAMILY OF STRANGERS
THE SECRETS OF CROMWELL CROSSING
SINISTER STONE
THE VICTIM
WALK AROUND THE SQUARE

NewCond.   'V/4   v/ 1975

£2.

THE
Death Watch

Daoma Winston

PIATKUS

Copyright © 1975, by Daoma Winston, Inc.

First published in Great Britain in 1986
by Judy Piatkus (Publishers) Limited of London

ISBN 0 86188 517 1

Printed in Great Britain
by Mackays of Chatham Ltd

For Murray

PROLOGUE

"Good to the last drop, and I sure mean that," Al Kelly said as he drained the plastic cup, then cumpled it in his gnarled fist. "I don't know what I'd do without you, Daisy. You and your emergency rations. An old man like me . . ." He shrugged meager shoulders. ". . . . An old man like me, he needs something to go on."

Daisy grinned. "Old man like you . . ."

"Sixty-three," Al said. "Widowed twice. Five grandchildren. Retired from the police force eight years ago."

"Is that a fact? Why, nobody would ever believe it. Sixty-three, you say?"

It was a conversation they had had many times before. But neither of them minded. A few words here and there helped pass the long quiet hours of the night.

"Sixty-three," Al repeated, puffing out his chest and squaring his shoulders. He took two long limping strides to the trash bin to dump the plastic cup. He wiped his coffee-dampened hand on his thigh, and turned back to Daisy. "I guess that seems old to you. Only it goes by fast. You better believe me, Daisy. It sure as hell goes by fast."

"You don't seem old to me," she said. She smoothed

her pale green uniform over her round hips. "And it's all in how you feel, anyhow."

The sweet courtesy was as much a part of her as her high round hips, the dimples set deep into her saffron-colored skin; as much a part of her as her kinky copper hair and off-color gray eyes.

She was mixed black and white, he supposed. What they used to call mulatto, or maybe even quadroon, back in New Orleans when he was a boy.

And when she smiled at him, he didn't feel old. She put him in mind of some very good nights he had had. Nights he almost thought he could have again, with her.

He looked quickly, guiltily, away from her smile, hoping she wasn't a mind reader. Daisy Trunnel was a good, respectable, hard-working girl. She had two kids, and a construction-worker husband. They were trying their damnedest, squeezing their guts to beat some shape into their lives. And even if none of that were true, even if she were fancy free, she wouldn't have anything to do with the likes of Al Kelly, an old, beat-up man, with nothing to offer. He was entirely ashamed of himself for what had been going on in his head.

But back in the old days he and his friends would have licked their lips and called it poontang and gone after it as hard and fast and often as they could. Because poontang was supposed to be 'specially good. He could still hear the snickering voices talking about it, still see the wet-lipped smiles.

But he was long gone from the old days, the snickering voices, the wet-lipped smiles. And Daisy Trunnel was not poontang, not even in his mind.

If she had been following his random thoughts, nothing showed on her face. She said, still smiling, "You don't look as if you want to go. How about another cup of coffee?"

"I guess not, Daisy. Too much gives me the heartburn. But thanks." He looked down the dimly lit hall. "Quiet night, isn't it? Who's on emergency?"

"Dr. Harner."

"Oh, yeah, that's right. I saw him when Dr. Stevens came in, him and his daughter. I wonder what all that was about."

Daisy shrugged. "Search me."

"A funny time of night to be visiting. If it *was* visiting. She didn't look like she wanted to, anyhow, the way he was dragging her along. And I don't much blame her. You wouldn't find me here on a Sunday night. Not if I didn't have to be."

"Nor me," Daisy agreed. "Hours drag slow, real slow." She went on, . . . "Now you take last night . . . I tell you, we were running from seven on. And I mean running, too."

"Yeah, they were pouring in, weren't they? The Saturday routine, same as always. Like when I was on the force. The calls hard and fast: shootings, knifings, fist fights, accidents. I guess some things never change, only get worse . . ." His voice trailed off. Back in the old days, he had been in the thick of it. It still went on, but now he was on the sidelines, watching the ambulances spin up the emergency entrance driveway, red lights blinking, the last moan of the siren dying away.

"Regular flood of them, and tonight so dead . . ." Daisy laughed softly. "I tell you, dead or no, more nights like last and old Gorman is going to have to find himself some ground for a new wing. We're about to bust out at the seams."

9

"He's got it to find." Al glanced at his wrist watch, sighed. "Well, I've got to be on my way."

"You come back later on. I'll fix you some more coffee. If it gives you the heartburn, I've got something for that, too."

"I'll be back, Daisy." He straightened his shoulders, smoothed his gray uniform jacket. "A quick check of the lots, a look-see at the grounds, and I'll be back, trotting out the pictures of the grandchildren."

He limped down the hall, favoring his left leg. At the door, he stopped, turned to wave a mock salute. But Daisy, her nose already buried in a book, didn't see it.

The heavy plate glass door whispered shut behind him. He went down the driveway, through shadows cast by still-young cottonwoods. A night wind from the mountains stirred the leaves overhead, and underfoot, the shadow broke and re-formed.

Gorman Memorial Hospital was the newest one in the city, and the most modern one in the state. It was six stories high, U-shaped to fit the crown of a hill that had once been a public golf course. There had been a five-year hospital drive; at the end of ten years, state and federal funds became available, and the hospital was built.

Gorman Memorial had been designed by a well-known architect, recommended by a younger member of the Gorman family who had met him in San Francisco during one of a series of lost weekends. Now, eight years later, the cast concrete and steel and glass had weathered well, but its size was diminished by the black range of mountains that crested miles away yet seemed much closer. Still, it had a look of solidity and power which suited a forward-looking community; the City

Council, the Gorman family, the hospital drive committee, each took the credit for a job well done.

Al Kelly clocked in at his first station, and turned to look up at the building again. He thought it most impressive at night, with the lit windows of the fire stairs streaking long ribbons of pink from floor to floor, and the pale glow along the bottom of the drawn shades throwing narrow reflections on the concrete walls. Impressive, and still. Peculiarly still.

A slow shiver trailed along his spine.

He frowned, shifted his cap.

Tires hummed on the road just beyond the grounds. He watched the headlights fading past distant trees.

He turned in a small circle, squinting into the shadows. But he saw nothing except the blurred dark outlines of scraggly cottonwoods. He made himself grin into the empty night. He was an old cop; old hackles were rising on his neck. It just happened to be a peculiarly quiet Sunday night.

He went back to the triangle at the foot of the driveway, and then on to his second station. He was alert, listening, and at the same time annoyed with himself. He was too old to be developing a case of nerves. It was downright ridiculous that his left hand had automatically gripped his big flashlight and his right hand had somehow dropped to the regulation gun clipped to his belt. Telling himself that he was just an old fool, he headed for his third station.

The car was a long gray bulk in the darker shadows. There was nothing unusual about seeing an automobile in a parking area; except that it was the only one there and it was slewed around, covering three slots. Al went past his call station, and walked slowly around the big gray car. It seemed empty. He flicked on his light for a look at the license plate. The physician's insignia explained it: somebody in a hurry to take care of somebody's big trouble. He grinned with relief. So much for an old cop's hackles.

But the mountain wind seemed colder suddenly, and his gnarled hands were sweating. He cursed himself, but played along, flashing his light inside.

He froze at the open window. At first he didn't know what he was seeing. When he did know, he couldn't believe it.

And when he did believe it, he moaned, "Oh, Christ, sweet Jesus Christ! Christ, no! no!" and turned away, dropping to his hands and knees, the flashlight spinning away from him with a clatter to land against a rubber tire, the beam sluicing along the ground where he retched in great wracking coughs.

Later, he would say, "I don't know what happened to me. And I'm an old cop, too. You know that. I've seen everything there is to see and more than that. I just don't know what happened, but it hit me wrong." And he would rub his eyes to wipe away the remembered sight, and rub his mouth to wipe away the remembered taste of vomit. He would tell it over and over again, to the police, to Daisy Trunnel, to anybody who would listen. Most people would hear him out at least once, because he had been there. Al Kelly had been there and seen it first of all.

At the time, heaved out, bone dry, sweating, weak, he dragged himself up. His bad leg jerked in small spasms and his wiry body shook, but he got the torch, and staggered across the dark parking area and up the driveway to the heavy plate glass doors, mumbling,

THE DEATH WATCH

"Sweet Jesus! And on Sunday, too!" He fought the door, pushing when he should have pulled, and cursed, and finally got himself inside, calling ahead in a gravelly whisper, "Daisy, Daisy, get Dr. Harner and whoever else's in emergency! And call the cops, Daisy. For the love of God, get the cops out here!"

CHAPTER 1

Joe Stevens awakened with a peculiar sense of displacement.

Morning sun rimmed brocade drapes at the picture window. The faint golden light touched mahogany and marble, and glittered on brass. But he looked at the familiar surroundings with a stranger's eyes. For long unpleasant moments, he was no more than a body and a consciousness, a thing without name, identity, profession, or will. A man lost and hungering, burdened with the recollection of time gone that would never return and selfhood squandered that would never be regained.

Then, in the twin bed across the large shadowy room, his wife Ellen sighed and stirred, and murmured out of untranquil sleep, "What's the matter, Joe?"

He was instantly and totally himself, centered in the world, the life, the home he had made as part of what he liked to think was the rational man's response to chaos. Himself again, he wryly noted that odd awareness of hers which once had charmed him and now annoyed him. In the eighteen years of their marriage, it had become an invasion of privacy and a burden. More lately it had become a challenge. Very briefly, because he didn't want to waste time thinking of her, he wondered why she didn't change.

Her voice, still blurred, plaintive, came at him again. ". . . the matter, Joe?"

"Nothing, Ellen. Go back to sleep."

"Leaving now?" She was actually quite wide awake, watching him carefully from beneath a lowered fringe of thick brown eyelashes. She knew that something was bothering him, and just because he wouldn't talk about it, she wanted to know what it was.

He rose up on one elbow, nylon pajamas as unwrinkled and fresh as if he had just taken them from a drawer. His short sandy hair, shot through with gray, looked already brushed. Even the morning shadow of beard on his long narrow jaw seemed under control. He said, "I'll be leaving in just a few minutes, Ellen. I have a long day ahead of me."

She knew it was no use. There was nothing more to ask him. She mumbled, closing her eyes completely, "Then see you later, Joe."

"Yes. I don't know exactly what time."

"Of course. When do you ever know?" She could hardly be held accountable for what she said when she was scarcely awake. And it wasn't a reproach. He must know that she would never reproach him.

She sighed again, and stirred, settling herself against the heaped-up pillows. Her long auburn hair was spread out on her white shoulders. Her arms were flung wide and welcoming, and so were her legs. Her whole body seemed soft and ready, revealed by the dubious cover of a yellow lace gown.

He was up now, gray nylon clinging to lean flanks and shoulders. He gathered up his clothes, moving with quick grace. He was tall, just under six feet, with narrow, well-tended hands, and slim, high-arched feet. His eyes were set wide apart over high cheekbones, and somehow suggested candor and attentiveness; people who knew him well had learned to watch his hands rather than his wide-open blue eyes when trying to determine either.

With a quick sideways glance at Ellen's soft and ready body, he wondered, again very briefly, if she were really asleep this time. Or if, with that peculiar awareness of hers, she was shamming, yet at the same time offering herself to him. Did she expect him now to cross the thick blue carpet to her bed, and to throw himself on top of her?

He dismissed the question, and her, and headed toward the bathroom. He thought of those long unpleasant moments when he had first awakened. It amused him to recognize the symptoms of an old and familiar malady. He was, he diagnosed—though he had often said that a doctor who treats himself has a fool for a patient—suffering from the forty-five-year-old itch. He knew it, understood it, accepted it. He was amused because he once would have thought himself immune to that particular disease: he had ordered his life; he was a rational man. But presumed immunity was irrelevant. He was also human and male. He had to consider it natural, therefore, that he should be subject to the ills of men.

He shaved, then showered with habitual economy of movement. In a little while, he was dressed. His suit was pale blue, immaculate and freshly steamed. His shirt was white, his tie dark—a Sulka silk that Ellen had had flown in for him from Neiman-Marcus. His black shoes were elegantly cut and stitched, and showed off his unusually well-shaped feet, the single small vanity he allowed himself.

It was eight o'clock by then. He supposed that he would soon receive the morning check-in call from the Medical Service. He went through the silent house along the carpeted corridors, skirting the big living room that looked out on the enclosed patio and swimming pool, to the empty kitchen.

It was huge, with one wall of fieldstone that had been brought in from the north on flatbed cars. Long trays of miniature cacti bordered the three wide windows. The morning sun warmed the chill, slightly stale, air-conditioned air. The floor was of polished terrazzo, rose pale. The furniture was birch, satin smooth. The breakfast bar of honed cedar was set for him: a glass for orange juice, a cup for coffee, a plate for toast. A pink linen napkin. He frowned suddenly. There was a milk-stained glass where no milk-stained glass belonged.

He took for granted the accessories of his life. He had always had them, and always would. Taking them for granted, he noticed, and loathed, disorder. He put the glass firmly into the huge pink sink, turned the flame up under the coffeepot, and checked his watch again.

Tula was late. She should have been there to remove the dirty glass, to pour his orange juice, to start the coffee perking. The absence of the small services bothered him less than the failure of routine. It seemed to him that Tula was too often late. She was the daughter of Lupe, who had worked for his parents as long as he could remember, and still worked for them. The difference between Tula and Lupe was the difference between the two generations. The old days and the new. He poured juice, and drank it down quickly, planning his schedule. He knew, even then, what he was going to do.

He was a man who didn't believe in discontent. He prided himself on getting what he wanted. It never occurred to him that sometimes it was impossible for a man to have what he wanted; he never wanted what he couldn't have, or take.

But Thursday was always a big day. The muted telephone buzzer seemed to hum constantly in the hush of the pale yellow reception room. The heavy door closed only to open again moments later, admitting thick gusts of dry heat. The people coming and going, waiting and whispering. Neither speculation nor experience explained why it was that way. Neither foresight nor determination changed it. So since Thursday was always a big day, it took a combination of happy circumstances and careful planning to make possible a two-hour break in Joe's busy schedule.

By four o'clock, he had taken advantage of the happy circumstance, and accomplished the careful planning, and he had his two free hours. It was a neat trick for a much-in-demand doctor, but a man who prided himself on getting what he wanted had to learn how to manage neat tricks.

As his long gray Cadillac surged through the narrow street with the indifferent arrogance of a light-footed panther slicing through jungle shadow, he grinned into the brassy August sunlight. He thought that the familiar malady was bearable, even vastly enjoyable, if only a man knew how to cope. And he was a man who did.

Poor Bess Bradford had been almost tearfully apologetic, her white cap awry as always on her gray head, crying, "Oh, Doctor, I'm terribly sorry. I just noticed that those two emergency appointments you took this morning have cancelled out."

"Yes. While you were at lunch, Bradford."

"Oh, really . . . some people. You shouldn't have answered the phone."

"They wouldn't have shown up anyway."

"And just when you were running ahead. The first time in I don't know how long. You would have been able to—"

He said, "Don't worry about it. I can stand a couple of hours off, can't I?"

Running ahead had been the happy circumstance. The cancellations had been the result of planning. He wrote the appointments in before Bradford arrived at the office, and cancelled them when she was out. Thus two hours off for him.

"Of course you can stand a break, Doctor." Her washed-out blue eyes, slightly discolored at the lids, were filled with anguished adoration.

She had looked at him that way the day he hired her, and the fifteen years since had apparently left her illusions intact. He was not at all surprised.

It was a fact of life that nurses always adored the doctors with whom they worked.

He didn't know that she had silvered her hair because silver was chic. He didn't know that she discreetly wore eyeshadow, and dieted rigorously, and hated every empty hour of time off. He also didn't know that she was wondering about those cancellations, and wondering about the change she had noticed in him, a something different but not precisely new, although she didn't know exactly when it had first begun.

She said, "You ought to go out to the house and have

a swim and some sun. But I suppose you won't."
He had grinned then, "That's right. I won't."

Now, as he guided the car around a series of pot-
holes, feeling the power of it in his well-scrubbed hands,
and enjoying it with his whole body, he forget Bradford. The next two hours were exclusively his. His and
Claire's. Claire Manning . . . the answer to a forty-
five-year-old man's discontent with routinized relation-
ships and a routinized life; the answer to the sudden
resurgence of a need that went back to when he was
twenty-six and a resident in a Miami Beach Hospital.
He had fallen crazily, impossibly, in love with Belena
Sommers, and thought that she loved him too for a
single mad month before she drifted away on the play-
girl tide to Acapulco. He had realized soon after that
his misery was his good fortune, but he never forgot
her. He supposed that no man ever really forgot his
first love, and it seemed to him, somehow, that in having Claire he had found Belena again. Not that he had
ever been foolish enough to tell Claire anything like
that, any more than he had ever told Ellen. But Ellen,
of course, had known.

They had grown up in the same circle in the city, and
had always known everything about each other. He
could swear that he remembered her when she wore
her hair in short bright braids, the color then an awful
carrot red, and his recollection remained unshaken although she insisted that she had never had braids at
all. It was part of her peculiar awareness, so strong
even then, that she, having known about Belena, had
looked in his wallet on their wedding night, found the
picture of Belena there, and taken it out and destroyed
it without mentioning it to him. They had never spoken

20

of it, nor of Belena. He supposed they never would.

A light guiding touch brought the car close to the curb. He got out, taking his small black medical bag with him. It wasn't safe any more to leave it unattended anywhere, and even less safe on Rojas Lane.

For an instant, Joe felt the familiar irritation. He had expected, at the beginning, that Claire would eventually allow herself to be persuaded to move to a more suitable location, but that had never happened. They had argued about it so often in the past year. He still didn't see why she insisted upon staying on the dismal Old Town street: a huddle of adobe-walled compounds, once private homes but now broken into separate apartments, that had deteriorated into a hangout for completely disreputable types. Bohemians, beatniks, flower children. . . . He wasn't sure of the currently fashionable appellation, and didn't care to learn it. The whole new vocabulary that had grown up around him in the previous few years disgusted him; the attitudes that vocabulary represented disgusted him too.

Rojas Lane was distinguished only because from it one could see the black ridges of the mountains looming over the flat-topped roofs, and that was not, in Joe's opinion, an adequate substitute for the neat, clean, concrete and glass condominium, complete with all the amenities, he had offered and she had refused. He supposed that she knew what she was doing, but he still didn't understand it. Though he never mentioned it to her, there was one advantage to her living on Rojas Lane: there was considerably less chance of his seeing anyone he knew there than there would be elsewhere in the city.

Except, he thought, there was always Gilly. Gilly could

be anywhere, any time. Gilly was his daughter, seventeen now, and when he permitted himself to think of her, remembering what had happened and knowing what might happen, he experienced a sense of helplessness that only she could cause him to feel.

He couldn't resolve the problem of Gilly while he stood in the silent sunny lane. Perhaps he couldn't resolve it at all. He locked the car, and went into the compound.

As immaculate now as when he had left home that morning, brushed, scrubbed, and well-shaven, he didn't show the mounting excitement he felt. He had a long, quick stride. It suited his lean body. His obese patients often stared longingly at his narrow waist while he told them to stick to high-protein diets and insisted that self-indulgence was really self-destruction. He himself ate whatever he wanted, yet remained as slim as his very spare mother and father, both of whom preferred to take their calories liquid and let their livers go. While enjoying every symbol of wealth and refinement, they raised their eyebrows in Puritan rejection of gluttony, and spent days in the country club bar, bidding their restaurant-bound friends good afternoon at lunch time and good evening after dinner. Joe neither approved nor disapproved, though it was a way of life on which he had deliberately turned his back long before.

Within the compound there were patches of fading crab grass and stands of wilting hollyhocks, unplanned reds and pinks dusted with the ubiquitous sand of the surrounding mesas.

He picked his way around a litter of empty beer cans.

Claire's door was open. A young man stepped out, said something Joe couldn't quite hear, then slammed the door.

Joe catalogued him quickly: young, between twenty and twenty-four; blond hair a little too long; tight chinos hugging narrow hips; cracked moccasins; a yellow turtleneck sweater.

They passed, and exchanged a quick, hard, headlong look.

Joe paused involuntarily, a response to a sudden shocking image. Claire and this boy, arms and legs entangled, shining with sweat, writhing on the king-sized bed that was her only real luxury . . . mouths glued, hips heaving . . . Claire crying out at the last. Claire.

The boy kicked a beer can and the hard, startling sound cut through the sunny silence. Somewhere a radio blared a single chorus of frenzied trumpet and then there was stillness again.

On the sidewalk, the boy hunched his shoulders, hooked his thumbs in his pockets, and turned back with sudden recognition. He swung away, wondering.

Joe took a long, calming breath, the quick hot shock, the unwelcome mind picture, fading, replaced by wry amusement. He and Claire had been lovers for almost a year. She, coming into his life when he had needed her, had asked very little of him, and he had asked little of her. There had been no reason to discuss constancy. Jealousy was decidedly out of place here, he told himself. He knocked at the door.

Claire called, "Yes? What now, David? I told you before . . ."

So the boy's name is David, he thought, as he pushed open the door. "David? David, Claire?" he said.

From where Joe stood he could see straight through into the bedroom; he could see the tousled sheets on the king-sized bed. Once again he was assaulted by the vision of the two of them linked, writhing.

"Oh, it's you, Joe," Claire said. "I didn't expect you."

She was sitting at the desk, turned sideways, so that he could see her long legs. She wore a pair of white shorts cut so high they were almost bikini pants. A sleeveless yellow turtleneck pullover hugged her high breasts. A sketching pencil stuck rakishly behind her ear poked through her short dark curls like a small antenna. There was a smudge of black on the end of her up-turned nose; another, almost a thumb print, at her left breast.

The yellow pullover was a twin to the one the boy she called David had been wearing. Before he could stop himself, he asked, "Who is David, Claire?"

She raised the sketchbook, and held it away from her, cocking her head critically. "I don't know. . . . It just doesn't look right. Maybe . . ."

"Claire!" he exploded. "Who is David?"

"What?" She shot Joe a look over the edge of the sketchbook. "David? Oh. David Tiller. He's a kid from down the block. Sculpts. Talented, but . . ."

"I thought you'd be alone," Joe said.

"Did you?"

"I told you when I called that I'd get here as early as I could."

That's right, you did, didn't you, Joe? But after all, it's not Monday night, and it's not Friday, and how was I to know that you'd call, or even that you'd make it after you *did* call?"

"I said I would."

24

"Oh, yes, you did. But, as I mentioned, it's not Monday, nor Friday, and so . . ."

He had to admit that had been the routine. Of necessity even his love affair required a certain degree of order. How was she to know of those long unpleasant moments this morning?

He said, smiling, "I couldn't wait until tomorrow, Claire." He paused. "I'm afraid we don't have too much time."

She dropped the sketchbook on the desk, and leaned back in her chair, her pixie face tilted up to him. "We never do."

"All the more reason for not wasting it."

Her amber eyes narrowed. "Then put down that silly bag of yours, and take off your jacket. Make yourself at home. Have a drink, or some soda, or coffee, whatever you want. Don't just stand there staring at me as if I'm a freak. Look alive and do something."

"You're not a freak."

He put the black bag on the floor near the door. He took off his jacket and hung it in the closet near the bedroom. He stole a quick look at the tousled bed as he loosened his tie.

"It took some doing to get here."

"That so?"

He decided to drop it. The only way to handle Claire, or any woman, was to allow her to work her own way out of her moods.

He sat down on the sofa. It made a loud, twanging noise.

The room was small. It had an Indian fireplace built into one corner, its adobe mantel sooted with years of use. There were red curtains at the two windows. A faded blue and red serape hung on one wall. On another, there was a tattered travel poster of a castle in Spain. The floor was a scrubbed splintery brown.

A bee hummed along the broken screen in the window. The refrigerator clicked on, then off. He looked again at the bed, still visible from where he sat. He said, "It's getting pretty hot in here, isn't it? I wish you'd let me buy you an air conditioner, Claire. Or let me move into a new place on the other side of town."

"No thanks."

"But really, Calire, why not?"

"I don't want to be bought, Joe."

"Why do you put it like that?"

"Because that's how it would be. Then you'd have the right to feel the way you already do feel. The *right*, Joe."

"What are you talking about now?"

She knew she was spoiling it. She could feel the precious minutes ticking away with the beating of her heart——wasting time when there was so little of it. But she couldn't help herself. She said, "You expect me to be here, waiting for you. Don't you? Not only waiting here, but waiting and ready, too. Maybe all naked and stretched out on the bed, with my legs wide open, and and my pills safely swallowed, and all of it so cut and dried and——"

"Don't be crude," he said.

"Crude? Oh, do forgive me. I forgot I was talking to the eminent Dr. Joe Stevens."

He laughed, "Hey, Claire, come on now . . ."

"The successful, in control, oh-so-smooth doctor."

"Not so smooth apparently."

"No."

She looked at his mouth, wanting to kiss him. She wished that there were some way to touch him, to force him to see her: a whole woman who had turned twenty-seven and suddenly saw her life slipping away from her. She wished he would see her as she was, not just as the girl he slept with when it was convenient, in hungry search for a lost youth.

He said, "Besides, you weren't actually waiting for me, so what's all this about anyhow?"

"You came through the door asking, 'Who's David?' with every possible insinuation in your voice. And your eyes going straight to the bed, checking it. Checking me, Joe."

"Is that what's wrong?"

"Yes."

But it wasn't. Not really. Or at least that was only part of it.

He grinned. "Then I'm sorry. I admit to a slight twinge of jealousy. Okay? Is that good enough? Or do I go down on my hands and knees?"

"Oh, shut up, Joe. You jealous of David Tiller? He's not even twenty years old!"

"And you're not even twenty-eight. And I'm . . ."

Sudden tears burned her eyes. She turned her head away. "I just want it to be different," she whispered.

And in that moment he wanted it to be different, too. But it couldn't be. There was Ellen, and Gilly. His standing in the community. He was a rational man now just as he had been when Belena wanted him to throw everything away, to allow himself to drift into the life on which he had deliberately turned his back. It couldn't be different. But he wanted Claire. He said her name softly.

"Oh, I know. I always did, didn't I? I can't say you've tricked me, or lied to me. Oh ńo. I went into it with my eyes wide open. But just the same, Joe, I wish . . ."

There was nothing he could say.

"It doesn't seem right. There's Lori. Look at Lori."

Lori Manning, Claire's young sister-in-law. Joe's patient.

"Lori, with so much to live for, and Mike . . ."

Mike Manning, Claire's older brother. Once Joe's patient, too. It was through Mike that Joe had first met Claire.

"Mike. Eating his heart out, Joe. And here I am . . ."

There was no way to talk to her when she kept shifting ground. From herself, to Lori, to Mike, then back to herself.

Lori. Mike. Joe stiffened. . . . What was Claire really saying? He had done everything a man could do.

He said, "Yes, here you are, and I'm looking at you."

"Don't you care about anybody, Joe?"

It had gone far enough. He now wished he had followed Bradford's advice and spent his two free hours at the pool. "Is that what you think?"

"I wonder," she wispered.

He rose. "Then I'm sorry, Claire."

Suddenly she was out of the chair, flashing across the room to burrow into his arms. "Joe, don't leave! I don't know what's the matter with me!"

The hot relief he felt sickened him. It was too strong. It made a lie of the kind of man he thought himself to be. But he found that he was grinning, holding her so tightly he could hardly breathe. "Maybe it's that time of the month for you."

"Damn you anyhow! I hate your being a doctor, Joe!"
But she turned in his arms, and led him into the bedroom.

They came together hungrily, reaching for each other
while they fought the clothes that separated them, until,
flesh to flesh, they dropped to the tousled sheets. It
didn't matter than that the pillows showed the cumpled
marks of what might have been two heads. Nor that
Claire and David Tiller had been wearing identical
yellow pullovers.

Joe wanted to drown in her sweet warm body and the
man it made of him, and in drowning, to obliterate
that momentary glimpse of a self he had never known
before: that self that had risen to leave, yet, if she
hadn't spoken first, if she hadn't come, to him, would
have stayed, waiting and helpless, until at the last he
would surely have gone to her.

And she wanted to enwrap him in such quick ardor
that everything she had said before would be burned
away forever and, helpless in his hunger, yearning and
demanding, a timeless and mindless man animal, he
would be hers. For it was only then that he was truly
hers.

Allowing the secret woman inside her a new freedom
she spun a veil of passion around him with crooned
words that begged and urged and adored. She led him
with bites and kisses, and he sought out her sweet secret
places, loving all of her, loving that wanton heat that
brought back the memory of Belena. And then he
dismissed it, for it wasn't the memory of Belena that
mattered, but Claire.

Her long slender legs, her mouth warm and moist,
her eyes wide with supplication. . . . It was like the

first time they had been together. Her cry . . . his senses reduced to a single point of swooning pleasure . . . the slow current slowly shifting, straining, rising.

"Ah yes, Joe.

"Yes. Yes.

"More.

"Joe . . . Joe . . ."

Tightening thighs . . . nails raking his shoulders . . . rolling hips, her breath quickening . . .

"Joe. . . !"

The phone rang. The swift shrill cry raced through his body, quick cold ice daggers. Time . . . . Time.

It rang again.

Plunging still, he gasped, "Don't answer it."

"Oh no, no, no . . ."

"Don't, Claire."

And it rang again.

"Joe, I have to."

There was anguish in her amber eyes. Her scissored legs loosened, her hands thrusting at his chest, her hips sunken away and stilled.

"No, Claire. Don't answer it." But already he was wondering who, why, as the heat receded from his groin.

"It could be Mike, Joe. I have to."

Another swift, shrill cry.

Joe was at its mercy, as always; it was the summons to the life he had chosen.

Their flesh seemed unwilling to part. But the icy daggers of sound still sliced through his nerves. She pulled away from him, and slipped from his arms, and the movement of withdrawal brought on the sudden cresting sensation and spasm. He fell aside, an involuntary cry on his lips, semen spilling wasted on the body-warm sheets.

She darted across the room, through the doorway and snatched up the phone. Sunlight streaming through the red drapes at the windows turned her nude body gold and glowing.

Her voice, still husky with love: "Yes? Yes? Oh . . . Mike . . ."

Joe listened and thought of Mike—Big Mike Manning. Joe thought of that dark night three years before. Mike . . . the big body limp, yet the pulse pounding, the heart striving . . . struggling to survive. Big Mike Manning, down, and Joe, with the shadow on him, reaching through . . .

"Oh, Mike. I know." Then, "But listen, it might not mean a thing. Not a thing. Don't you see, Mike? Really. . . . He's not? You tried the office? The house? Well, keep on trying. And leave your name, Mike. You did? Then he'll call you. I'm sure he'll call you, Mike. I promise he'll call you." She said softly, "Do you want me to come? I can be there in a little while. All right, yes, I'll wait. But call me back. You *will* call me back, won't you? Mike? Take it easy. Just try to. . . . It's . . ." She whispred, "Mickey, you have to. For Lori."

The phone replaced, Claire appeared in the doorway. Her dark head was bent, twisting on the slim stalk of her throat. Although the sunlight still touched her, the golden glow was gone.

"It was Mike," she said, as if Joe couldn't have guessed, as if he hadn't been listening. "He's frantic, Joe. He's been trying to call you. Bradford said she didn't know where you were.

"Of course she doesn't know," Joe said. "Do you think I'm crazy enough to give her this number? I told her I'd call in, as usual, and I will."

"I felt so awful . . . not telling him . . . And here you are."

Joe was sitting up now. He had smoothed his close-cropped hair. "It doesn't matter that I was here. What difference can that make to Mike, or to Lori? To anyone?"

"Certainly not to you."

"Claire!"

She shivered. "Listen, Joe. Go call him back. Right now. He's at the hospital. I tell you, he's frantic. Something about a patient being moved out. He thinks. . . . Listen, Joe, don't just sit there——"

"Do something," he finished for her. "But if I call him immediately he's going to realize something funny is going on. Maybe he won't realize it now, today, but some time, when he has a chance to think beyond Lori, then——"

"I don't care."

"You have to. And can't I ever get away from the phone? Its demands? Can't I ever have an hour, two, just for myself? Is there ever an end to——"

"It's *Mike,* Joe! You have to do something."

"But suppose there's nothing to do?"

"Oh God, Joe . . ."

"Yes. Oh God."

She stood straight and still at the foot of the bed. Her body was taut, breasts high and full, hips curved, thighs long. The source of all succor and joy. But her pixie face was stony. "You have to help him, Joe. He's at his strength's end."

"And there's still a way to go."

"How much of a way?"

Joe's voice was hard, raw-edged. "I don't know. Nobody knows that."

Her eyes beseeching, she stared into his face. She didn't know that he was lying to her.

"Nobody could even guess," he said.

But he could. Soon now. Soon. Lori fading, sinking, then drifting into sleep, and from sleep into——

"He can't take any more, Joe."

"He'll take whatever he has to. That's how it is. surely you're old enough to realize that, Claire. People always take exactly what they have to. Some react well; some badly. Some cry. Some curse. Some——"

"Some don't care."

Her voice was husky, but no longer with sex. Why? *Why?*

"I did everything I could, Claire—everything anyone could."

"Except . . ." A faint hesitation. "Except care."

He didn't answer her.

"They have so much." she cried. "They had so much together, Lori and Mike. Not like most people. Not like . . ." She stared into Joe's face. "Oh, they don't deserve this!"

"Nobody does. Not ever." Then, immediately sorry, he opened his arms to her, offering what comfort he could. "Come here."

"Now? Now?" Misunderstanding, her unsatisfied longing an ache, she trembled. "You can't mean now."

"But . . ." His arms dropped. "Just to hold you. Because even so, life goes on. We have to take what we can."

"Take our little—our little interlude. Not life, Joe. No, it's not life. Just an interlude. An hour you give me, or maybe yourself. Twice a week, hiding away. Or maybe three times, if you can manage it. A small nightmare inside of a larger one. A small nightmare. Yes, and somehow, some time, I'll have to wake up. I *will* have to wake up, won't I?"

He sighed, rose. "I suppose I should have known it wouldn't be any good. After all the good luck and planning, the omens were sour from the minute I walked into the compound."

"That was your fault."

"I admitted that. And I said I was sorry."

She shook her head. "Oh, just call Mike. That's all I want."

But first he washed and dressed. He wished that he had a change of clothes. He didn't like putting on a worn shirt, trousers not freshly pressed. But Claire wouldn't allow him to leave anything in her apartment. He supposed that was one more symbol of her feelings of guilt at their relationship.

He felt no guilt at all, he knew. Then suddenly the memory of that glimpse of his other self returned, and he experienced real fear. To want her that much was to give something necessary to himself away. But he brushed the recognition aside, and smoothed his gray-flecked sandy hair. Immaculate again, taking long quick steps in the narrow shoes just wiped with tissue, he came out of the bathroom.

She sat huddled on the bed, her pixie face still stone, her hands clasped between her knees, her curved body now golden in the sunlight. He felt a swift return of desire.

She whispered, "It's so awful, Joe: But right now, even while I'm thinking of Mike and Lori, I want you so. I'm so ashamed." She swallowed hard. "Here I sit, wishing I hadn't answered the phone, wishing we were still . . . still . . ."

The quick image of her wanton body clinging, pumping, writhing, hot wet kisses, crooning words. . . . "Then you know what I meant when I asked you not to take the call."

"I knew then, Joe. But I was so sure it would be Mike. And still, I want you, and I'm ashamed, and——"

"It's done. We'll have other days."

He called Medical Service first. Joe was a stickler for detail. It was through the Service that he was supposed to get Mike's message. The message received through proper channels, he hung up, and then dialed the hospital. After a moment, Mike's gruff whisper could be heard.

"It's Joe. You were trying to reach me?"

"Listen, are you coming in? Something has happened I don't understand."

"What's happened?"

"Not now, Joe? You're too busy to talk? Okay, give me your number, and I'll call you back in a little while."

For a split second Joe didn't understand. He wondered if granite Mike had broken. Then he realized that Mike couldn't talk freely in front of Lori. Joe said, "You don't have to call me from someplace else, Mike. I'll be down at Gorman in a few minutes. I'm on the way right now."

He hung up quickly. He wasn't going to have Mike call him at Claire's.

She was standing in the doorway. She had put on the

yellow turtleneck pullover, the white shorts. "What's the matter?"

"I don't know. I'm going in to see him, and I won't know until I get there."

Her taut body seemed to wilt. "I'm sorry, Joe."

"Me too."

"Thursday's nice. Different."

He picked up his bag.

"You'll let me know?"

"Of course."

"Joe . . .? Are you mad at me? I didn't mean . . ."

"Of course not."

"Then . . ."

"Yes?" he said crisply, impatiently.

"Then aren't you going to kiss me good-bye?"

He went to her, and pressed a quick hard kiss on her raised and clinging lips, annoyed with himself at the abrupt hunger that rose in him.

"Better. But somehow you still look . . . you know . . ."

"Aren't you used to my professional face yet?"

"Not yet."

He kissed her once again, the black bag swinging against her hips, and then he left.

She watched him walk across the compound and disappear through the opening where the gate had once been. She hugged herself, shivering suddenly in the heat.

The phone rang. She ran to answer it.

Mike said, "Claire? I got hold of him. He's coming in."

Yes. I know. "Should I come too, Mike?"

"No. Not yet."

"You'll let me know?"

"Sure."

"Mike . . . take it easy. Joe's doing everything—everything he can."

"Sure."

But she thought that she heard some reservation in the gruff assent. She said, "Don't doubt it, Mike."

"I've got to go now, Claire."

"You will let me know?"

"Sure," Mike told her.

The receiver fell out of his sweaty hand and banged jarringly against the wall of the phone booth. He swore as he caught it up and slammed it into its cradle. A big man whose barrel chest and wide shoulders needed plenty of space, he hurriedly made his way out of the phone booth.

He wore an old brown suit, a fraying lightweight worsted baggy at knee and elbow. There were buttons missing at the waist and sleeve, marked by straggling black threads. His hair was very dark, an uncompromising crew cut that needed a barber's attention. He had dark eyes, black straight brows, fair skin weathered by wind and sun and pulled too tightly across high cheekbones. There were new wrinkles lining his forehead, bracketing his mouth. The lips were thin, but always ready to smile, and that smile was warm, melting what in repose was a craggy rock of a face with a jutting nose and squared jaw. A long white scar climbed out of his collar at his tie knot and swung upwards to end in a pucker under his left ear. Straight on, it looked like the result of a shaving mishap. From the left side it was a great ragged tear, healed but scabbed with evil memories.

THE DEATH WATCH

He went down the green hallway, his long legs swallowing up the yards. He skirted an early dinner cart, almost choking on the odor of food cooling in its own steam. He swiveled past a preoccupied nurse. The flutter of the white nylon uniform, the dip of the white nylon cap were in response to him, but they went unnoticed. His attention was fixed ahead, on a particular door.

But when he reached it, he stopped. He looked at the small sign: Lori Manning, f., 25. He hated the small sign, its slightly soiled pale yellow background, the pale green panel to which it was taped. Pale green . . . supposedly easy on the eyes. Voices, footsteps. . . . He heard nothing.

He stood there for another moment. Then, taking a deep breath, he touched the door and pushed it slowly open.

CHAPTER 2

He had done the same thing a couple of hours earlier, the 8:00 A.M. to 4:00 P.M. shift behind him. Behind him, too, was the daily disgust at all that wondrous, taken-for-granted, abused good health wasted on the vicious, the stupid, and the useless, whom he hunted and questioned and listened to and dealt with. Whines, bravado, terror, promises; the car doors slamming; the phones ringing; the paper work piling up. And lies, lies, lies. He had put in those eight hours the same man he had always been, but with a new disgust controlled, a new rage sublimated. He had worked with his whole heart gone from him to be with Lori at Gorman. And then, stopping in front of the door, pushing it slowly open . . .

It had closed behind him with a too-familiar asthmatic wheeze. He took a single step into the pale green stillness of the room, stared unbelievingly at the empty bed.

It was stripped of sheets and blankets, revealing the pressed ridges of a shiny mattress cover. Two bare pillows were carelessly crumpled at one end. There was nothing on the night stand, nothing on the kicked-over footstool below.

For a long moment he was lost in mindless terror.

His dread had become reality and no one had called to let him know in time. The pale green walls of the room seemed to recede behind shimmering dark curtains. The breathless silence was the silence of the grave.

He relived in his mind how it had been every day for so many days: Mary Jensen's welcoming grin, the rouged and powdered face rising up from the stacked pillows, the kohl-lined eyes winking brightly at him, the sweet cloud of expensive scent enveloping him. Her high thin voice would cry, "Hi, Mike, you're right on time. We're waiting for you. She's had a pretty good day, everything considered. You have, haven't you Lori?"

He imagined all that in a single breathless instant, and realized that the empty bed was Mary's. The collection of stuffed animals was gone, and the plump velvet pillows; the line-up of fat bottles and thin ones, of glittery boxes, and crocheted caps. Gone.

He considered it, accepting the implication, but there was room in him for only one terror.

Mary Jensen, age fifteen, living on strangers' blood and hurrying adolescence and young womanhood with scents and creams and satins lest telescoping time deprive her of them forever; like the little boy who celebrated his last Christmas in July. But Mike's feelings had one focus.

He went on then, past the empty bed, to the one where Lori lay.

She was so slight that her body made hardly a rise under the coverlet. He had first met her one year and nine months before. She had been small: just an inch over five feet, with her chin raised. Small, yes, and compared to his own excessively robust bulk, even fragile. Narrow-boned, with fine wrists and tiny feet, yet, strangely, curved and compact and all woman. Small enough to be mistaken for a child, but all woman. Hips to hold, round perfect breasts with nipples sweet to the taste and velvet to the touch. Her hair, bronze as clover honey, had fallen in a silken sheath to her waist. Now, shining still, but cut short for easy care, it feathered around the small triangle of her face. The small white triangle of her face had once been golden, dimpled. The bitter months had burned the dimples away, singed the golden cheeks, and left blue bruises beneath her sunken eyes still the bright clear color of Navajo turquoise. The bitter months had spread small pale stains, a dozen different bruises, on the corded throat, the bony shoulders.

He stared at the slight rise and fall of the coverlet. She was asleep, or, if not, then shuttered away from awareness so that the fabric of pain that constantly enwrapped her was laced with rest. Grinning lest she suddenly open her eyes and see him in an unguarded moment, he took his usual place in the deep leather chair beside her bed. The holstered gun he wore dug into his left side and when he shifted to adjust its position, the chair heaved a deep and lonely sigh.

She fluttered pale fingers at him. Her lips moved slightly. "Mike?"

"Don't wake yourself up, Lori. I'm going to be here." But he waited, hoping she would open her turquoise eyes, wanting at least a brief glimpse of their jewel brightness. She fluttered her fingers again but her face remained still, closed against him, against what they both knew must come.

At last, after what seemed a long time, she said, "Mike, it's really going to happen."

His denial was hard, quick "Nothing's going to happen, Lori." He took a deep aching breath, fueling

41

for more denial. "You're going to get well, and pretty damn soon all this will be nothing but a bad dream that I'll make you forget."

"Is that how it'll be?" Her voice came out in a thin unbelieving whisper; the words were slow, falling like tiny pebbles into the pond of silence that filled the room.

Drowning in that pond, he fought, chest hurting, and gasped, "Yes. That's how it'll be."

And he damned himself for his denials, which were as much for him as for her, because he didn't dare acknowledge otherwise. Yet those denials, so necessary to them that for six long months they had lived by them, those denials robbed her of some final honesty to which she was entitled; some dignity that it was not his right to withhold from her. But cowardice compelled him.

"Thank you," she said. Her pale lips turned up in a faint smile. The bruises, all those pale splotches that were withering capillaries, rippled and spread as she moved her shoulders.

He got up, walked around the bed to the window. The venetian blinds were drawn tightly against the August sun. He said, "I don't know why they keep this room so dark. How about if I let the sun in?

"No, Mike, don't." Her hand fluttered off the coverlet, hung in the air above her face before it dropped down again.

"Okay. Sure." He agreed hastily, knowing from her face-shielding gesture that she didn't want him to see what had happened to her in the past few days, or was it the past few hours? "Just the same, if it didn't bother your eyes, Lori . . ."

"No. But I keep dozing off, and . . ."

"Okay," he repeated.

He went back to his chair. The holster annoyed him again when he sat down. He wished he didn't have to wear it, but there was no safe place for him to put it. He didn't want to take the time to go back to the apartment before coming to the hospital. The glove compartment of his car was no good; a police special got a good price in the market. So he wore the gun, though off duty. He adjusted his bulk and leaned back.

"You're tired."

"No."

"Your day?"

"Okay. The same as always."

He thought about the time he put in, eight hours out of the day wasted because he wasn't with her. The first morning stop had been a grocery story break-and-entry: small cash gone, wine gone; a withered old man wringing his brown hands. Mike was glad as always, and even more than usual that his partner was with him. Miguelito knew the lingo; he could question the old man in Spanish. The two of them, big Mike and little Mike, had been partners ever since they had come off the patrol car stint within the same month over five years ago. Miguelito, sensitive as a woman, quick as a cougar, knew what to ask, what not to ask, without being told. It was he who had gone in three weeks before to arrange for the eight to four shift indefinitely instead of the usual once a month deal; the hours of Lori's day when she needed Mike most were thus reserved for her. Mike hadn't wanted to ask; Miguelito had simply done it. And only that morning, Mike had learned, from somebody else, that Miguelito had volunteered to take the same stint so that the partnership would go on. Except for that new piece of knowledge, the day was the same as always. Always the bitter taste of seeing good health wasted. Miguelito described it differently. Shrugging, he said, "Every man suffers in his own way. They're up and walking, sure, sure, only do they look good to you? Do they look happy?" But it didn't help.

Lori whispered, "You there, Mike?"

"Sure. Of course."

"Special cases?"

"What, Lori?"

"Your day, Mike."

"Oh, I didn't follow. No. Nothing. Dog-day doldrums. The usual."

"Miguelito?"

"He's okay. Maybe he'll be by tonight."

"Good."

"I was thinking today, how did I manage to grow up in this town and not learn Spanish? It seems wrong. I ought to have."

"No need, maybe."

"I ought to have though."

She didn't answer him.

He waited for a little while, watching her, then asked, "And how about you? Your day?"

"Nothing."

"Did you have a transfusion?"

"Very early—daylight. I think they had to wake me up. Running behind from last night, I guess."

But at least they had taken the time to clean her up. Two weeks before he had come in several hours after she had had a transfusion to find her weeping silently, weeping

44

out the meager strength the fresh new blood might have given her.

"Look at me," she whimpered. "Mike, I'm like a vampire. It makes me sick, Mike."

She had been left in blood-stained sheets, her arms and face crusted and scabbed. She had been left to stare at the dark puddle on the floor beside the bed, to breathe in the fetid odor.

He sponged her face and arms, and soothed her, and when she was quiet again, he went out to the nurses' station.

There were four of them, young, shapely, a drift of cigarette smoke hanging over their crisp caps. As he approached they made quick, casual shifts; coffee cups were slid beneath papers, and ripples of movement wafted the cigarette smoke away.

He said very quietly, "I want somebody in there, right now to get my wife cleaned up and changed. And if I ever find out that she's been left that way again, there's four of you going to be sick, too. There's going to be some untransfused blood splashed around on these walls."

"Why, Mr. Manning . . . we had an emergency, you see. And we just couldn't . . . I mean . . ."

"Coffee emergency," he snapped. "Now move."

They scattered. Lori was attended to, and lay smiling at him from fresh sheets.

The next day Joe said, "What happened here, Mike?" Mike told him.

"You shook them up, Mike."

"I meant to."

"But you gather more flies with honey, Mike."

"That was Joe's way. Not Mike's. And what he had

45

said to the nurses that night had helped—more than the transfusion itself. Two weeks ago, after her tears had dried, she smiled at him. Today. . . . He said, "But it *has* picked you up a lot, hasn't it?"

"Oh, yes."

Only it hadn't. They both knew it.

He said hastily, "I see Mary Jensen went home. We'll miss her, won't we?"

"I was hoping you wouldn't notice."

That stopped him. But he had to say something. "Well, now . . ."

"They *say* she went home." Lori's fingers trembled. "But they put her in a wheelchair. They stuck all her stuff in a suitcase, and packed up her makeup, and took her out in a wheelchair."

"Sure in a wheelchair. That's how it's done. When you go home, I always——"

"But dressed, Mike. And she wasn't. She wasn't."

"Oh, they probably just didn't want to disturb you. They got her into her clothes down the hall."

Lori didn't answer.

"The room smells different, doesn't it, without Mary's silly perfume?"

"I won't miss her. She made me ashamed of myself. She . . . I was jealous."

"You? Jealous of her?"

Lori's whisper was weaker still. "She has more time left, Mike."

"Why, Lori, don't——"

"Don't, Mike."

He floundered. "Then you should have told me. I would have had you moved. I never dreamed she bothered you. I thought she was good company: a silly

46

fifteen-year-old kid, wearing makeup like an old whore."

He was trying to think. He didn't know if she were right; if Mary Jensen's being moved out meant something. He didn't know. Maybe they really had dressed her down the hall and sent her home. Only maybe they hadn't. And if they hadn't . . .

Lori whispered, "I guess I don't really mean it anyhow. And talking is so . . ."

"Rest now, Lori."

"So useless. Don't you see?" She paused. "But it was good, what we had. That part was all good, Mike."

"And it will be for a long time to come, too. It will be forever." His gravelly voice sounded certain. "Yes, Lori."

She finally turned her head and opened her eyes.

Clean bright deep turquoise—direct, knowing. Beneath the straight look were the deep blue thumb prints of sickness.

He tried not to shrink under the impact of her knowing. The peculiar part of it was that although he knew and understood and accepted, somehow there was still something in him that didn't believe it.

"You're going to be lonely. I wish I could have left you a baby, Mike."

It was a good place for him to take over. He could widen his fixed grin and tell her that maybe the future would provide for that. And if it didn't it wouldn't be because they hadn't tried. He knew that was the right way to answer her. He almost believed it himself in that peculiar part of him that still pretended, since it was as necessary as breathing to pretend. But somehow he could only look at her, trying to keep the faint grin on his lips, trying not to break down in tears.

47

"A little girl," she said dreamily. "Because daughters are close and loving."

"Lori, rest now."

She closed her eyes, nodded. "A little girl, Mike. But maybe you'd rather have had a boy. Men always want boys."

And then he was saying it, "Not this man. A girl it is. Small, blonde."

A faint smile touched her lips.

He sat very still, watching her, and thinking about Mary Jensen, wondering where she was. Home? Or in some other room? He thought about that, and he thought how impossible it was that anything that had begun in such sweet certainty, the way it had between him and Lori, must end as it was ending.

He couldn't let himself dwell on that. He rose, the leather chair sighing again.

"What, Mike?"

"I thought you had dozed off. I'm going down to stretch my legs, okay?"

"God knows I don't mean to hurt you, Mike."

"Oh, Lori, love . . . you don't."

She fluttered her fingers. "Go stretch now. I'll wait for you."

He dodged whole companies of steaming dinner carts. He wanted to kick them over, smash, tear, destroy, demolish. But that would be childish, and it wouldn't help; and he was thirty-two years old, and felt a hundred and two.

The nurses buzzed around the station. At his approach, there was a shift and stir. They were bracing themselves for him, he thought: Mrs. Meenahan, Mrs. O'Connor, Miss Dacey coming to starched attention because they had diagnosed him as an unmanagable type, definitely brutal and possibly violent. It didn't occur to him that they were simply reacting as women to the presence of a good-looking male.

The moment he had left Lori's room, he dropped the aching false grin he always wore for her. But now he arranged his haggard face into what he hoped might be pleasantness, and leaned lightly against the high counter, and asked, "Say, what about Mary Jensen?

"She was moved downstairs today, Mr. Manning." Miss Dacey made herself spokeswoman for the others. Single but experienced, she believed she knew a good stud when she saw one.

"Mary didn't go home?" Mike had straightened up. A muscle began to quiver in his right thigh. His big hands curled into fists. He asked again, "You mean Mary didn't go home?"

"No, Mr. Manning. She's not ready for that yet."

"Then why? How come they moved her out? What does it mean?"

Mrs. O'Connor and Mrs. Meenahan put their heads together, conferring in shrill whispers over a stack of charts.

The experienced Miss Dacey took a step back. "I'm afraid I don't know, Mr. Manning. You'd have to ask Dr. Stevens."

As Mike swung away, heading down the hall toward the elevator, he imagined the three nurses as slaughtered pigeons, trailing white wings crumpled, necks wrung, beady eyes closed.

He found Mary Jensen's new room easily.

When he tapped at the half-open door, she cried, "Well, come in. I'm dying for company."

He felt a twinge. The word hurt him. Dying. He couldn't help it. He supposed it was natural.

He grinned the false grin that pained his face, that seemed to have become a permanent part of his features. "Just wanted to see how you're doing, Mary."

"You're a doll, Mike. An ever-loving, ever-lasting doll. I thought I'd surely never never see you again."

Already the air was saturated with her sweet expensive scent. Stuffed animals sat on the bed and night table. Atomizers and creams and powders were lined up, waiting and ready. She nestled in a circle of bright pillows, her gray eyes staring out at him from peepholes of false lashes and beady mascara and great smears of green shadow.

"How come they moved you, Mary?"

"Search me. Just one of those things, I guess. You know how hospitals are. Whatever you want, they've got some reason for saying no it has to be a different way. They just came in, told me, 'Let's go. You're going home.' And the next thing I knew, I and all my possessions were here, and that was that. Lori's okay, isn't she?"

"Sure. I just wondered . . ." He gave Mary a wider version of his phony grin. "I thought maybe you found my company too trying. Hanging around from four until closing . . ."

"Oh, Mike, you're crazy! Why, you've always been the best part of the day."

"Good, then I'll stop in and see you again. Okay?"

"You bet it's okay." She blew him a kiss, a puckering of scarlet. "Don't forget."

He went straight to the phone booth, called Joe's office. He tried a couple of more times before he went back to Lori.

She asked, "Find her, Mike?"

"Who?"

"Mary."

He made the mistake because he just couldn't think fast enough. He said, "She's gone home."

"Don't lie to me."

But he was stuck with it. He insisted, "She has, Lori."

Lori opened her eyes, gave him a long look, then turned her face to the window.

He waited, hunched in the big chair that was too small for him.

She seemed to have drifted off to sleep; she didn't stir when the phone rang. Still, he didn't dare talk to Joe. But Joe wouldn't let him go out and call him back. Mike wondered where the hell he was that he couldn't have a call come in for him, but he wondered only briefly. It didn't really matter. Joe was coming in.

A nurse's aide brought in the dinner tray, and left it. Lori roused, and he rolled her bed up. He fed her slowly. She ate a little of this and that to please him, then drifted off to sleep again.

He went out to call Claire, remembering suddenly that he had promised he would. Claire had said not to doubt Joe. Not to doubt him . . .

Now again, the door wheezed automatically as it closed behind him. And now again, he stared at the empty bed.

They had moved Mary Jensen to another room, and told Lori that Mary was going home. If they were going to lie to Lori, why hadn't they bothered to make it look convincing? Why didn't they care what she thought? He gave the empty bed a last look, and then, just as before, he went on past it, fixing that terrible false grin on his lips.

Nobody had come to take away the dinner tray. It sat where he had left it, the barely touched food cold and hardening, smelling of grease and stale boiled potatoes. He picked it up, started out.

"Where now?" Lori asked.

"To get rid of this stuff."

"Good."

The cart was just outside the door. He dumped the tray and shoved the cart with his foot—hard, so that it went scudding wildly away.

Inside again, he settled into the leather chair.

Lori moved.

He said, "Come on, rest now. Take it easy."

"Joe coming?"

"He always does just about this time, doesn't he?"

"I guess so."

"Does something hurt? Do you feel worse, Lori?" Anxiety drove the painful grin from his lips. Strain deepened the new lines on his forehead. "Lori?"

"No. Don't worry. It's going to be all right."

"You asking about Joe . . ."

"Wondering, Mike."

He was remembering how it began.

He was in the kitchen. Not in that big sunny bright dream kitchen he had planned to give her some day, but in the tiny one with the old stove, gasping refrigerator, and cracked linoleum—the kind of kitchen you got on a cop's pay. It was small, old, everything wrong that could be wrong with it, but she had managed to make it something good. Dotted swiss curtains and fresh paint and shining pots covered a multitude of scars. They were there together. He watched her quick movements at the stove. When she turned sideways, reaching for the toaster, he blinked.

It was February when they married. Now a hot August wind fluttered the dotted swiss at his back. He had looked at her every morning for six months. He could swear he'd never taken his eyes off her, except when he was at work. How come, then, that he hadn't seen it before?

She put eggs and steaming black coffee before him.

He studied her deft hands, then her waist. His voice, always rough, was especially hard. "Lori, you were never very big. I mean, a handful sure, but not big. Only now, aren't you getting downright skinny?"

By then, she was sitting opposite him. The shining sheath of hair hung down her back. Her paper-thin fingers played with a bit of toast. A laugh began in her eyes, but was never completed. Her face went taut, and her color faded, and her eyes widened in astonishment.

Without thinking, without knowing what he was doing, he was on his feet and around the table. But as quickly as he had moved, he was too late. She had tipped sideways, crumpling to the floor. He scooped her up and felt the trembling in her body, and the echoing tremors in his own.

He set her carefully in a chair, and held her with one hand on her shoulder, the other reaching for a glass of water. Small kitchens did have their advantages.

She said, "Mike?"

"Easy. Here, take a sip. Don't move. I'm going to call a doctor."

"But what happened? I didn't faint, did I? I couldn't

possibly faint, Mike. I wouldn't even know how to."

"You don't need to know how." Standing over her, he was anxious, sure, but not in a panic. He had already noticed how thin she was. They would just have to find out what was going on, and do something about it.

"Don't hang over me, Mike. Really, I'm okay now. And your eggs are getting cold." She swung the long shining hair away from her face, and smiled. "Come on. Eat."

Her color had come back, and she was smiling, and she looked wonderful. By God, how wonderful she looked to him!

"Still, you can't be all right and have that happen, Lori."

"I can't? Well, I am, and that's not all. I'm hungry, too."

He wasn't. His big morning appetite was gone, but to please her he stuffed the breakfast down, watching her uneasily. "I can call in sick," he said finally. "I'll take you to a doctor."

"Don't be silly. I'm okay."

As he was finishing his coffee, he saw the beads of sweat on her upper lip. He burst out, "Lori, what's wrong with you?"

"If you'd just stop fading away," she whispered. He was halfway to his feet when she smiled and said, "Oh, I guess it's a virus. Stop acting as if I'm so fragile. I hate for you to treat me like a glass doll. Go to work and make a buck, Mike."

When she said "doll," he thought of it. Suddenly he was very nearly joyous. He raised his dark brows. "Say, Lori, do you think that maybe . . ."

"You've got an awfully short memory for a cop. Remember last night, and the night before? Sorry, I'm not pregnant."

He rose. "Then what is it?"

"Virus, I told you." She got up too. She stood on tiptoe to plant a kiss on his mouth. "But you wait, one of these days . . ."

He held her in a quick hungry hug. "Nothing matters as long as I've got you."

"Don't start what you can't finish, boy," she grinned.

He started to the door. "If you don't feel better, call me, and call a doctor, too."

"Like who? I'm a stranger in town and I'm not used to being sick."

"Who?" he was stuck for a minute. "Joe Stevens," he said then. "You call him. He's in the phone book. Tell him you're my wife."

"All right, Mike," Lori said. "If I need to."

"Dizzy spells! Fainting! Skinny!" Mike's voice was gravelly again. "Listen, Lori, you're okay, aren't you?"

That was how it had begun, with a ridiculous bid for reassurance. He didn't realize then how quickly he would learn to be afraid.

Now he sighed, checked his watch. He hadn't looked at the time when Joe returned his call. He couldn't guess how much time had passed since Joe had promised to come in. He only knew it was taking too long.

Lori was still, her face turned to the window.

He suddenly found himself moving backwards in ime again, to a night . . . one year and nine months ago.

He sat in Las Placitas, an Old Town restaurant, waiting impatiently for Claire to turn up.

She was late as usual, that sweet, crazy sister of his with her fashion artist job, and her serious painting on the side, and her mod clothes and mod friends. She was twenty-five years old and single, and if she had a steady man on the string, she kept it to herself.

He would liked to have seen her safely settled down with some decent guy, and a couple of kids to keep her busy, but he couldn't say much about it to her. After all, he was pretty free and easy himself. He had had marriage up to his ears. It had been a disastrous two years with Francie, when he was in his twenties. He took it as long as he could, and then threw her out. But he was a long time mending. He figured a man who fell for and married a nympho must have something wrong with him, and a cop who couldn't recognize whore signs when he saw them must really have something wrong with him. So he remained foot-loose and fancy-free, Francie free, and glad of it. He was a hit and run type, a slam-bam-thank you, ma'am type. No sweat, no strain.

It was just the two of them——Claire and him, going their own ways mostly, but sometimes meeting for a drink, for dinner, for a little impersonal talk.

Las Placitas had a dark beamed ceiling, tiled walls, and paintings. He concentrated on them, ignoring the hovering waiter who seemed to think he ought to have a drink, or two, or three, to justify his presence there. Mike would have enjoyed a drink, but he went on duty at midnight. He was getting itchy, beginning to wonder if Claire could have forgotten the appointment, when suddenly there she was, looming over him, smug as a kid making off with the last cookie.

He saw immediately the reason for the smugness. She had gone back to trying a bit of matchmaking. For a while, he had stuck her with it, and she had stuck him the same. Then they had decided to leave each other alone. She had broken the truce, and what's more, was pleased with herself. That was okay with him; he didn't have to buy every piece of merchandise he was shown.

Sliding into her seat, Claire said, "So sorry I'm late. Got tied up." And then, "Lori, sit down. He won't eat you." And to Mike "Mike, this is Lori. She models, and she's working for me now. Children's clothes. Would you believe it, Mickey?" And back to Lori, "Oh. Great. What a backwards introduction that turned out to be. Lori, this is Mike. My big brother Mike."

Claire grinned widely, spilling excitement over them. That "Mickey" was the tip-off. Mike wondered what it was all about. Surely just getting him and this girl together wasn't reason enough. He knew he'd find out some time, and for now he dismissed it.

Claire said, "Lori's new in town, Mickey. I want to help her feel at home. It's awfully hard when you're young and on your own, and . . ."

He looked across the table at Lori. He was a little surprised at Claire's unaccustomed lack of perception. She ought to have known that he wouldn't go for a girl who was an Old Town type. He sized Lori up. Old Town style, definitely. Golden hair to her waist. A black skirt. A bright red shirt. High boots. Then he looked into her eyes. They were clear bright challenging turquoise, and he realized that he was seeing a great deal more than he had expected, and realized, too, that she knew it and was amused.

Claire chattered, still riding that high crest of excitement, as if she already knew what was going to happen.

But he, cautious, hostile, watched himself. Then, midway through the meal, Claire suddenly flashed a look at her wrist watch, groaned, and excused herself. "Forgive me? Be right back." She returned, but she didn't quite settle down. She was restless watching the time. Mike wondered, until finally Claire said, "Listen, would you think I'm too awful, both of you, if I were to slip away? Something's come up, and . . ."

Mike and Lori agreed that they would somehow manage.

Alone, Mike and Lori looked at each other, and burst out laughing.

"I wonder who," Lori said. "Though it's none of my business."

"And I wonder why," Mike retorted. But his hostility was suddenly gone.

"I may model as a child—I can't help that, I just didn't grow very tall—but I'm not a child, and I hate being treated like one."

"Are you accusing me?"

"Claire." A grin flashed across Lori's tanned face. "Forgive me if I seem agressive, but I tell you, to look like me at almost twenty-four is . . . well, damn it, it's just plain boring, Mike."

"I thought women always wanted to look young."

"I'm different. And argumentative."

"Fine," he told her. Strangely, he, too, knew what was going to happen then. This time Claire had actually brought it off.

He forgot he was a slam-bam-thank you, ma'am type. When he had to take Lori home early because of the midnight shift, he considered it a personal plot against him. The first thing he said when he met up with Miguelito was, "Say, listen, there's this friend of Claire's . . ."

Miguelito grinned. "So it's finally happened."

"Something's happened," Mike agreed, his mouth still

sweet with Lori's good-night kiss. He didn't know that his craggy face was alight, and that Miguelito, seeing the glow, hoped Mike wasn't in for another hurtful ride on the roller coaster.

Mike considered time away from her wasted. He saw her every night that week. On their Sunday picnic, they had chicken sandwiches they forgot to eat. On the way home she said, "It was a lovely day, Mike, a lovely week. But . . ."

"But what, Lori?"

"This is when I say good-bye."

He pulled the car off the road, stopped with a jerk that shook them both. "What? What are you talking about?"

It was a few seconds before she answered, a lifetime to him. "It's too much, too fast. For both of us. I know how to get hurt. Don't play with me, Mike."

Twilight. Blue hills spreading around them. The highway still and empty. He reached for her, whispering, "Lori, Lori," and kissed her until they were both shivering with passion. She pulled away from him.

"Not here. Not now, Mike."

"Where then? When?"

"Maybe nowhere. Maybe never."

"You want me as much as I want you, Lori."

"Is that an accusation?"

It could have been; he could have been remembering Francie and her hot urgency. But it was as if there had never been a Francie in his life.

He growled, "Damn it! Don't you know me at all, Lori?"

She grinned then. "It's time to go home."

The next night, in his apartment, with lamp light aglow in her hair, her body golden in his arms, she was all his. And he was somehow afraid, holding back: a thirty-year-old man suddenly timid, too conscious of his size and strength and hunger. Cherishing her, he was afraid, and the fear shriveled him until she cried, "Mike, it's no good! I'm not fragile. I won't break. But you hold me as if I were a clay doll. I'm a woman, Mike!"

A woman, yes. There had been none like her before, and none since. A woman. All pride and desire, all giving.

It took him three months to persuade her to marry him. Behind his back, at headquarters, the men called her the child bride. Except Miguelito, because he knew, just by looking, what the others didn't know: that Mike had found a woman to meet the man in him. She was small, yes, gentle, too—but with all the violence and joy in love that he needed, so that nothing was ever too much, or too soon, but only good, always good.

Six months of marriage, and then the morning that he realized she was ill. And then the next six months while she went every two weeks to Joe, and took vitamins like a pregnant woman, and talked about rest and fresh air, and about other things, too, that Mike wouldn't let himself think about now. The day before their first wedding anniversary, Joe sent her to Gorman—for tests, he said.

"But on our anniversary!" Lori cried. "It's silly—I'm not that sick. What difference does a day or two make? Oh, please, we were going to go out, and . . ."

When Mike saw the look on Joe's face, he told Lori, "No use putting it *off*. We'll celebrate afterwards."

Later, alone with Joe, he asked, "Dr. Stevens, what are you looking for?"

"I don't know yet, Mr. Manning."

From then on, it was "Joe" and "Mike."

Four days later, he phoned and asked Mike to come to the office and the big hard man began to crumble inside.

Joe told him what they had found.

"How long?" Mike asked.

"Nobody knows. We'll try to keep her going. If it works out all right, she'll do pretty well for a while." Then, "I'm sorry, Mike."

"But you said before she was just run-down, and . . ." He swallowed hard to hold down the sickness. ". . . adjusting to marriage, and all that. Don't you remember?"

"There was no reason, then, to think otherwise. And it wouldn't have mattered. Even if the process had begun by then, and I'd seen it, nothing would have changed. It would have given her six months less of normal life, that's all."

Mike, leaning forward, elbows on the desk edge, whispered painfully, "You saved me, Joe. Don't you remember? You've got to save me one more time."

Joe didn't answer him. Maybe he was remembering the night that Mike and Miguelito got out of the car and were cut down by a hail of bullets. Miguelito got it in the leg, but Mike had taken one through the throat, a long angling rip from his Adam's apple to a place just under his left ear. He fell, with the stars spinning above him, and the night wind whispering good-bye. Joe, driving home from the country club with his wife beside him, saw it. He gave Mike breath when he couldn't breathe, and dammed the flow of blood, and, not waiting for the slow ambulance, held Mike in his arms while Ellen drove them to the hospital. Mike thought that maybe Joe, too, was remembering that night.

But Joe didn't answer him.

Mike had to accept his silence.

Heavily, he got to his feet. "You'll have to tell me what to do—how to handle it."

"Don't do anything."

"And Lori?"

"Time will do the handling. You'll see what I mean."

Mike nodded, started for the door.

Joe said, "I'm sorry."

"I know you are."

Outside, in the cheerless sun, he stopped. He didn't know where to go, or what to do. He wanted to weep, to curse, but he couldn't. He wanted to get sodden, sick, unconscious drunk. Instead he went to Gorman.

Lori was up, dressed, smiling. "Did you talk to Joe? Can I go home?"

"Right now, Lori."

She grinned joyfully, all shining hair and dimples, but then her turquoise eyes darkened. "What's the matter, Mike? Are you tired?"

"Yes. I guess so. A little."

"Now that I'm going home it'll be better." She shook her head. "Oh, Mike, it's been awful. I know that. But now everything's going to be okay. You'll see. I'm getting better. Soon we'll be back to normal." Her voice was husky. "I can hardly wait."

"You won't have to." That was when he learned that he could grin, if he tried hard, if he forced it. "Believe me, Lori. You won't have to wait."

For a few weeks, she was up, laughing. Then, suddenly, she was down. Her first transfusion. Then there were others. She said, "I must have the blood of every cop in town running through me by now, Mike." She said, "It's funny that I have to have another one, Mike."

62

She said, "But you know, I feel so much better today, Mike."

She was in and out of the hospital, where she met Mary Jensen, and a nurses' aide told her all about it. "Poor Mary, the bravest child in the world. Or else she doesn't know. She hasn't long. She's living on transfusions. If she didn't have them, she'd die tomorrow."

Mike, walking in to hear just enough of it to understand, but too late to stop her said gruffly, "Why the hell don't you shut up?" and the aide went scurrying away to complain tearfully to the supervisor that Mr. Manning had cursed her.

But Lori seemed not to have heard. Looking thoughtfully out of the window, she said, "When I get home this time, let's go on a picnic up in the hills, Mike. Promise?"

He promised, and they did.

After six months, Joe's words seemed unreal, something Mike had dreamed, and almost but not quite forgotten. What was real was the routine: those weeks when Lori was at home, Mike hurried back from the job to see her, anxious to know if he would find her as he'd left her; those weeks when Lori was in the hospital, Mike was on the eight to four shift so he could be with her when she needed him the most. What was real was the game they played between them: this visit to the hospital was the last; this transfusion would do it; all that rich red cop blood in her would do the trick; she was getting better. But her dimples had slowly burned away, and her long shining hair had been cut, and she was back in Gorman Memorial.

And now Mary Jensen was gone from the room, and

so were her bottles and scents and satin pillows, and her giggles.

Mike gave the empty bed a yearning look. He wished they hadn't taken her away and left Lori alone.

She whispered, "Mike, you there?"

"Sure." He moved closer. "Right here."

"Time you ate."

"Not yet."

"It's late."

"I'll get something after a while."

"Joe come while I was dozing?"

"He's on the way. It hasn't been long since he called."

"Mike? Could you . . . would you mind . . ." She paused for breath.

He got up, leaned closer, a great rock looming over a tiny pebble. "What, Lori? What do you want?"

She used too much breath in brief laughter, then, "Oh, if I told you what I want . . . if I said it here, now, you would . . ."

He put his hand over hers. Her thin fingers entwined themselves in his.

"Yes," she whispered.

"Yes?"

"You're just teasing me. You know"

"We might create an incident." He forced the usual grin to his lips. "Can you imagine what would happen if you and I . . . the two of us in that narrow bed, and Joe . . . with maybe a nurse or two——"

"Oh, I love you, Mike! It's ridiculous how I love you."

He put his hand lightly on her breast, and was rewarded with a faint smile. "Ridiculous how you love me?"

"And wonderful," she said.

His hand still on her breast, his other hand entwined in

hers . . . he saw the simpering face of death peer at him, bare skull and empty eye sockets, a mirthless fixed grin.

He was transfixed with pain.

She opened her eyes. ". . . wonderful to love you."

As he bent to kiss her he heard Joe's voice just outside the closed door.

CHAPTER 3

"Let me see it," Gilly Stevens said. "I mean, if you really think it's so hot, and you're so proud of it, then how come you keep saying I have to wait?"

David sighed. He rubbed his hands on his yellow pullover, leaving a trail of gray stone chips. He flexed his fingers. He had already explained three times. He would have to explain three more, or thirty-three more, or maybe even thirty-three hundred more. That was Gilly.

He said patiently, "Sorry. Not until it's finished. I want it to be perfect."

"For me to look at?"

For you, but for the show, too. Listen, if they take it, do you know what that means? If they do, then, God, Gilly, I'm on top of the world!"

"Because of a statue of me?"

"Yes. Because of that."

"Then let me look, David. If it's that important, I want to look."

He sighed again, and bent over the heavy table. He puckered his lips, blew gently. A fine mist rose and drifted away. He took up his tools: a small wooden mallet, a small chisel.

"David!"

66

"You can see it from over there."

"No I can't. Not really. To see it I have to be close. I have to touch it. A statue. . . . You have to touch it."

"That's right," he agreed. He adjusted the chisel and gave it a tentative tap. "Only not yet."

She prowled from corner to corner, from the bare window to the broken chair. She was tall, very thin, all angles even though she was seventeen. She had on faded blue jeans torn off raggedly just below the knees and a man's white shirt, one of her father's that she had stolen, tucked into a heavy silver conch belt which had been hammered out by Navaho Indians sixty years before. Her hair was long, unbrushed, a dull dusty chestnut in color. It was drawn back from hen face and twisted into a tight braid held together in a red rubber band that had come off a bunch of celery. Her blue eyes were large, and set wide apart over high cheekbones. Her mouth was sulky and sensual.

Her aimless prowl became purposeful. She edged closer to David.

Without looking up, he said, "Get back, Gilly. Come on, please."

"I want to see."

"Please, just stop talking for a minute, will you? Stop talking, and stop prowling around. I want to get done, Gilly. I have to get done, don't I?" The small mallet went tap, tap, tap. His lips puckered and he blew out carefully.

"I won't hurt it. I promise. I won't touch. I just want to see."

He sighed again. "Do me a favor. Just leave me alone. I can't help it, Gilly. It's the way I am. Don't spoil it now."

"And that's the way I am."

"Spoiled," he muttered. With the careful tap, tap, tap, and even as he answered her, he thought of the man he had seen going into Claire's house earlier. Carrying a small black bag, a fairly tall, slim man, oh, so spruce with shoes like mirrors on dusty Rojas Lane, went into Claire's house. A man with wide apart blue eyes. David knew: Gilly's doctor father. No question. Only what the hell was Gilly's father doing at Claire's? "Yeah, that's it," David said aloud. "Spoiled."

"What?"

"Always have to have it your own way."

"Always, David?"

"Just about."

"No. Really. Is that what you think of me?"

"That's what I think."

She chuckled. "Then give in. Let me see it."

He flung the mallet down, but not the chisel. It had a delicate blade. He had to be careful of the chisel. "Gilly! For God's sake, leave me alone."

"Is that what you want?"

"No, that's not what I want. But do you have to be such a kook?"

"We're all kooks."

He grinned. "I guess so."

"Can I see it?"

"No!"

She chuckled again. "I don't believe you've even done it. I think you're just pretending. I'm not there in that stone. You've been snowing me, and now you're scared I'm going to find you out . . . ."

"Okay. You'll know different in a couple of days."

"But that's how things always are, David. Just one great big fat snow job after another."

"Okay. Only not with us. Not between you and me."

"Really, David?"

"How do you want me to prove it to you once and for all?"

She licked her lips, gave a quick hard suggestive bounce of her flat hips. "Don't you know?"

"Hey, Gilly."

"Come on. Let's do it, David."

"I've got to work."

"You'll be working."

"On the statue."

"You'll be doing just that," she giggled, "if you work on me."

"Gilly Stevens! What would your mother say?" he demanded, mock horror in his voice and his lips pulled back in a wide grin, and all the while, the mallet went tap, tap, tap.

"And my father, oh boy, my father."

"All of them."

"The whole stinking, lousy, rotten, phony bunch. Damn them, David. There's only you and me, so . . ."

"And the rest of them, remember," he said gloomily, thinking of Gilly's father going into Claire's apartment on a bright Thursday afternoon. "And all I need is fifty bucks. That would take me the rest of the month, and . . ."

"Did you ask your friend?"

"Claire? Sure. Sure I did. She said she didn't have it."

"Some friend."

"She was afraid of what I'd spend it for."

Gilly hooted, "That right?"

David grinned. "So help me, I'm positive. Cross my stone heart!"

"Why should she care?"

"Beats me."

Gilly prowled. Bare window to broken chair to corner to corner.

It was a small room, once a stable. The floor was a cracked concrete block. The walls were whitewashed adobe, webbed with ancient settling gaps. The table, two chairs, the single day bed were all ten generation hand-me-downs and looked it. There was a two-burner hot plate in one corner, an open, half-unpacked suitcase in another. That was David's room.

Gilly said, "I wish you'd pay attention to me."

Something in her voice made him put down his chisel and mallet. He straightened up, rubbed his back. Eyes still on the small stone piece, he asked, "What's the matter, Gill?"

"Everything. *Everything.* You know."

He itched to take up his tools, but he didn't let himself do it. If he did, he knew that Gilly would be all over him. He had gotten her off that wanting-to-look-at-the-statue kick—he wasn't sure just how—and off the sex kick, too. He wasn't sure about that either. But he didn't want to remind her. And besides, she was entitled to some attention. Maybe the sex was a good idea. But if he got involved now. . . . Not that he didn't want her. He could feel the heat growing in his groin. He always wanted her and always would, and he didn't intend to fight that, not ever. But he had to get the piece done, and starting with Gilly now, when she was feeling restless and something else that he didn't quite know how to describe, starting right then would mean the last part of the day gone, and the evening gone and the night gone, and that would leave the Gilly statue unfinished. So he gave her the attention she was asking for, and hoped that would do and he could get back to work.

He looked at her. "Gilly, light some place, and tell me what you're talking about. Everything's wrong? No, it's not. We're together, aren't we?"

"I don't mean that, David." She went to the window and leaned her arms on the broad sill and peered out into the walled garden.

He thought about her father again. Except for the wall, she might see dapper Dr. Stevens drive away from Rojas Lane.

"Then what do you mean?" David asked.

"We're together . . ." she said. "That's right, isn't it?"

"Sure we are. Just the way we worked it out."

"Fooled them, didn't we?"

"I guess so." He made himself laugh, wishing that he had heard at least some small trace of amusement in her voice.

"What *they* want . . . their ways . . . their ways. That's all, David. Never mind me. How I feel. Never mind nothing. Just be their Gilly Stevens." She swung around, cried defiantly, "But I'm me. I'm my own girl. I am. I am!"

He grinned at her. "So what else is new?"

And that was right. Suddenly she was grinning, too. "That's got a real ring to it. Throw it on the counter and it hums. 'I'm my own girl.' " She sobered suddenly. "But you, David. . . . What about your folks?"

Somehow he managed to make the transition with her.

71

She was back on the money situation again. "My folks? Hah. I'm cut off, Gilly."

"For good and all and forever?"

"I guess so."

He knew so. They were finished with him, and he supposed he was finished with them. Sometimes in the empty night hours when he couldn't fall asleep, he tried to remember how it had been when he was a kid, and he and his parents and his younger brother Paul had been together, a family, caring about each other. But it seemed a long time ago, though it wasn't actually so very long in years. The divorce had come when he was thirteen, Paul eleven. The two of them with their mother, his father was three thousand miles away across the country, having gone as far as he could go without drowning in the big water: checks, occasional letters, rare telephone calls; six years of meaningless empty contact. His mother fed them bitterness with every hamburger; his father, indifference across the barricade of miles. He and Paul were too close. Paul clinging, cuddling, scared, tender; David the strong one.

Suddenly he was grown, at college. His mother was relieved—only one more at home, one more to go— but at the same time she clung to Paul. The clinging, cuddling, scared, tender boy was a delicate and lonely seventeen. He sought the father he had lost, the brother he had lost. Paul, rouged lips, bleached hair, was trapped and undone. He was shamed and hounded, and they wouldn't let him see David, let David visit him, help him. They blamed David for it all. And finally, Paul was a suicide at seventeen. Dead.

That month David left school, wandering up north to

Taos. His father sent him twenty-five dollars a month, his mother twenty-five. David supposed they had worked it out between them in a couple of strained phone calls. But then it was six months since Paul died and they decided he had had enough time. He must have recovered. He had to return to college or else. Or else starve, be drafted, disappear forever, so that they wouldn't have to worry about him any more and talk to each other across the barricade of miles.

He couldn't go back. School seemed as trivial and empty as his mother's smile, as trivial and empty as his father's cold clear distant voice.

And besides, there was Gilly.

Spring. A cool wind off the snow-tipped mountains. Green just beginning to frost the cottonwoods. A great arch of unblemished blue sky. Mud in the lanes, mud in the adobes and in the outhouses. Mud, blue sky, green frosting, And Gilly, suddenly, having arrived from nowhere, with nothing. Gilly, clean-limbed and laughing, and immediately his.

Two months: May, June. Bowls of boiled beans, Coffee. Day and night talk. Climbing in the cedar-scented mountains. Loving under the great arch of the sky.

When her mother came, fire and ice, tight-mouthed and beautiful, and took Gilly away, he packed his suitcase with extra chinos and skivvy shirts and tools, all that he owned, and followed. He stood at the side of the road, sweating in the early July sun, thumb out, until a Texas tourist gave him a lift. South on one ride. Then another, then another.

The tiny room, once stables, in Old Town was home now. Home. And Gilly was in his arms again. The tall thin awkward breathtaking Gilly that he had captured in stone. It would be his beginning, his life. She was his luck. Gilly.

He looked down at the table, at the cold stone Gilly: lithe limbs, sweet narrow hips, tight belly button and bottom, sleek head shaped to the tangle of sleek hair; cold stone and burning Gilly.

She said, "Okay, so it's awful, David. But screw them all. I'll get you your fifty bucks."

"Such language! Remember, you're a member of the upper classes, sweetie. You're a privileged type. You have responsibilities. You are——"

"Screw them all, I said."

"Is that a way to talk?"

"A member of the lower middle upper classes, David. That makes it all right, doesn't it?"

He grinned, "If you say so."

"I do. Besides, you think you've got troubles? At least your parents are a long ways away. Now you look at me. Did I ever tell you about Joe? About Ellen?"

"Yes, I think you've mentioned them to me a couple of times."

Gilly went right on, "That perfect man. Dr. Joe Stevens. That's my father. He's upper upper-middle high class. Or maybe he's lower lower sub-lower upper class. That depends. And Ellen! Now!"

David forgot to listen. Eyes on the cold stone Gilly not yet quite brought to life, instead of on the warm demanding Gilly who was very much alive, he reached for mallet and chisel.

"When can I see it, David?" she demanded instantly.

He gave a tentative tap.

She prowled closer, angling in. "If you're not going

to work, and you haven't been, not really . . . oh, yes, tap, tap, tap, but I don't mean that. You weren't, not until just now. So if you're not going to, then how about a little . . ."

He kept his head bent, his eyes on the small Gilly. He blew gently. "Oh, come on, Gill. Is that all you think about?"

"Almost."

"How come?"

He sensed her approach, and put down the tools.

She stopped, chuckled. "It makes me feel good. That's how come. When did you learn how to do it, David?"

"I don't know. I can't remember."

"You can't remember! Hey . . . hey, you're lying to me."

"No, Gilly. Cross my stone heart." But he *was* lying. He couldn't admit that the first time for him had been with her.

"I remember. I was eight. It was at the club swimming pool. And they were in the bar whooping it up over early cocktail hour. I mean *early*. Two o'clock. My mother and some of her friends. My father was out playing hero, like always. So then, a kid named Jonah and I decided to swim naked. The guard didn't pay any attention. He was licking up on a big girl—fifteen, I guess—back of the locker room. Jonah got out of his trunks, and I got out of mine, and out of that silly ruffled blue string that was the bikini top. We played, and played and played, and we figured it out. I mean, it's not all that complicated, is it? Anyhow, we figured it out. He got it in and I liked it. Don't ask me why."

"What hadn't seemed very complicated to her had

seemed very complicated indeed to him, David thought. Which was why it had taken him so long to try it, he supposed. He asked "You didn't get caught?"

"By who? The lifeguard? The grownups? They were too busy working at their own things, you know? And even if I had been caught, so what. . . . They couldn't have stopped me after that, David. I liked it. I mean, really, and I didn't know it was wrong or anything. I even asked my father to do it to me that night. I mean, I wanted to get close to him."

"Sure, I know."

Gilly laughed. "I tell you . . ."

"I can imagine."

"Oh no you can't. My father got quiet, gave me that clinical look—sort of taking my temperature and peering down my throat just with the expression on his face. But something else was in his eyes, something that was a funny kind of laughter. And at the same time, he was saying how I was such a smart little girl, one hundred seventy I.Q. and all, that I could understand him when he told me that that was for later, for being married, and not for now. And I was so smart, I could understand how he expected me to be perfect. And not doing that, not doing it, David, that was being perfect." She crowed, "Get it? Not was perfect. But my mother, she just listened, and her face was blank and her eyes were blank. Not clinical outside, not laughing inside. She was hating me. And I knew why even then: she never got enough of it from him for herself; she wasn't about to share any with me."

"Hey, Gilly, what would you expect, anyhow?"

"What I got. Exactly what I got."

They were quiet for a minute, and he looked down at the little statue, but he didn't touch it.

"David, let's go back to Taos."

"She'll come and get you again, Gilly."

"I know. Only it's no good here, David. That house. Them. It's just no good."

"Give it a little more time."

"And then?"

"You turn eighteen, Gilly. We'll get married. They won't be able to do a thing."

"I don't want to get married."

"Hey, come on, Gilly."

"I don't. We don't have to. What for? That's what spoils everything. Being married."

He didn't answer her. They had been through it before. When the time came, he would talk her into it. He knew he could. She was just afraid. It would all come out okay, if only he had enough money to keep on going . . . if only . . .

He sighed. "Why the hell does everything have to boil down to money?"

"Screw money," she giggled. "That is, if you won't screw me."

He winced, but he had already brought up the language subject once. He wasn't going to make her mad by bringing it up again. Most of the kids sounded off. "Screw everything," because that was saying it all. Only it wasn't her, and coming from her it sounded wrong.

She prowled closer. He grabbed up a torn flannel shirt, threw it over the tiny incomplete image.

"David, I guess you don't have any pot, huh?"

He shook his head. "What do you think? I don't have any money."

"That again."

"It's what you need to get pot with, Gilly. And liquor, and plain old-fashioned cancer sticks, and food, too."

"Not always."

"Hah."

"I know where to get some, David."

"Some what?"

"Money, cash, bread. And I will." Suddenly he didn't like the look on her face. Her long mobile mouth had become sly. Her wide blue eyes had narrowed maliciously.

"I will," she repeated, coming closer to him.

He opened his arms to her. "Hey, Gilly, I know something better."

Claire opened the door so quickly that David thought she was must have been standing there, waiting for someone to knock.

When she squinted into the blue twilight, her disappointment obvious, he knew he had been right. He said quickly, "Listen, I'll only be a minute. I just wanted to ask you to keep your ears open. . . . I mean, if you hear about a job, anything that I can do, and I can do almost anything. I mean. whatever kind of thing that turns up . . ."

She didn't ask him in. He could see she had changed from shorts and pullover to a red skirt and a matching red blouse, and she looked very good. It surprised him how good she looked, considering that she was old—in her late twenties—but she really got it across.

"But what about your work, David? You don't have very much time. And if you're not finished, they won't look at it. You won't have a chance."

"I'll finish. I've got until next Tuesday, and it's really

almost done now. Just the touches and the polishing. But I'm going to need a job. I mean, right away. So I thought, maybe, if you or your brother . . ."

He had decided that he had to do it. It was Gilly's talking about how she wanted to go back to Taos. Ever since she had been dragged home, given a new convertible as a bribe, settled, hopefully, into what her folks wanted her to be, something had been happening to her. It scared him. She was restless, angry, and at the same time, held in tight. He just didn't know what she was going to do next. Maybe she didn't know either. But it scared him. Her wanting to go back to Taos. . . . He couldn't, not until he had some money. A few days work, and he'd have enough. He could get the two of them away from her folks. She wanted to get away from them.

Claire said, as if she were thinking of something else, "Okay, David. I'll keep my eyes open. I'll try to call around."

He thanked her, trying to conceal his disappointment. He knew it was childish, but in the back of his mind, he had hoped she would tell him that she already knew of something, and he could start right then.

She must have read his thoughts on his face. "I mean it, David. I'll really try."

He thanked her again, and started to turn away, but something stopped him. He was back again in that brief moment earlier in the afternoon. He came out into the sunlight, and passed that tall, slim, dapper man, and they both paused, caught, somehow, and stared at each other. Sandy hair touched with gray, the wide open candid blue eyes, the clean perfectionist look. . . . He had to say it. "Before, there was a man here. I thought . . . I mean, could I know him?"

"I don't see how."

"His name . . ." David felt himself blushing. "I mean
. . . listen, wasn't that Dr. Stevens?"

"What if it was?" Claire asked softly.

"Hey, Claire, I only meant . . . I mean, I know his
daughter Gilly, that's all."

"Oh? Do you?"

David nodded.

"Small world," Claire said.

"Well, then . . ." Again he started to turn away.

"Wait, David. I'll get busy right away seeing if I can
find something for you. Okay? And meantime. how
about a loan?"

He understood immediately. He said slowly, "You told
me you didn't have any money before."

"I can't go to fifty bucks, but I can give you five."

He mentioned Gilly's father, and suddenly Claire decided to lend him five bucks. He didn't like it. "No,"
he said, "no, it's okay."

"But you have to eat. And you do want to finish the
piece before Tuesday."

"I'll make out."

"Sure you will. But meanwhile . . ." She left him in
the doorway and hurried across the living room into the
bedroom. When she came back a moment later, she
stuck a five dollar bill into his hand. "Okay?"

He thought of Gilly, that quick restlessness, her wide
blue eyes narrowing with malice. Five wasn't fifty, but he
could get her eased down. He whispered "Listen, Claire,
I didn't mean. . . . But thanks a lot."

When he had gone, she closed the door.

She had always known that somehow, somewhere, she

and Joe would get caught. It had never occurred to her that Gilly, wild, spoiled, trouble-prone Gilly, would turn out to be somebody David knew. Yet when she'd first met David, she'd heard that he had just come down from Taos. And wasn't it just about the same time that Joe had been so upset because Ellen had had to go looking for Gilly, and finally found her up in Taos?

Claire shivered. She told herself that it didn't mean a thing. Still . . . still, David had mentioned it, and she had given him five dollars. She'd realized as soon as she spoke of the money that she had made a mistake. David hadn't intended anything of the kind. But she'd gone through with it anyway. The only thing was, since she had gone through with it, she should have gone all the way and asked him not to mention seeing Joe to Gilly. But it was too late now . . . too late. She looked at her wrist watch, and promptly forgot David and Gilly.

There had been more than enough time for Joe to get to the hospital. Surely he had gone straight there. Surely he had seen Mike. Then why hadn't Mike called back as he had promised?

Something was happening. She knew that something must be happening. While she stood there, waiting, waiting, waiting, something was happening to Mike and Lori.

It seemed to Claire, then, that the whole nightmare of the past six months had been building up to this moment. She remembered Mike's voice, taut, despairing, frightened beyond belief. She couldn't imagine Mike frightened, not ever. But it wasn't for himself. He was frightened for Lori. That night when Claire brought them together, she hadn't really planned matchmaking. She had simply been sorry for Lori, who was new in town, and somehow seemed shy. But seeing them together, Claire had known they were perfect for each other. They had had just these twenty-one months . . .

Claire suddenly spun around and darted into the bedroom. She gave her hair a quick brush, then grabbed up her purse. She kept her eyes carefully away from the bed where she and Joe had been together. She didn't want to think about that now; she refused to let herself think about that. She glanced at the telephone, giving it one last chance, then went out to the car.

A tiny sliver of red moon edged one great black hump of the mountains. Later it would rise, full and silver, to hang against the dark nighttime sky. She backed out of the compound, heading down Rojas Lane.

The hospital grounds were crowded. Claire hurried inside. As she stepped off the elevator, a thick heavy silence seemed to descend upon her. She sped down the long dim hall, past the nurses' station.

One looked up.

Claire remembered the face, but not the name. "Is Mrs. Manning all right?"

"Dr. Stevens is there now." The nurse gave a bright approving smile.

They all liked him. Joe was that kind of man. Nurses . . . women. . . . Lori, from the first time she went to him, had liked him too. She had trusted him.

Claire hurried on. She tapped on the door lightly, then opened it.

Joe was standing next to the bed, at its far side.

Mike sat deep in the leather chair.

Lori lay between them, barely more than a shadow.

". . . and we'll see tomorrow," Joe was saying, his voice deep, noncommittal, but at the same time, comforting.

"Tomorrow," Lori whispered.

"It's just me," Claire said brightly. "I thought I'd pop in for a minute. All right?"

"Sure. How are you these days, Claire?" Joe said, as if he hadn't left her just a little more than an hour before.

"I'm fine, thanks." The answer was set by the rules of the game they played. Moving closer, she asked Lori, "How's today?"

"Claire, honey." Acknowledgment, nothing else.

Claire swallowed a lump of bitter understanding. Lori wasn't trying any more. Acknowledgment, not reassurance. "Claire, honey." Not, "I'm pretty good." Not, "I think I'm better."

Claire looked at Mike. She noticed for the first time the empty bed. Mary Jensen should have been there. . . . The bitter lump of understanding took Claire's breath away. She suffocated on it, fought it, finally managed to breathe again.

Joe leaned over Lori. "Rest well." His deep voice was full of the strange confidence that was his power.

Claire asked herself if he were saying good-bye. She asked herself why he didn't stay, why he didn't do something.

She went to stand behind Mike and put both hands on his wide shoulders. She clung to him and offered him support at the same time. "Have your supper yet?"

"Later."

"I'll bring something in."

"Make him eat," Lori whispered. "Make him take care of himself, Claire. A favor, for me. . . . He needs a button sewn on his sleeve . . ."

"Don't worry," Claire said. "There's nothing wrong with our Mike."

But something was wrong.

Joe tapped Mike's shoulder. "Take care."

"Did you tell the nurses?" Mike asked. "I don't want any arguments."

"It's okay. But not after ten, Mike. That's already stretching it by two hours."

"Sure."

Claire thought about the fact that it hadn't always been that easy. They didn't like to have visitors around after hours. Something about routine. Joe had once explained. But now, tonight . . .

"I'll get you a sandwich, Mike. Be right back," Claire said. She looked at Lori, but Lori's face was turned away. Claire whispered "Be right back."

Joe held the door open for her, closed it carefully when he had followed her out.

"Joe . . ."

He shook his head, touched her elbow, led her down the hall.

Careful Joe Stevens, she thought, and she wondered why it mattered then, that night. Because she understood. She knew.

Still, at the elevator, she asked, "What is it, Joe? What's happening?"

He didn't answer her.

She said, "I'm scared."

"I know. But you have to be strong to help Mike."

She suddenly remembered the first time she had seen

Joe. Late at night, it was in a hospital corridor then too, but on the first floor—Gorman Emergency wing. He came out of surgery, his pale green gown stained with Mike's blood. "Miss Manning? You are Mike Manning's sister?" She had nodded, unable to speak, so sure in that awful moment that Mike was dead. But Joe had smiled. "He's going to be okay." And the hall was misty, and she felt herself falling. He caught her, held her. "Easy, easy," he said. She whispered. "Oh, Doctor, thank you." He told it had been the surgeon's work, not his. He had only been lucky enough to be where it happened, to get Mike to the hospital in time.

But later, days later, Mike said Joe had saved his life, Joe and Ellen between them. The Department feted him. They Police Superintendent, the Chief, the Head of Detectives, they were all on the platform when the Mayor awarded Joe a gold lifesaving medal. Joe had remained imperturbable in the face of the honor and the attendant publicity; unmoved, modest, and so startlingly attractive to Claire.

She had thought she would never see him again, and she hadn't, not until she bumped into him on the street years later. It was just a month or two before she introduced Mike to Lori. He bought Claire a drink. Again she thought she would never see him again, but he called her. They went out together. And suddenly she was waiting to hear his voice, the scattered, far-apart dates too important to her. Then, a year ago, they had become lovers. Mike never knew . . .

Joe' was saying, "Claire? Claire, you're not going to go to pieces, are you?"

"I'll get Mike's sandwiches and coffee."

Joe nodded.

"And then I'll go home." Her rusty voice had a question in it. She heard it and hated herself, ashamed to be asking Joe now, *now* . . .

"You'd better, Claire."

"You mean that they'll want to be alone now, don't you?"

"I'll wait for you in the lobby," he said only, and they rode down together.

It took her just a few minutes to pick up ham sandwiches and coffee from the cafeteria. She brought them up to Mike. He seemed not have moved since she left him.

He thanked her when she put his dinner on the bedside table.

She asked, whispering, if he wanted her to say.

He said he'd rather she didn't.

She bent over Lori. "Good night, sweetie. Sleep tight."

Lori's eyes opened, clear cool turquoise. "Tomorrow, Claire. You're so pretty in red."

"I'll wear it tomorrow, too," Claire promised, and turned away, her eyes filling with tears. When she told Mike good night, he nodded wordlessly.

He was relieved to hear the click of the latch as the door closed behind her.

Lori's eyes were closed again. She seemed even smaller now, the narrow bed growing wider around her. She fluttered her fingers at him. "Eating, Mike?"

"Sure, what do you think?" He crumped a sandwich in his big fist. The wax paper was noisy, convincing. He carefully put the soggy mess into the wastebasket near him.

But she knew. "You cheated, Mike." Her fingers crept toward him.

He shifted closer, put his hand over hers. All bone, a thin layer of cold flesh, a slow slow pulse. He leaned down and laid his face against her arm, but carefully, gently, allowing no weight to burden her, just the warmth of his chin in the crook of her elbow. He felt the slow slow pulse there, too, and the quiver of response at his touch.

She said, "I tried, Mike." She took a long shallow breath. He waited in agony. Finally she went on, "Going back to Joe. How I hated those visits. I liked him, still do. But the questions. You. Me. Remember? I've told you all about it, haven't I? All those questions. And as if I were too dumb to understand. And underneath, the hint that I wanted to be sick . . ."

"You did tell me all about it, Lori. I haven't forgotten. Don't talk now."

". . . wanted to be sick. And all the time it was in me. Working away. Six months of doubting myself. You. Love. Time wasted. And just when we had so little time."

"Lori, no." He wouldn't let himself remember that part of it now. Later. Later.

She said suddenly, "I wish we'd had a baby, Mike."

"Maybe we will." He got the words out, hating himself for them. It was wrong, wrong.

Yet she smiled. Not a faint curling at the corners of her pale lips. A wide bright smile, and the dimples he loved were suddenly there, in the thinness of her cheeks.

"We might," she agreed. "Staying with me?"

"Sure."

"Even when I fall asleep?"

"Sure, Lori."
"Say it for me, Mike."
"Love you, Lori."
She moved her arm against his cheek.
"I'll be right here," he said.

CHAPTER 4

Joe had other patients to see in the hospital, but having spent those difficult forty-five minutes with Lori, he felt as if he had done a full day's work on top of a full day's work. He decided to skip the others and go home. But as he raised his hand to punch out the light next to his name on the call board, the metallic-voiced intercom paged him.

"Dr. Joseph Stevens, third floor, please. Dr. Stevens. third floor."

He let his hand drop. He tried to think of whom he had on the third floor. For a moment, his mind was completely blank. Oh yes, Mrs. Taylor, scared, spoiled, struck down by mycardial infarction in late middle-age after sixty-eight years of self-indulgence. Though recovering now, the habits of a lifetime were making her progress to normalcy even more difficult than it had to be. He sighed. Just about the last patient he wanted to see then was Mrs. Taylor.

He saw Claire get off the elevator, a gay, gallant figure in bright red: long legs beautiful, the contours of the high round breasts showing through the snug blouse, dark hair brushed into a helmet of curls. Perfect from head to toe—and his. Really his. He went to meet her.

Close up, she looked gay and gallant no longer. Her eyes shone with unshed tears. Pallor was a pale background on which her careful makeup looked splotched and smeared.

She said, "I still can't believe it, Joe. Are you sure? I mean, are you absolutely certain . . .?"

"I'm not sure of anything. And I think you ought to go home, and get some rest, and try not to worry too much."

He had intended to do exactly that himself. Instead, he went on, "I'll meet you there in a few minutes."

"You'll come back to my place, Joe?"

"For a little while. I have to go upstairs first. It won't take long."

"You mean you'll really come back?" she asked.

"Claire! I just said so."

"Sorry." She smiled at him, a stranger's smile for the benefit of the others in the lobby, others who might be looking at them. She had remembered where she was, who she was.

He was glad to see it. But every moment that concerned Lori and Mike became sour for them. It was always like that, had to admit to himself. Ever since she had learned that he had sent Lori into the hospital for bone marrow tests and the whole work-up, something had come between Claire and him.

Yet he knew he had done everything he could. Those first six months it had been obvious that what was troubling her, to the point of a physical reaction, was something in her marriage to Mike Manning. She was small, and fragile, and startlingly beautiful with those extraordinary eyes, that long golden hair. He knew instinctively, the moment she was shown into his office,

90

that she was childlike, delicate, one of those shy, sensitive women who needed the pampering of a tender man.

And there, towering over her, was Mike Manning, craggy face stony, dark brows flat, voice hard as flint. "I guess maybe you remember me, Dr. Stevens . . ."

Claire was saying now, "Then I'll see you in a little while." When he nodded, she turned away.

He watched her go toward the glass doors.

A watchman in uniform, wiry, with a bad left leg, somehow managed to leap to hold the door open for her, an old man's tribute to her tall slim figure.

Joe grinned. He couldn't remember the man's name, but he knew him: an ex-cop, friendly if given any encouragement. Joe never gave him any.

Still smiling, he got on the elevator. But thinking of the night watchman had reminded him of Mike, and Joe's smile faded.

When he first knew Mike, those hours when life was a thin graying thread for the big man, Mike had been dependent, a shrunken hulk struggling to maintain itself, and later, through the weeks of convalescence, hospital-gowned and flat on his back, he had been full of what seemed to Joe an almost childlike trust. But a few months later, seeing Mike at the medal-awarding banquet, Joe had thought that he was seeing a different man. He saw Mike the cop, not Mike the patient. And everything about Mike the cop repelled Joe. From those huge feet in unpolished shoes to the rocklike, barrel-chested body in baggy clothes, to the raw, craggy, somehow unsymmetrical face, Mike seemed all barely leashed violence.

Mike gave him the gold medal and shook his hand,

and Joe smiled modestly and didn't expect to see him again. But he had, when Mike had brought Gilly home.

He got off the elevator, stopped at the nurses' station. The nurse smiled at him as he reached for Mrs. Taylor's chart.

"You heard my call then? I thought perhaps you'd gone."

"I heard it. What's the trouble?"

"The usual. She's scared, I suppose."

Joe wished he could remember the nurse's name. But it didn't matter. "All cardiacs are as they recover."

"Save me from them," the nurse said.

"Busy otherwise?"

"Too busy. It's going to be one of those nights. I'm glad I go off at twelve." Her white-capped blond head was tipped up, her glowing smile directed right at him.

He wondered briefly if there had been a thinly veiled invitation in her words. It didn't matter. He wouldn't take her up on it, nor even acknowledge it, although he had already noticed that she was shapely enough to tempt the most discriminating—which he was. A man who saw as many bodies as he did was bound to be discriminating, if he weren't surfeited—which he wasn't. He grinned to himself, thinking of Claire.

With the chart under his arm, he went down the hall, knowing that the nurse watched him all the way.

Mrs. Taylor gave him a sad smile, said in a wan whisper, "Oh, I am glad to see you, Doctor."

He sat beside her, giving her the appearance of that calm and unhurried attention to which all of his patients were accustomed. In fact, he was able to listen to her, and at the same time to think his own thoughts.

She was some kind of cousin to the Gormans, a woman

of wealth and position in the city, of the same generation, life style, and standards as his own mother and Ellen's; the same life style, and standards, and expectations to which he, and Ellen, too, had been born.

Though he didn't often think of it that way, they were, all of them, the elite, old settlers who had owned the great empty areas that surrounded the city, the inheritors of the cedar-dotted mesas. When, with the Second World War, the air fields and factories suddenly burgeoned on the great red flats, the change had had varying effects on the parents and their children. Some had become, after the war was over, globe-trotters, and later on, jet-setters. Others interested themselves in increasing their holdings. A few developed a taste for art and music. Still fewer devoted themselves to new philanthropies. Joe's parents had become feverish pursuers of their simple pleasures—gold, fishing, and gin.

Having weighed them and found them wanting while still in his early teens, Joe decided to study medicine. He'd had a faint heart murmur since early childhood which kept him out of the Army. He chose medicine over other possibilities. He had always had a wry attitude toward illness, but he gloried in being needed, in the sense of power it conferred on him.

Now he half-listened to Mrs. Taylor, nodded at her, and gave her the looked-for reassurance. She was smiling happily when he rose to leave.

On his way downstairs, he ran into Sam Upson, a specialist in chest surgery.

Joe listened to an old joke, chuckled dutifully at the punch line, then made a Sunday afternoon golf date with him. Sam was a big man, larded with rolls of fat, whose voice was as loud as his ties and sporty suits.

He was a relative newcomer to the city. He didn't take himself or anyone else seriously, although his patients spoke of him as if he were a saint. At least Luke himself.

Joe did not consider him a saint, nor a master of healing, but he was, like Joe, somewhat more master of his time than most of the physicians Joe knew. Chest surgeons do not make house calls, and Joe, as an internist, made only rare ones.

Sam Upson told one more joke. Again Joe dutifully chuckled. Sam's idea of humor was not very acute.

With the golf date confirmed, they parted in the lobby.

Bess Bradford saw the elevator door open, and Sam Upson and Joe come out together, pause for a moment of laughter, and then separate.

As Joe came towards her, she edged backward, seeking a sheltering spot behind a concrete column. From there, unseen, she watched him stride toward the big glass front doors.

She knew it was a silly thing for her to do. She had no real reason to hide. She had a right to be at the hospital if she wanted. Should Joe see her, she could always say she was visiting a sick friend. What friend? Well, if he asked how come he hadn't heard before about her sick friend, then she would have to think fast. But, of course, she knew that if Joe did see her he would ask absolutely no questions. He would give her that wide white wonderful smile of his, and say, "How are you tonight, Bradford?" and then go straight on, without waiting to hear what she would answer.

So it was silly of her to duck behind the concrete column. In fact, the whole thing was silly. Her being there, watching for him, having gotten dressed up, having thought her thoughts. . . . Why, he probably wouldn't even recognize her if he did see her. If he ever thought of her, outside the office, he probably assumed that she had been born in a white nylon uniform, umbilical cord the belt.

He didn't see her. His tall, lithe form paused at the wide doors, and that skinny watchman who had long before begun to recognize her and say hello—Al Kelly was his name, she had learned—he pulled the doors open for Joe and touched his cap in a gesture of respect. Joe nodded and went on, oblivious to her as always, to disappear into the dark.

She told herself that she was going to go home, now that Joe had made his appearance and gone. Since she was going to go home, there was no hurry. But just the same she made a dash for the doors.

It was a precarious dash, her feet unsteady in the three-inch purple pumps she wore that evening. Her purple skirt exposed two inches of plump thigh and long thick legs in lavendar stockings. Her waist was cinched by a wide purple belt that was edged with narrow rolls of flesh. They showed clearly through the tight purple pullover, and rose, old molding on woodwork, against the outlines of her breasts.

She saw the lights go on in Joe's car, and she hurried to her own. She didn't intend to follow him. She had never done that before. But somehow, when he pulled into the traffic, she slipped in a few cars behind him.

That was when she decided that something was wrong with her. It just didn't make sense to do what she was doing. The rest of it, all right, maybe that wasn't so bad. It wasn't really so crazy for her to almost always go home right after the office was closed and change to a pretty dress, and then hurry to Gorman Memorial just in time to see him after he made his evening rounds there. The nights were so long, and she was so lonesome. There wasn't anything wrong in wanting to see him for a few minutes more at the end of the day.

But to go after him, slipping through the dark like she was doing? Still, instead of turning off for home, and bed, and a bottle for company—which is what she usually did, and what she supposed she would do eventually—she just drifted along behind him.

The long gray Cadillac was easy to keep in view. She didn't have to worry about him spotting her; he didn't know what kind of car she had, or if she had a car, for that matter. She was sure she had told him once, but she was just as sure that he hadn't listened. And why should he listen? He didn't care about her. Even after fifteen years, he had never called her anything but "Bradford," as if she didn't have a first name. She supposed it was better that way, but after fifteen years, better or not, she couldn't bear it that he never called her Bess, nor acknowledged her as a human being—as a woman. She just couldn't bear it. But of course she didn't really expect anything different. How could she? She wasn't a pretty woman, nor had she been a pretty girl. But she had a sympathetic face, a sweet face, she had been told. Maybe she didn't look her age, but she was forty years old. Forty wasn't all that old, of course. Not if a woman kept busy, and up to date, and alive and outgoing. Not if a woman didn't let herself go. She hadn't, of course. She didn't dare let herself go. Joe would notice, and he wouldn't approve, and the next thing that would happen was——

She squinted against sudden tears. She knew she was

being ridiculous even to think of it. He wouldn't fire her. They had been together for fifteen years. He had only been practicing for three years when she took over from that silly what's-her-name who was working for him and married Dr. Sloane from down the hall, and got pregnant so soon that it was downright unrespectable. That silly what's-her-name had three children now, and looked hardly a day older than when she had twitched her round bottom out of Joe's office for the last time, leaving the files in a terrible mess and the supplies so low that Bess had taken weeks to get everything straightened out to her satisfaction. And they had been together, she and Joe, ever since. They would always be together, Bess and Joe. Those days in the office . . . she carrying out his unspoken orders, he appreciating her help even though he didn't acknowledge it in words. And she understood: they were too much to each other to require spoken gratitude, compliments, or vows.

The long gray Cadillac turned into Central Avenue, gleamed briefly under distant street lights, and disappeared. She drove straight ahead, saying aloud, "I'm awfully glad I ran into you tonight, Joe. I was thinking about you just a few minutes ago. Let's go home now, shall we?"

The ritual of evening fantasy had begun.

"I guess Sam Upson was telling you another one of his terrible jokes," she said, smiling archly. "Probably one you couldn't even repeat to me. I saw how the two of you were laughing when you got out of the elevator. Like small boys exchanging smut. Oh, I know about that, you can believe me. A girl doesn't grow up on a ranch with four brothers without hearing more than you can imagine. But still, that Sam Upson is such a coarse man, a loud-mouthed coarse man. It's very good of you to put up with the likes of him. Not everyone would. And that plump little blonde sow he's married to . . ."

Bess chuckled hoarsely. To her it sounded like a low thrilling laugh. "Oh, you're so right. Of course it takes all kinds. But does it have to take *that* kind, too?

"But then, what can you do? You're too fine a person to hurt anyone, Joe. We can just forget all about the Upsons now, can't we? And how was your day, Joe? Did you enjoy yourself during your couple of hours off? You looked like a small boy playing hookey—mysterious and happy. I hope you found it relaxing. You certainly can stand a little relaxation. Why, if one more new patient comes to you, Joe, I don't know what you're going to do. It's different now, isn't it? That's what I always tell my father. It's not like in the old days when he was driving that rickety old sedan over the hills. A G.P. didn't do a whole lot more than drive and drive then, and still he couldn't keep up with it. And after all that, look what he's got, Joe. Nothing. Nothing. He's an old man now, my father. I mean, just an old man with gnarled hands that delivered I don't know how many kids, and set I don't know how many bones. So there he sits on the front porch with those gnarled hands in his lap, criticizing everything about the way things are now. You'd think he'd have better sense. Honestly, Joe, you can't imagine how many times I've told him off. An internist works just as hard as he ever did. House calls? Well, nowadays, with all the equipment you need for proper diagnosis, and the millions of tests that have to be done and whatnot, the hospital is the best place for a sick person.

She maneuvered skillfully around a double-parked car, made the left turn into her street, and slowing down, said, "We're almost there now. And I have the loveliest pitcher of dry martinis ready and waiting for us. Just what you need at the end of a hard day, Joe."

She parked, locked up. She went along the walk, and up the four steps into the building's foyer.

A neighbor said something to her. She nodded brightly, but didn't answer.

She got out her keys as she climbed the steps, unlocked the door, and hurried into the empty silence. But she didn't notice. As she went from lamp to lamp, filling the dark room with light, she chattered joyfully. "Now come right in, Joe. Sit down and relax. I'll rustle up those martinis right away, and while you're having your first one, I'll just change into something more comfortable."

Smiling brilliantly, she ducked into the tiny kitchen. She mixed a tall pitcher of gin and ice and small parings of lemon. Joe liked his martinis very dry, and so did she.

She set a copper tray with two fine cocktail glasses, delicately etched, and polished until they shone. They were the only two she owned. She had bought them for her and Joe. She filled a tiny silver dish with red pistachios, and another with shelled blanched almonds. The cocktail napkins were orange and lavendar striped, and the same orange was in the floral cover of the big sofa to which she returned, tray in hand, still smiling brilliantly. "There, that didn't take long, Joe. Now you go right ahead. Don't wait for me. I'll be back in a minute."

In the bedroom, she pulled off the skirt and blouse she had worn for him hoping, although she had cowered behind the column in the hospital lobby, that he would see her. She drew on a filmy black lace gown, then a peignoir, also of black lace, that floated delicately around her white plump body.

She had found it after a long and diligent search through the city's three big stores, explaining unnecessarily to the indifferent salesgirls that it was a gift for a young friend and certainly not for herself, knowing that the salesgirls hadn't believed her and didn't care anyway.

Now Bess brushed her silvered waves, fluffing them softly around her cheeks, and darkened the blue eye shadow, and affixed great sweeping fans of false lashes that tickled the side of her nose when she batted them at herself in the dresser mirror.

Pasted to that mirror were pictures of Joe Stevens: Joe receiving the gold medal after he had saved Mike Manning; three other pictures just like it carefully cut from newspapers of that time; a snapshot of Joe stepping out of the office, smiling into the sunlight; another of him on the golf course. These last she had taken herself on occasions manufactured for that purpose. "Oh, Dr. Stevens, I just happened to have my camera with me," and "For goodness sakes, look who's here!" and, "I'll just up this last one on you, Dr. Stevens, and then I can have the roll developed." They were pictures of Joe she had laboriously collected over the years. The clip from his college yearbook had been a lucky find. She had rescued it from the wastebasket where he had tossed it.

But now she looked at herself, not at the pictures of Joe. He was in the living room, in the flesh, waiting for her.

She drew a heavy pouting mouth with her lipstick. She touched ears, throat, elbows, the backs of her knees with perfume. *Fascination!* The tiny crystal vial was unbelievably expensive, but nothing was too good for Joe.

Finally satisfied, she returned to the living room, sank down into the sofa, and took up her glass. "To you, too, dear."

She gulped the drink, warmth spreading through her, and immediately refilled her glass.

"Thank you," she said softly, her brilliant smile turning shy. "Thank you, Joe. I'm glad you like it. I bought it for you. After all, Joe, I came down from the hills a long time ago. Why? Can you imagine me staying there, Joe? My father aging, my four brothers watching me as if I were . . . oh, I don't know, Joe. Brothers are just funny, I guess. And nursing was the natural thing for me to go into. Though I must say I hated the training. So much discipline. And I never did like hospital work. I guess a year or two of that was all I could take, and then private nursing, and then, when I saw your ad . . ."

She drained her glass, refilled it. Her voice was growing husky.

"Wasn't it lucky that I did, Joe?" She smiled at the empty orange pillows. "Oh, yes, it was for me, too. I always knew how it would be. From the moment I saw you, I was committed to you. I don't mind the way things have been. I knew they couldn't be different, Joe. And I'm grateful for what we've always had.

"Chances? Well, of course I did. Still do." She giggled as she finished her drink and leaned forward, black lace swirling around her, to raise the pitcher with both hands and tilt it carefully over the glass. "Benjamin? My goodness, Joe, you don't have to be jealous of Benjamin. That's the funniest thing I ever heard. You, jealous of him! But darling, just think, could you picture me married to him? Really? After knowing you, how could I ever care about poor Benjamin? A great big coarse ignorant baby, always wanting my constant attention. Why, if I even mentioned your name, Joe, he just . . . well . . . he just . . ." She smiled archly. "We can forget Benjamin. And the others. They were the same. If I ever mentioned you, the office, they just . . . Oh, I don't know, Joe. It was always you and me, that's all. I never wanted anybody else. I know you're glad, darling. I know you are. I know you want me, and only me, and we have to be brave and accept things the way they are."

She got the half-full glass to her mouth and sipped at it until it was empty. She set it down next to the orange napkins, and it made a small ring on the cocktail table. Ignoring that, she tipped forward, her head spinning, to raise the pitcher again. When the glass was overflowing, she leaned forward further to sip from it. Giggling, she said, "Joe, you know how I feel? Just wonderful that's how, Joe." Tipped forward still, sipping between giggles, she emptied the glass. Then, with her arms wide, reaching, she fell into the heap of orange pillows and lay there, heaving, hugging herself, one hand clutching her round breast. In a little while, she whispered, "Joe, let's go into the bedroom now."

Her arms still wrapped around herself, she staggered to her feet, and made her way across the brightly lit, empty room to her brightly lit, empty bed. She fell into it, crying, "Oh, Joe, Joe, I love you! I love you. Lover, I love you," and struggling to remove her black lace gown. After moaning through long busy moments, she fell asleep.

THE DEATH WATCH

The long gray Cadillac swung around the house and pulled up to stop at the three-car garage. Its lights went off. A match flared as Joe lit a cigarette. He blew the flame out, dropped the match into the dashboard ashtray.

There was a yellow gleam seeping under the edges of the drapes that covered the game room windows. He wondered if he had forgotten some entertainment that Ellen had planned. But the only cars there were Ellen's and Gilly's, so he was all right: he hadn't forgotten this time.

He was glad to be home. The past two hours at Claire's had been grueling. He hadn't intended to go back there in the first place, but she had seemed to need him so much, and though he didn't admit it to himself now, he had needed her, too.

He looked past the big adobe house to the dark hulk of the mountains, the star-dusted arch of the sky that was the shimmering backdrop for the white moon.

Claire. She had had sandwiches and coffee ready for him when he finally got there. He had a quick silent snack, hoping that she wasn't going to start talking about Lori and Mike. There was nothing more to say, nothing more to do. It wasn't that he didn't care. He had wished he could do more for Lori from the beginning. But there were still great gaps in medical knowledge. So much could be done and that was all. Still, the laymen, insisted on believing in miracles, and each wanted his own: looking into Joe's eyes, demanding miracles. Like Claire, watching him, her face pale, her eyes awash again with tears, whispering, "Joe please. What about Lori?"

What about Lori, he asked himself as he had done from the first time Mike brought her into the office. Mike, big, tough, gravelly-voiced, the prototype of the hard, demanding, aggressive male; Lori, so delicate and frail that it seemed she must break if Mike's shadow fell on her. Joe, accepting them both as he saw them, was certain that he understood the problem.

Lori, so recently a bride, was just too fragile for so robust a man. She was using illness, weakness, dizzy spells, self-induced weight loss, to slow Mike down.

Joe had any number of women like Lori as patients. They came to his office for attention and sympathy, for a good listening ear. They couldn't all go to psychiatrists, and few of them actually needed that. They just needed to be given tiny doses of stimulants, and large doses of reassurance. Within a few months, a year, they adjusted to their over-bearing husbands. He was sure that was the Lori who had first come into his office.

But suddenly, after many visits, after about six months, she sat across the desk from him and said, "Doctor, do you know, I think I'm a lot worse." And something happened inside of him. He felt a quick, questioning wrench, and cringed inside with recognition. A foul smell flooded his nostrils. He knew that he was looking at true, real, desperate illness, not a case of early marital maladjustment.

He got busy. Lori went into the hospital for the first of the diagnostic tests, but he was certain even then; there would be nothing he could do. And over the past six months, he had seen how wrong he had been about her. She was brave, gallant. She was strong. If ever there was a woman made for the Mike Mannings of this world, then Lori was that woman. And Joe had done what he could, for Lori, for Mike. Even for Claire . . .

He sighed, put the cigarette out, and left the car. He went up to the house, remembering his hands on Claire's breasts, his lips on hers and her strained words, "Oh God, I want you, Joe. But I can't. I just can't." He remembered how before he had had time to leash his desire, it had died, and when he left her, she had whispered, "I'm sorry, Joe."

As he let himself into the house, Ellen called to him. He went into the big living room.

She was sitting on the edge of the deep green sofa, hands clasped around a tall glass. She had on her face that expression of patient waiting that had always been a reproach to him, and always would be.

He said, "All right, Ellen. What's the matter now?"

"She wants fifty dollars, Joe."

"Gilly? What for?"

"How do I know?"

"You asked her, didn't you?"

Ellen sighed. "Of course I asked."

"Then?"

"She wouldn't tell me."

Joe accepted that without comment.

Ellen asked, "Do you want a drink?"

He nodded.

She got up, moving stiffly. Her yellow sheath dress clung to her, almost but not quite too snug. She mixed him a tall Scotch and soda, added a single ice cube, and brought the glass over to him. "It would have to be tonight," she said.

"What's special about tonight?"

"Thursday's bridge club. And you know it." When he looked at her, obviously not understanding, she went on, still patient, "Gilly started in on me while I was dressing. She got me so rattled . . ."

He grinned. "And the ladies are so serious about it. Okay, how much did you lose?"

"It was less than fifty dollars," Ellen retorted, sipping her drink.

She had been sitting before the vanity, thinking that she didn't really look forty-three years old, when Gilly's face suddenly appeared in the mirror.

"I want fififty dollars," she said. "I want it tonight."

"Fifty dollars? For what?"

"I just want it, Mother," Gilly said, that mulish expression pulling her pretty face awry.

Ellen, suddenly tense, the golden lipstick tube trembling at her lips, retorted, "That's no explanation. I think you'd better tell me why you want it."

"When I had my own bank account I didn't have to answer for every single penny I spent."

"And you know what happened, Gilly."

"I don't want to talk about that."

"We have to."

"No, we don't," Gilly answered, her patience obviously strained. "Really. What's the point of always making everything so complicated? All you have to do is write a check for me. That's simple enough, isn't it? Just write the check."

Ellen carefully re-capped the lipstick tube, carefully put it back in its place in the golden tray. "I don't think we ought to discuss it now, Gilly. I'm expecting three tables of bridge in about thirty minutes."

"We have to discuss it, Mother. I need it now."

"Why don't you ask your father?"

"Because I'm asking you."

"But you ought to ask him."

"What for? So he'll be the one to tell me no? Why are you always passing the buck?"

"I've already said no, haven't I? If I haven't, then consider it said."

Gilly's eyes narrowed until they seemed lost between taut folds of pale flesh. "Maybe the thing for me to do is go out to the club. Go ask that kid—what's his name again?—Oh, that's right: Bud Slater. Maybe I ought to ask Bud Slater."

Ellen swung around to face Gilly. The mirror's second-hand confrontation had suddenly become frightening. "Gilly, what on earth is that supposed to mean?"

"You know, Mother."

"I know? Why should I know? Why should he give you money? Anyway, which one is Bud . . . Bud Slater, is it?" She knew instantly she had made a mistake. She oughtn't to pretend she didn't remember Bud. Everyone at the club knew him. She went on quickly, "Oh, Bud. You mean that tall blond boy . . ."

"That tall blond boy," Gilly agreed. "And you know exactly what I'm talking about. I've seen the two of you together. All that gay girlish laughter from you."

Ellen felt the heat rising in her cheeks, tension creating tight iron bands at her temples. Gilly's implication was ridiculous! Of course Ellen had laughed with Bud, talked with him. Everyone did. He was a likable boy, good-looking and personable, and very friendly. As the tennis pro, he was around the club all the time. That was all there was to it, of course. She might once or twice have wondered what it would be like to ruffle his golden hair, to put her head against his broad chest. . . . But she had never, never. . . . And then she realized that what Gilly was saying was really blackmail. There just wasn't any other word for it. She said carefully, "Gilly, it's hard for me to believe that you're serious. Bud Slater is young enough—almost young enough, anyway, to be my son."

"He *is* young enough. So what?"

"And for you to imply . . ."

"Mother, I've *seen* you."

"What you have seen was always perfectly innocent, and I'm certain that you know that as well as I do."

But Ellen knew that although there had been nothing between her and Bud Slater, nothing except her own silly thoughts, he had had affairs with other women at the club. So many of the marriages were shaky. She wondered what had happened to them; she wondered what had happened to her and Joe. Ellen prided herself on a certain deep basic honesty, however, and she told herself that nothing had happened to her and Joe, that was the trouble. She had been second choice when he married her.

She remembered their first night together. She was dressed in satin, her bridal nightgown, waiting for Joe to join her, and she had gone into his wallet for something so trivial that she no longer recalled what it was. There, smiling up at her, she had found Belena. Belena . . . Ellen had carefully taken the picture out, torn it to shreds, and thrown the shreds away. Joe had never mentioned missing it; she had never mentioned destroying it. But she hadn't forgotten Belena's smiling face. Ellen had known then, as she knew now, that she was second to Belena always, and then when Gilly came, to Gilly. After Belena and Gilly, there were all of Joe's patients, unnamed, unknown to her, but still before her in Joe's heart . . .

She felt a hard hot spasm in her throat, and a tightening of the iron bands at her temples.

Gilly sighed. "All right, Mother. Whatever you say. But what about the fifty dollars?"

"Sorry. No."

"You shouldn't have dragged me back from Taos."

"You shouldn't have run away either."

"Why not? I want to live my own life."

"It's not time for that yet."

"When does it happen?" Gilly demanded. "When I'm ready? Or when *you* decide I'm ready?"

"You're just seventeen, Gilly."

"Old enough."

Ellen made herself smile. "You only think so. Some day you'll understand and thank me."

"You only think so," Gilly retorted, mimicking her, and ran out of the room.

Ellen swung around to face the mirror again. She looked forty-three, and more. She finished making up her face, and went into the living room as the first of the bridge club guests arrived.

But she couldn't concentrate on the too-serious bidding, on the fast moves. She kept thinking about Gilly, and Bud Slater. It was all mixed up in her mind. And buried deep was the feeling that maybe . . . maybe . . .

The girls finally departed, Doreen Upson chirping, "What's wrong with you tonight, Ellen?" and Ellen left everything in the game room as it was, even the lights on, for Tula to clear up in the morning. She retreated to the living room, where she tried to dissolve the iron bands at her temples with quick nervous sips of Scotch, and waited for Joe to come home.

And now he was saying, "I guess I'd better talk to her. Where is she?"

"In her room, I suppose."

"But why just suppose? Why don't you know?"

Ellen answered sharply, "I can't watch her every minute, Joe."

"Every minute isn't necessary, but——"

"Never mind that. What are you going to tell her?"

"Oh *I'm* to decide, is that it?"

"That's right."

"But she's *our* daughter, Ellen."

"That's right."

"Then . . .?"

"I've already told her I wouldn't do it."

"But why?" He sipped his drink. "It isn't really all that much, and if it keeps her satisfied . . ."

"Fifty dollars is quite a bit. And you know what Dr. Richards said."

"Oh, Ellen, all psychiatrists are half crazy."

"Maybe. But he's right about that: as soon as she gets the money together she'll take off again. I don't want to go through that twice, Joe. I just can't go through it twice."

"You found her and she was all right."

"All right, Joe?"

"You know what I mean."

Ellen knew. Gilly had been alive. Alive, and not pregnant, and not diseased. So Joe assumed that she was all right. But Joe had never understood how it was.

It was Ellen who had gone, shivering with humiliation, to ask for help, finally. Ellen who had had to describe Gilly; her clothes, her . . . her style, her interests. At last, despairing that the police could help her, it was

Ellen who had started the search that took her wandering through Haight-Ashbury in San Francisco, and down the coast to Monterey, and then, desperate, returning alone, she had heard someone mention the flower children of Taos. Taos. Just one hundred and sixty miles from home.

She drove there, and found Gilly living in a squalid adobe, going barefoot and dirty. She found Gilly living with a tall blond boy named David. Gilly cursed her and clawed her, but finally, threatened with the police, she came home, to remain ever since a stranger, though more docile now, which made Ellen wonder. Gilly docile? Why?

Joe didn't know how it had been. He was saying, "And if we don't give it to her, you know what could happen."

"She didn't do it for money, Joe. We all agreed on that. And she said so herself."

"But this time she could."

"I don't think so."

"But you can't be sure."

She remembered the beginning of it, very nearly two years before. She remembered the ring of the doorbell. She was home alone, as usual. She went to see who it was, uneasy as usual. Somehow she was always uneasy. She put on the foyer light and peered out. Gilly was standing there, and there was a man with her—a big, broad-shouldered man who somehow seemed familiar. She flung the door open.

"Gilly? Why didn't you come in . . ." Her voice faded away. Something was obviously wrong. The big man's rugged face was lined with painful embarrassment.

He cleared his throat twice. "Mrs. Stevens, I'm Mike Manning. Do you remember me?"

She knew him finally: the policeman she and Joe had found wounded and taken to the hospital. Somewhere in the house they had pictures of the Mayor giving Joe a medal. Joe had looked as detached as always, as if Mike Manning's life hadn't mattered. Then it hit her. Mike Manning was a policeman, and he was holding fifteen-year-old Gilly's arm, holding it tightly.

Ellen asked, "What's the matter, Mr. Manning?"

Gilly cried, "He's sticking his big nose into my affairs. I never asked him for any favors. If there's anything I hate——"

He gave her a little shake. "You've said more than enough, Gilly. Be quiet now." To Ellen he said, "Listen, is Dr. Stevens in? I think he should be here."

"No," Ellen responded, thinking that of course he wouldn't know that Joe was rarely at home. Not that he couldn't be, of course. Joe didn't make house calls, but somehow, even without that burden, he managed to spend his time away. He managed to absent himself in body, just as he always absented himself in spirit when he was there; so it didn't matter all that much. And she suddenly thought that there was something else she ought to remember about Mike Manning. It fluttered through her mind and was gone before she could seize it. Suddenly, recollecting herself, she cried, "But come on in. Why are we just standing here?" She stepped back. "Come in, Gilly."

Gilly seemed to brace herself. She was shorter then, very thin. Her hair was cut into bangs that hung wildly about her wide defiant eyes.

Mike Manning gave her another shake. "Let's go," he said, in the voice he must use so many times on his job that it was second nature to him. It had to be, for him to use that particular tone with Gilly.

She grimaced, "You brought me home, so now why don't you leave?"

He walked past Ellen, hesitated.

"Straight ahead," she told him, closing the door behind them.

"You can let me go now," Gilly demanded.

He dropped her arm. "Look, Mrs. Stevens, I think your husband should be here too. I'd feel better about it."

"It doesn't make any difference," Gilly cried. "I know what you're going to do."

Ellen went to the phone. "I'll try to find him, Mr. Manning."

He nodded, sat down, stiff and uncomfortable in the petit point chair. "We'll wait for him."

And that was what they did. She plied Mike with questions, offered him drinks. He ignored the first, refused the second. Finally Joe came home . . .

Now Joe was saying, "I don't think she'll ever do that again, Ellen. But it's a calculated risk, isn't it?"

Ellen shrugged.

"If we give her the fifty she might run away again. If we don't, she might end up in Jasons stealing for profit instead of for kicks."

"She was fifteen when she did that."

"Is she any better now?"

Ellen shrugged again. "How do I know? Decide, Joe."

"Give her the check."

"I said I wouldn't. You'd better do it."

"It has to be on my shoulders, doesn't it? Anything that happens has to be because I decided, I took the responsibility."

"You're her father."

"And you're her mother."

"I sometimes wonder if somebody, somehow, somewhere, pulled a switch on me. If Gilly is really mine."

"You sound as if you mean that, Ellen." His voice was cold with reproof.

She wasn't supposed to feel that way, much less say it aloud. No matter what one's child did, one must stand behind her. Everyone said so. Mike Manning, Dr. Richards, the books . . .

"I just don't understand her," Ellen said. "She's brilliant, Joe. The tests all show that. She could do anything she wanted to. And she doesn't want to do anything."

"It's a stage."

Ellen tried to tell herself that they were right. Gilly was in a stage. She would outgrow whatever drove her. Gilly, suddenly, at seventeen and a half, or eighteen, any day now, Gilly would become a true daughter.

But trying to believe didn't create belief. Ellen knew that Gilly would always be a cool presence between her and Joe, pitting them against each other, exploiting their weaknesses and timidities, their shames . . .

Ellen said, "Do what you think best, Joe."

"I'll give it to her, and have a talk with her."

"And if she takes off, you go after her this time. Promise me that?"

He smiled. "If it makes you feel better, I promise I will. If I have to. And if I can."

"Don't qualify it. You mustn't qualify a promise, Joe."

"I'm afraid I have to this time."

She finished her drink, went to the sideboard to mix another. "One more for you?"

"Yes, please. Nightcap, and stage prop." He smiled

again. "It won't be so formal that way. The stern parent bit, I mean. When I talk to her."

Ellen didn't answer. She gave him the drink, not quite looking at him.

He knew what she was thinking—that he never played the stern parent bit with Gilly. She had never understood how he felt. Gilly was his daughter, his own, his flesh. He had made her. Of course Ellen had, too. But the difference in their natures explained the difference in their reactions. Ellen never felt that Gilly was an extension of herself in the way that he felt Gilly to be an extension of himself. Perhaps, in that, Dr. Richards had been right. Perhaps Joe had expected too much from her, expected what he would expect from himself, and perhaps, at the same time, he had indulged her too much. Still, he knew that some freedom wouldn't hurt her, would only help her grow. She had plenty of time yet. She could always go to college a year later. He just had to wait for her to get over the awkward age and she would be all right.

Ellen said, "Will you be coming to bed soon?"

"In a little while. I want to read for a few minutes after I've talked to Gilly."

He went down the corridor, tapped at the door.

Gilly mumbled something. He went in.

She was sprawled on the bed, staring grimly at the pink ceiling.

He said, "Hi," and smiled, and sat down beside her.

"Mother tell you all about it?"

"She told me what she knew."

Gilly groaned, "Oh, don't you start too. I just need fifty dollars."

"Your mother's afraid you're going to pull another disappearing act."

"I'm not going to."

"Promise?"

"I promise." She paused. "Not now, anyhow." She sat up. "Can I have it?"

"It's quite a lot of money."

She made a rude sound.

He felt completely helpless, and his tone was sharp when he said, "Gilly, can't you at least try to be a lady?"

"Sorry." But she was grinning. "You're going to give it to me, aren't you?"

"Yes. I am."

"Good," she chortled, and put our her hand. "Now?"

It was dawn when the phone rang.

Joe's arm was out, reaching, at the first sound. He fumbled the receiver, caught it, pressed it to his ear. "Stevens here."

He listened, spoke a few words, hung up.

Ellen stirred, whispered, "Joe? What is it?"

"Go back to sleep."

"Are you going out?"

"Just into the study to make a phone call."

"It's not Gilly, is it, Joe?"

"Of course not."

"Okay."

She was still again, sinking back immediately into drugged sleep.

He was glad. After the scene she had put on the night before, the headache she had gotten as a result, she needed her rest. He hoped they would both quickly forget those ridiculous few minutes.

He got into his robe. He washed his face with cold water before he went to the study.

Dialing, he wished there were some automatic way to notify the family. It was uncivilized that the doctor should have to handle that part of it, too. When the patient was gone, the doctor was done.

A buzz of sound began and ended swiftly. He pulled a deep hard breath into his lungs.

"Mike?" he said. "Listen, Mike, this is Joe Stevens."

CHAPTER 5

He had been partly dressed, lying on the bed, enshrouded by the noncommittal dark. The phone was nearby.

When he heard it ring, it was as if he had heard it ring a hundred times before. He was rehearsed, ready for Joe's voice.

Still, with the words said, the connection broken, he found that reality was no different from anticipation. He didn't believe it any more than he had believed it earlier.

He found his jacket and shoes, and put them on. He got his gun from the top drawer of the dresser, and slid it into its holster. He carefully checked the lock when he left the apartment.

He drove swiftly through the pale glimmer of dawn. With no memory of how he had gotten there, or how long it had taken, he parked in the hospital driveway. As he left the car, a glass door swung open.

Al Kelly strode out. He recognized Mike from years before, from those days when Mike had been a young cop, just on the beat, and Al had been an old one, too long on the beat. He began a friendly grin before he had a good look at Mike's face, remembering, suddenly, the time of day, and the many times he had seen Mike go in and out. Al's grin faded. He held the door open, and mumbled a tentative hello.

Mike's stony eyes touched Al briefly. He nodded in thanks for the courtesy, and in wordless recognition. He didn't know Al's name, but he knew the face. But by the time his long legs brought him to the elevator, he had forgotten Al Kelly.

Al, watching the big doors slide shut, considered briefly. He had been through it himself. Twice. He knew what it was like. He went into the phone booth.

Drifting upward, Mike found himself choking, and realized that he had been holding his breath. He had been holding it so hard that something hurt in his chest, and there was a strange sour ringing in his ears.

The elevator glided to a stop. The door slid open. He automatically began the walk down the long silent corridor.

He had gotten halfway when Miss Dacey stepped out of a shadowed recess, and gasped, "Oh, Mr. Manning!"

He nodded and kept going, his eyes on the door ahead, on the small yellow card.

She touched his arm. He broke stride, but went on. She trotted along beside him, tugging at his sleeve until he stopped.

"Will you wait back at the station, please? I'll call Dr. Barnham."

"What for?"

She looked at some point just past Mike's ear. "I assume you've heard from Dr. Stevens. I just want to say that I—we all are very very sorry."

Mike jerked his head once. "I heard from him. That's why I'm here."

"Your wife was very very brave, very sweet, Mr. Manning. It was a privilege to have known her."

"I want to see her," Mike said.

"Not *now*, Mr. Manning." The hand on his arm urged him back along the hall, but she might as well have tried to shift the mountains behind the hospital. "There are certain formalities, you understand. Please do let me call Dr. Barnham."

"Can he do anything now?" Mike asked.

Miss Dacey gave Mike a helpless look. The white cap nestled in her hair trembled like a frightened dove.

"I want to see her," he repeated.

"Mr. Manning, that just isn't possible right now. Things must be done. . . . Please. Please."

He went around her. The yellow card was no longer on the door. He stared at the empty bracket for the space of two breaths, then shoved the door open and went in. Miss Dacey was at his heels, though he wasn't aware of her then.

The empty room was full of reflected sunrise. The empty bed was stripped and bare.

He backed away and bumped into Miss Dacey. He apologized automatically.

"Oh, that's all right," she said, her voice full of professional cheer. "Shall we go back to the station now? I'll call Dr. Barnham, and he'll——"

"Where is she?"

"She?"

"My wife."

Miss Dacey was startled. She had been misled by his brief apology into thinking that he had become the usual tractable bereaved. She had even been prepared to offer some further cooing reassurance. Now she knew better. She said, "Your wife has been taken downstairs, Mr. Manning."

But his yard-eating amble had already lengthened into full stride as he headed for the elevator.

She raced along behind him on whispering rubber soles, murmuring, "Mr. Manning! Now listen, Mr. Manning. There's a routine. Dr. Barnham must talk to you."

He stopped, swung around. "Then why the hell don't you get him?"

She went to the station, picked up the phone, and her voice was a distant hiss, saying words Mike couldn't understand.

As he waited, he remembered that he had said to Lori, "Tell me about it tomorrow." Tomorrow was now; she couldn't tell him about it. What would she have said? Why hadn't he listened then?

He felt a hand on his arm.

"Mr. Manning, are you all right?" Miss Dacey was asking.

For the first time his stony eyes really saw her. Her white-lipped mouth was quivering. There were tears on her lashes.

His knees suddenly weakened. He let himself lean on the desk. He said slowly, "Sure, I'm all right."

At the sound of footsteps, he turned.

Dr. Barnham was young, brisk, a man in a gray flannel suit wearing a white tunic and white trousers and white shoes. He had a stethoscope hanging around his neck instead of an attache case under his arm.

He led Mike into a small, misty green office, and pressed him into a chair. He stated precise regrets, shuffled forms, and then took a deep breath. "Now then, Mr. Manning, this is your consent." He placed a card beneath Mike's hand, a pen in his fingers. "For a post-mortem examination to be performed on your wife."

"Post-mortem," Mike repeated. "What for?"

"We like to do it, Mr. Manning."

"You like to?"

Dr. Barnham said nothing.

"You know why she died," Mike said.

Spoken aloud, the words had a peculiar blinding quality. The misty green of the room darkened. There was no air for breath. Mike hung suspended in a conscious faint for what seemed like endless moments.

Dr. Barnham was saying casually, "Oh, yes. Of course we know why she died."

Mike found air to breathe and the blood beat hard in his veins, and his vision suddenly sharpened. He saw that Dr. Barnham was very young behind the ginger mustache he wore.

"Then if you know . . .?" Mike asked.

"There's a lot to be learned, Mr. Manning."

"You're talking about an autopsy to learn from Lori?"

Dr. Barnham sat a bit straighter. "It's just a——"

"Formality," Mike said. "The usual routine."

"So if you'll just sign at the bottom there . . . Then we can go on to the next——it won't take long at all. . . . I'm sure you're——"

"No."

"Mr. Manning," Dr. Barnham said, "I know this is a difficult time for you. You must, however, try to think of all the others who might benefit from what we could learn."

Mike shoved the form away from him. "No. That's final. She's had enough done to her."

"Mr. Manning . . ."

"I will not sign."

"We're not alone in this world. We owe——"

Mike rose, fists at his side. "If you're finished with me, then I want to see her."

"Sit down, Mr. Manning. We're a long way from finished."

"I'm not." But Mike did sit down.

Names, dates, histories. A hundred meaningless questions. A repetition of what had been supplied a dozen times before, entered on countless other forms and lost in them.

Mike signed the last one and rose. "I want to see her, Dr. Barnham."

"I'm sorry. That's not possible. This evening . . . at the funeral home . . ."

"Now. I won't wait until this evening. I want to see her now."

Dr. Barnham smoothed his ginger mustache, and got to his feet. "I'm sorry, Mr. Manning."

Mike beat him to the door. "What about her things?"

"The nurse on the floor will have them all ready for you."

Mike found Miss Dacey bent over her morning reports.

"All set, I hope," Miss Dacey said.

"My wife's things."

"Oh, yes. Of course. They've all been gathered together and sent down."

"Sent down where?"

"The Property Office, Mr. Manning."

"Where's that?"

"The second floor. I'm sorry that makes another errand for you. The aides automatically do it when they clear out the room."

He thanked her, turned away.

He didn't know she was thinking that it was too bad she'd never see him again. He was a lot of man, and she could imagine him in bed, and it wouldn't be long before he was thinking of that himself. She said, "Take it easy, Mr. Manning."

He swung back. "I guess I've been a lot of trouble. I'm sorry."

"I know," she told him.

He looked at the white cap nestling in her hair. "I don't know how you stand it."

"I have to. Just as you have to."

"Does it get easier?"

"For me? Or for you?"

"Either of us." But he knew the answer from her question. He didn't wait to hear what she would say. He gave her a last nod and got into the elevator.

On the second floor, at the Property Office, he gave his name. He waited through a long scurry among paper bags that echoed the whispering rubbed-soled shoes. One girl looked through the cupboards, two munched doughnuts and sipped coffee and peered at him over the rims of their paper cups.

He gave his name again. He gave the time of death again. At last a brown paper bag was thrust at him, a form to sign. He got to the lobby at the same time as Miguelito.

Miguelito said, "You were supposed to call me, Mike."

"I forgot." Then, "How did you know?"

"Al Kelly phoned downtown and got my number."

"Al Kelly?"

"The guard here. He saw you come in. He said you were alone. What about Claire?"

"I haven't let her know yet."

"We'd better, Mike."

"Soon."

"Let's get some coffee."

"Okay."

"And we'd better get over to the funeral home, too."

"I guess so."

"Mike?"

"I'm okay. Let's go."

"In here," Jerry Dormet said. He moved quickly, so that he could close the door behind them and seal away the terrible sound of a woman's shrieking.

The momentary silence had its own abrasive quality.

Mike sank into a deep chair. Miguelito stood beside him.

Jerry Dormet retreated behind the barricade of a highly polished mahogany desk, and said gently, "There are just these few questions I must ask you, and then you'll want to pick out a casket."

"I want to see her," Mike said.

Jerry Dormet looked shocked. "Oh no, not yet."

"Now."

Miguelito growled, "Mike, listen . . ."

"This afternoon," Jerry Dormet said quickly. "Say . . . four o'clock. Yes. Four o'clock, Mr. Manning."

Mike subsided, clenched fists on his thighs. "All right. What questions?"

THE DEATH WATCH

David came awake hard, the breath rough in his throat, his mouth dusty dry, his heart trip-hammering at his ribs.

It wasn't the first time he had fought his way out of sleep. He supposed it wouldn't be the last. If there had been a dream, it had gone now and he didn't remember it. He was quite willing to leave it forgotten.

He licked his lips and waited to feel like himself, to shed awareness of the unwelcome stranger who dwelled within him. Slowly, too slowly, the shadowed room settled. Morning sun rippled on the whitewashed adobe walls and streaked the concrete floor. A bee hummed at the broken screen, was silent during its successful invasion, and then did a loop-de-loop near the ceiling. A haze of dust drifted near the window. The half-unpacked suitcase spilled a waterfall of garments. Gilly had been at it, rooting for something of his to wear for sleep. She'd settled finally on an old red plaid shirt, and hadn't worn it long.

Beside him, she sighed and stirred and was still again.

He thought hungrily of breakfast, but didn't move. It was good to think ahead. Honeydew melon. Bacon. Eggs. Rye bread and whipped butter. Coffee with cream. A glass of milk.

He had bought a few absolute necessities with part of that five dollars from Claire. Now he wished he hadn't spent it. He should have given her the money back right then. She would have understood that he hadn't intended to mention the money and ask about Gilly's father in the same breath. It had simply happened before he could stop himself. Maybe Claire would really find him a job. Then he could pay her back and it would be okay. The crazy thing was he could have managed without Claire's money after all.

THE DEATH WATCH

Gilly had come back the night before, grinning at him over a sack of groceries. Honeydew. Bacon. Huge tomatoes. Beautiful stuff, but not necessities. She'd pouted when he pointed that out. The fifty dollars had to go far, far, far.

She'd said, "Oh, don't spoil it, David."

"How much do you have left?"

"Twenty dollars."

He groaned, "Gilly! Gilly, you mean this stuff cost you thirty dollars?"

"Haven't you heard about inflation lately?"

"Oh, come on, Gilly."

She grinned at him. "The truth is, I held back a few bucks. Just for myself, David. And I'm not going to give them to you."

"It's your money," he shrugged.

"No it isn't. It's my father's money."

And that reminded David of the day before again. Joe Stevens going into Claire's house . . .

"Did you have trouble getting it?" David asked her.

"Not much." She grinned again. "I know how to ask."

"Is it all right for you to be out now?"

"What do you think?"

"I'm wondering, Gilly."

She demanded in a thin cold voice, "Am I in your way, David? If I am, just say the word. I'll take off. I'll go so far nobody'll ever find me again."

"Gilly, hey, Gilly . . ."

She giggled, "I'm going to stay all night, David."

He knew better than to argue. He hugged her close, eyes going to the covered statue. He'd still have Friday, Saturday, Sunday, Monday, Tuesday. There'd be time. There had to be time.

127

Now she said suddenly, "Like it was in Taos, waking up beside you."

He turned his head. Her wide open eyes peered at him. Blue, pale pale blue, with odd points of light. Diamond eyes.

"I didn't know you were awake, Gilly."

"I know you didn't. I've been lying here, watching you and feeling you."

"Long?"

"Not so very long."

"Aren't they going to worry about you?"

"Probably."

"Maybe you ought to call."

"No."

"Why not? We don't want to make trouble now, Gill."

"We're not going to."

"If you don't turn up . . ."

"Oh, I'll go home, and they can see me, touch me, yell at me. But later." She stretched and sighed. "I don't want to think about them now, David."

"Okay," he yawned. "Think of me."

"I am."

"What're you thinking?"

She was suddenly too still. It took her too long to answer. He rolled on his side, one elbow tucked under his cheek. "Gilly?"

"It won't last," she said softly. "You and me. The two of us this way. We won't be able to make it."

"Tell me that in ten years, Gilly."

"No, David. I can feel it."

"Hey, Gilly."

"They'll wreck us. Somehow, between the two of them, they'll smash us to pieces."

He rose up over her and pressed his lips to her still-moving mouth. Her hands cupped the back of his head, and her words became small quick breaths at his searching tongue. Their bodies melted together as if there were no barrier of skin between them, no separate flesh and tendon, no individually activated bone. They lived on a single beating heart. He supposed that was why, how, she knew. Why she so suddenly turned her head aside and shoved him away.

But he asked, "What's the matter, Gilly?"

"You're not thinking of me here. You're thinking of me there."

"There?"

"On the table. That me."

"I ought to work."

"I know. I *know*." Shrill, angry, she flung back the sheet so hard that her hand, continuing on, slammed into his chest.

He caught her wrist. "Hey, Gilly, take it easy."

But suddenly she laughed and rolled over on him, her fingers playing piano on his ribs. "Skinny," she said. "You are too goddam skinny. Why don't you eat more, David? Why don't you fatten up? I like fat men."

"Come on," he yelped, thrashing and reaching for her. "Come on. Quit that." Captured, hands in his, body between his legs, she went limp, the light of laughter fading from her eyes. "Give in?" he whispered.

She nodded against his chest.

"This is the way it'll be with us, Gilly. When we're married."

"We're not going to get married."

"Sure we are. And it won't be long."

"I don't want to, David. I just want to be with you.

This way its right. But not with a ring. Not with a noose around my neck and yours."

"No nooses, I promise."

"You can't, David."

"I can. I do."

"No," she said.

He let it go. When the time came, he'd be able to convince her. He'd make her see the small gold ring he'd put on her finger was necessary to protect them both against the interfering world.

"You're thinking about it again," she whispered.

"Not yet. But I should."

"Please don't, David. Not today. Let's just be together today. Don't think about it."

"I have to, Gilly. It's for us. You know it is. I explained it all."

"Will you let me see it?"

"Not yet. But pretty soon."

"I want to see it, David. It's me, isn't it?"

"Only the facade, the form. You're more. If I could only show how much more."

He was thinking about the day. First, he'd return the five dollars to Claire, and he could remind her about the job.

Gilly chuckled suddenly.

"What?" he asked.

"You're sweet." Her tongue made a small moist circle on his chest. "My, you *are* sweet David. Chocolate, and licorice and strawberry shortcake."

"Thank you." His arms tightened around her. "I tell you what. You take a shower first, and I'll start breakfast. I'm so hungry I'm growling inside."

"I don't want a shower."

"Why not?"

"I don't want to be clean."

"But it feels good to be clean."

"You're so straight, David."

"Me?" he laughed.

"You. Be clean. Be good. Be married. You're just like *them*."

"Me?" he repeated.

"You," she laughed.

"I'm just trying to get by. And using my head to do it."

"Exactly like them," she told him, and the laughter was gone. Something old and terrible peered at him from her eyes. "You should just try to *be*. And use your heart to do it."

"But it's just part of living, Gilly."

The old and terrible something to which he had not dared put a name was suddenly gone from her eyes. She chortled, "And here's another part," and pressed against him.

His heart expanded inside him. He rolled with her, thighs twined, the bones of her hips sharp and sweet, her small breasts below his heart, the two bodies now a single heaving unit sweating in quickening rhythm.

While something within David sang, Gilly suddenly raised her head, grinned, "There's nothing like a good screw to make you forget you're hungry."

The singing in David soured and stopped. He went still. "Damn you, Gilly. You're just trying to be disgusting. And you are."

"*We* are disgusting," she said, grinning again.

"Gilly, no."

"David, yes." Mockery in her whisper, but tears in her eyes.

He held her close to him, their bodies still melted together, but their hearts beating singly now, and he knew he had never felt more alone in his life. "Why, Gilly? Why did you do that?"

She rolled her hips under his.

"No, Gilly. Why do you have to hurt me?"

"I didn't mean to. I only wanted to show you that we're machines. You. Me. Everybody. We're all just machines. Press a button, a spot. Touch it, lick it, stroke it. Press that button and see what happens?"

"No," he whispered.

"I didn't make it that way. Don't blame me, David. You just don't want to believe."

"I can't."

She rolled her hips again. "You want further proof? Give me a minute."

He pulled away from her. "I'm going to give you breakfast."

"David," she wailed. "Don't."

"It's done."

He threw the sheet over her. But she came out of it, arms reaching through the tangle, and caught him, and wrestled him down with her. Surprisingly strong for all her thinness, and eager and agile, in a moment they were joined again, her tears salty on his lips, the tangle of her hair veiling her intent face, their bodies striving together for release and finding it.

And moments later, while the pounding stilled, he

heard her say, "You know what I wish, David? You know what I want right now?"

"What, Gill?" he asked sluggishly.

"Some pot. That's what I wish I had. That's what I want. Right now."

"You had better put in an appearance at home," he said over bacon and eggs.

"I suppose," she agreed.

"Because if you don't, they might call the police."

"Maybe," she agreed again.

"We don't want any trouble now, Gilly."

"No. I guess not." Then she looked at him sideways. "But that's not what you're thinking about. Not really. You just want to work on it. And you want me out of here."

"I *do* want to work," he admitted.

"When can I see it, David?"

He groaned, "Gilly, hey, not that again."

"But I want to, David."

"When it's finished, Gilly."

"And when will that be?"

"Soon." He grinned at her. "Can't you even wait until 'soon'?"

"I don't want to."

"It won't be long."

She was quiet for a little while. Then she said, "David, we ought to get back to Taos. Now. While we can."

"But we can't now. That's the thing. Do you think I don't want to?"

"I don't know, David. I wonder."

"Don't wonder. I *do* want to, Gill. But we have to know what we're doing."

"Head instead of heart," she mocked him. "Do you think we know what we're doing, David?"

He said, "Yes. Yes. I know what we're doing." But later, after she had gone, he kept wondering about that.

CHAPTER 6

"I got some money last night after all," David said, putting a five dollar bill into Claire's hand, "so I thought I'd bring this back."

Her swollen amber eyes regarded him blankly. Her slim throat worked, convulsing around soundless words. She was wearing a black shirt and a black skirt, and with them, she seemed to have put on a veil of age. There were new lines in her face, and her mouth had a curious tucked-in look.

He had always thought of her as older, of course, though conspicuously attractive at the same time. But now a malicious brush had painted a few harsh strokes, and what had once been attractive was not.

He took a step back, stammered, "I mean, since I didn't really need it, I thought I'd return it. And then, about the job, maybe if you get a chance today . . ."

She nodded, but continued to stare at him blankly. "It's okay. Thank you, David."

"I hope I'm not bothering you. If I am, I'll go . . ."

"No."

He asked unwillingly, "Is something wrong, Claire?"

"Its Lori. My sister-in-law. She died this morning."

This time it was David who swallowed convulsively.

Died. . . . Pain corkscrewed through him. His brother's painted face, plump and placid, all hunger and horror pumped and waxed and colored away. When David found breath again, he asked, "But what happened?" The same question he had asked when they told him about his brother. But what happened?

"She was sick," Claire whispered. "She died."

"I'm sorry." A sudden blush burned his cheekbones. Gilly's father had been there the day before. Claire's sister-in-law had been sick. Maybe he had had something to tell Claire. Maybe he. . . . "I'm sorry," David repeated. "Can I do anything for you?"

Claire shook her head.

"Maybe you want me to take you some place?"

"I'm waiting for a call. I don't know where he is—my brother, I mean. I don't know what's happening. I don't know what to do."

"Your brother?" David repeated.

"Mike."

David shook his head helplessly.

"Miguelito said to wait here, so that's what I'm doing. He always knows. That's how he is. And he said stay here. But it's awful, being alone like this. Wondering . . ."

David edged back another step. She seemed, suddenly, to have forgotten he was there. She was looking past him, out at the emptiness of the patio.

"Would you want me to stay with you?" he asked finally, his feet itching to be away and gone down the steet.

"No, thank you," she answered, and with that, she closed the door.

She leaned against it, her forehead on the painted

wood. She heard him sigh, heard the scuff of retreating footsteps. She supposed she hadn't been very kind to him, but there had been no kindness left in her.

Tears gathered in her eyes, and spilled down her cheeks. She wiped at them, and found she was still holding the five dollar bill he had returned to her. She opened her cold fingers, allowed it to fall to the floor.

Lori, gone now. Gone now, too, that last faint hope. The ridiculous hope that Joe could save her.

Where was Joe? Why hadn't he called.

A sudden sweat beaded Claire's brow and the short black curls grew wet. The adobe walls seemed to buckle and shrink, folding in upon themselves. Her flesh shrank, too, and trembled, and burned, sensitive nerve endings unable to discriminate between terror and lust. She stumbled to the desk, sank into the chair.

Where was he? Where was Joe?

It was Friday. Friday was their day—evening, really. Friday after hospital rounds was her time. Hers and his. Theirs.

She rose and stumbled to the phone to automatically dial the number she knew though she had never called it before.

Bradford said, "Dr. Stevens' office."

Claire swallowed and choked and was still.

"Dr. Stevens' office," Bradford repeated.

Claire knew her without ever having seen her, knew her to be a nonentity whose presence left no impact on Joe, so that he had never said her name to Claire, never described her. It was through Mike's eyes that Claire knew Bradford, through Lori's words that Claire understood her.

"Dr. Stevens' office," Bradford said for the third

time, sharper by then, suspicious, but still cool enough.

"Dr. Stevens, please," Claire managed.

"Who's calling?" Bradford demanded.

Claire swallowed again and whispered, "This is Claire Manning." *Okay, make something of that, you fat officious bitch!*

"Is this an emergency? The doctor is with a patient now."

"Manning," Claire repeated.

"Manning?"

Inflectionless, empty, without recognition.

"Lori Manning's sister-in-law. Mike Manning's sister. Surely you know that . . ."

"Manning," Bradford said once more.

"Put me through to Joe," Claire cried. "I have to talk to him."

There was a brief humming silence. It seemed for a moment as if the connection had been broken.

Then Bradford said, "Oh, yes. Manning. Just a minute, please."

And at the end of the same breath, Joe's voice came through, "Claire, what's the matter?"

She peered in astonishment at the phone. "The matter? But you know. You *do* know, don't you, Joe?"

"You mean Lori."

He sounded relieved.

She imagined his disciplined mouth saying the words. She pictured his wide open, direct, honest blue eyes. She saw his hands, lean and tanned, go tight with disapproval. She had known for a long time, she now realized, that his hands were far more expressive than his eyes.

She said, "Lori. Of course. Yes. That's what I mean."

"You must try to help Mike, Claire."

"But how can I? I don't know where he is. I don't know what he's doing. I don't . . ." Her voice shivered and broke. "Oh, Joe, what am I going to do?"

He sounded far away and cold. "There's not much you can do, is there?"

"Is he all right?"

"Of course."

"You saw him?"

"No. I called him. This morning. When it happened. There was nothing to see him for."

"But why didn't you call me, Joe? You should have. Did you think I don't care? Did you think it wasn't important to me? Or didn't you remember me at all?"

"I have a patient waiting, Claire."

"Yes," she said. "Of course. Bradford told me. I understand."

"But later perhaps . . ."

"You mean tonight?" Friday, Friday, Friday . . .

She wondered if Bradford were listening. She wondered if Joe were thinking of that.

"Claire? I want to talk to you about Mike."

Oh yes, she thought, Joe had thought about Bradford all right.

The knowledge was all that made it possible for Claire to say, "I don't know where I'll be tonight."

"Then I'll phone you."

"Yes," she said. "Do that, Joe. I really need to talk to you about Mike."

· As she put down the phone, she heard a sound from the patio. She went to the door.

139

THE DEATH WATCH

Mike was kneeling in the dust, big shoulders bowed, barrel chest caved in. He raised his dark, crew-cut head, and the angle of jutting nose and square jaw made him seem unaccountably sweet. He looked at her for a moment, then rose, a beer can in each hand.

"Mickey," she cried, "oh Mickey, what in God's name are you doing?"

"I don't know," he said, looking at her helplessly. "They ought to clean this place up some time. You don't have to live like this, do you?"

"Come in. Please. Please stop that and come in."

"It's all right." He bent his head, and the angle changed. His face hardened, but at the same time, it was suddenly alight with silent laughter. "I'm not losing my mind, Claire. It just bothered me, and I thought, 'What the hell, somebody's got to collect the debris. Why not me?' "

"You've been alone all this time, and Miguelito said he'd be with you."

Mike moved past her into the house. "I just left him. He had to go in. Time didn't stop when Lori died."

"Mickey!"

"Sorry, Claire." He stood in the middle of the floor, as if awaiting a cue.

"Sit down, Mickey. I'll get you some coffee."

"I've had more than I can drink of it." But he sat in the big chair and stretched his legs, making the habitual adjustment that settled his shoulder holster.

"What can I do, Mike?"

"It's all been done. But in a little while, maybe half an hour or so, I'm going back to the chapel. They said they'd let me see her. I haven't see her yet, Claire."

"Mickey, what's the use?"

140

"I have to."

"You look tired, Mike."

"It seems like a long time since Joe called."

"There's always a lot to do, isn't there? If only you'd let me help you."

"It was stuff I had to do myself, Claire."

She shivered. "Listen, Mickey, you . . . you're going to be okay, aren't you?"

"I think so."

It was not as firm a reassurance as she'd hoped for, as she needed, but she didn't know what else to say. And then, in the small silence, she heard the whisper of Lori's voice . . .

"Take off your jacket," Claire said.

He looked at her, dark eyes blank, dark brows lifting in a quizzical arch.

"Take it off, Mike. I want to sew those buttons on."

If he heard Lori's voice, he didn't say so. He shrugged the jacket off, handed it to Claire.

She found needle and thread and went to work. Head bent, with the first firm loop made, she asked, "The funeral?"

"Tomorrow at ten."

"And everything else?"

"Done."

"Clothes, Mickey?"

"Done," he repeated, wincing.

"You should have let me."

"Miguelito and I managed, Claire."

"Oh, Mickey . . ."

"You're too young."

"Mickey!"

She thought, for just a moment, that he would laugh.

141

She waited in terror for the sound of it, and for the sobs that must inevitably follow.

But he said, "I had to do it myself. I wanted to."

"You talked to Joe, of course."

Mike didn't answer.

She looked up from the needle and thread, her amber eyes full of unspoken questions.

Mike saw them and waited, but she didn't make the translation into words.

He said finally, "I talked to him when he called to tell me."

She looked as if she were holding her breath.

Mike noticed, just as he had noticed that she had had to say Joe's name. He filed both items away for future thought.

She said, "I thought maybe you'd seen Joe."

"No. I didn't see him. I didn't need him, Claire."

But Mike was certain she had lied, that she had known he hadn't seen Joe. It was one more item to be filed away.

She said unwillingly, "I guess there wasn't anything he could do."

Mike suddenly grinned. "You're learning. You may be all right. When you finally grow up."

She bit off the thread with an angry click of straight white teeth. "I want to go with you."

"What?"

"When you go back to the funeral home."

He paused, considered. "Okay. If you're sure."

"Of course, Mickey."

"I *am* okay."

"I know." She looked at him over the jacket. "I know, Mickey. But just the same . . ."

She thrust the jacket at him. "All set. Just tell me when you want to go."

He pushed himself to his feet. "Now, Claire."

The perfumed air of the chapel was anaesthetic, the dim hush a small preview of the sleep of death.

Lori lay in her casket, her face unbearably young over the pale blue of her burial dress.

Mike leaned over her, casting a pale shadow. He whispered, "I shouldn't have let it happen, Lori."

Claire touched his arm, protesting wordlessly.

He looked up at her. "Not dying. I couldn't have stopped her from dying. I know that, Claire. She had to die. People die all the time. But not this way."

"You did all you could, Mike. Lori would tell you. I'm sure she *did* tell you."

"That, yes. I let her tell me that. But not the rest. The important part. What it was like. What she felt and saw and knew. I wouldn't let her. I didn't have the guts to listen."

"You knew," Claire told him. "You were with her all the way. It didn't have to be said."

He wasn't listening then either. He said softly, his eyes on Lori's face, "It was all chance, you see. Just that, and nothing more."

All chance. He had been a healthy man all his life. He had known no doctors until the night he and Miguelito had been shot. Which was how Joe Stevens had come into his life—by saving it.

And it was chance again that had brought Joe back into his life a year later.

Mike and Miguelito had come into the station at midnight, both tired and thinking of home and bed. From

143

a side corridor, the vilest language he had heard in a long time spewed forth shrilly.

Shadows leaped and struggled against the frosted glass door.

Miguelito said with his cougar's grin, "It sounds like trouble."

"What's all that about?" Mike asked the man on the desk.

"You'd have to see it to believe it," was the unhappy answer. "And it looks as if you're going to see it right now." The wide red face was turned toward the door, wry with apprehension and disgust.

The door burst open. A slim teenager entered, pulling angrily at the restraining hands that clasped her wrists.

Mike caught a glimpse of wide-apart blue eyes and a high brow under chestnut bangs. He asked the desk man, "What's it about?"

"They brought her in three, four hours ago. Shop-lifting in a big way. A couple of leather coats, a bunch of other stuff. In two paper bags. She wasn't really try-ing to get away with anything."

"And . . .?"

"No identification on her. And she won't come across with a name or address. We've had a call in for Juvenile for two hours and some, but they're in the middle of a big night. So we have to wait. If we survive it."

Mike turned and looked at her again, remembering the small, unwilling, restive participant at the award cere-monies. Skinny, big blue eyes, chestnut bangs, a pink ruffled dress within which she had cringed. Now she was taller, but still skinny. And the eyes were still blue under chestnut bangs. She wore green hiphuggers and

144

a green shirt tied around a surprisingly tiny rib cage. Between shirt and pants there was a wide gap of smooth brown skin and a neat belly button. He was certain that even if he had never seen her before, he would have known her. She was so plainly Joe Stevens' daughter.

"Booked yet?" Mike asked the red-faced desk man over the shout of her curses.

"Jane Doe."

"Okay if I talk to her?"

The desk man grimaced. "Be my guest. If you think you can stand it."

Mike ambled over to her, Miguelito following.

Gilly, swearing still, hung between two detectives.

"Knock it off," one told her, "promise to knock it off, and we'll let you go."

She told him, graphically, what to do with himself. The words were oddly horrible falling from her pink lips.

Miguelito listened, his head cocked, his face expressionless.

Mike asked, "Do you remember me, Gilly? I'm a friend of your father's."

She spat at his feet.

He moved in closer. "I'm going to call him."

She shook herself loose and leaned against the wall. "Who invited you in?"

"I belong here," he told her. "You don't. Now tell me what this is all about."

"Nothing."

"You're not here for nothing. Nobody ends up here for nothing."

"You're no friend of my father's. I don't have a father. I don't have a name or an address or anything.

145

I don't belong to anybody, and I don't belong anywhere. So," she finished triumphantly, "all you can
do is put me away."

"Your father's Joe Stevens. He's a doctor. He lives
at——"

"Shut up," she screamed.

"I want to help you, if I can," Mike said softly.

She told Mike what to do with himself.

He restrained a desire to plant a good hard smack on
her thin cheek. He went back to the desk man. "How
about if I just take her home?"

"You crazy? What for?"

"She's Joe Stevens' daughter."

"Stevens? So what?" Then, "Oh, the doctor, you
mean."

Mike nodded.

"You'd be sticking your neck pretty far out, Mike."

"Remember how it was with me?"

"Yeah, I remember." A considering pause. A shrug.
"See if you can get her out of here quietly, will you?
And I'll put in a call to Juvenile again. They won't
kick about having one less to worry about."

Mike nodded.

Miguelito said then, "Mike, you better think this over."

"I have."

"Then I'd better go with you."

"I think I'd better do it aone."

"Then become more cautious than you usually are,
amigo."

Mike grinned and went back to Gilly. "I'm taking
you home now."

"Who asked you to mix in?"

"Nobody had to ask."

"But I don't want to go home."

"If you knew what not going home meant, then maybe you wouldn't say that so quickly. But I didn't ask you what you wanted. I told you what you were going to do."

His tone made it plain that she didn't have any choice.

She went with him. On the street, she suddenly gave a hop and a sprint and went sidewinding away. He snagged her without a break in his pace. From then on, he kept a hand on her arm, fingers loose when she relaxed, tight and bruising when she resisted. Mosly they were tight and bruising.

In the car, he asked, "Don't you want to tell me about it, Gilly?"

"No. It's none of your business."

"Sorry," he said. "It *is* my business. The law's business. Maybe I'm making a fool of myself. And doing you no favor. But this time, and just this one time, you're going to get a break whether you want it or not, or deserve it or not."

She laughed and scratched her belly button.

"I'm just trying to understand."

"You couldn't."

"How do you know if you don't try me?"

She swore at him.

He was relieved to deliver her to her mother, but not so relieved that he didn't do what he knew he must do. He insisted that Joe be called, and waited until he got there. Then, with Gilly sent to bed, Mike insisted that Joe and Ellen listen to him.

Ellen had seemed something less than shocked, Joe something more than resistant, while Mike laid it out for them.

147

They were both distant, courteous, and grateful, at the beginning.

In the end, they both agreed gracefully that Gilly must need help they couldn't give her. They promised to find the right man immediately. They thanked Mike for his interest and kindness. They bade him a pleasant good-bye.

Mike mentally crossed suspicious fingers, hoping that he had, in fact, been kind to Gilly, and to them, and went his way. He heard no more of Gilly, nor of Joe.

But they had been somewhere in his mind, and when Lori became ill, Joe was the doctor he thought of.

Mike sighed. Was that why he had taken Lori to Joe—because he just remembered Joe? Or was it because Joe owed him—owed him for bringing Gilly home.

One way or the other, it was chance . . .

"You try to do the right thing, Lori," he whispered. "But if you don't know . . ." His loving gaze shifted from her still face. His eyes suddenly narrowed, hardened, examining the thin hands folded on her breast. He looked sideways at Claire. "She's not wearing her wedding ring."

Claire breathed, "Oh God, Mike," and backed away, her eyes flooding. She staggered and fled across the lush carpet, through the dim perfumed hush, into the corridor beyond the velvet-curtained doorway.

"You ought to be wearing your wedding ring," Mike told Lori.

He listened to the words, waiting, empty-minded, for an answer that wouldn't ever come. Then he, too, left the chapel, left Lori alone there amid the great swoop of flowers and floating ferns.

Claire was huddled against a gray wall. He went by her without seeing her.

She said, "Mike, stop it!"

He didn't hear her. He tried first one door, then another, and finally, at the third, he found Jerry Dormet behind the huge mahogany desk.

"Her wedding ring," Mike said.

Jerry's sympathetic face dissolved with shock.

Mike thought that Jerry seemed easily affected for a man in his job. "My wife," he said patiently, "she ought to be wearing her wedding ring."

"Isn't she?"

"No. That's why I'm asking you about it."

"Then she didn't have it on when she was brought here."

"Are you sure?"

"How can I be sure, Mr. Manning?"

"Who would be?"

"Mr. Manning, I can understand that you're upset, but really, we don't know anything about your wife's wedding ring."

"How do you know that? You haven't asked anybody. You can't be certain of what anybody knows."

"I am sure, morally sure, that is, that if your wife had been wearing a ring . . ."

"She was wearing it."

"When she was brought here?"

"In the hospital."

"Then . . ."

Mike waited.

"Then, perhaps, in her effects. Do you have her effects?"

"The car."

"You should look there, Mr. Manning. I can assure you that if your wife was wearing her ring when she passed on and was brought here, then it would still be on her finger."

Mike jerked his head, started out, then turned back. He eyed Jerry Dormet fiercely. "What's the procedure?"

"Mr. Manning . . ." Jerry Dormet was pained, and apprehensive. He started to smooth his carefully combed patent leather black hair, then thought better of it and pressed pale hands on the desk. "Really, Mr. Manning . . ."

"I'm a cop. I can stand it. Just tell me what the procedure is."

"I don't understand."

"You ought to. It's your business. All I'm asking you is how it goes. Somebody dies in a hospital, right?"
Jerry Dormet nodded.

Mike went on, "There's a declaration of death. The family is notified. And then?"

"Then?"

"Mr. Dormet, either you're dumber than you look, or you think I am."

"The bereaved are not supposed to ask such questions," Jerry Dormet replied from behind an invincible wall of dignity.

Mike promptly demolished it. "Who picked her up?"
Jerry Dormet threw up his hands. "Check with the hospital. Check with the effects you have. If you don't find what you're looking for, and I'm sure you will —there's just been a small mistake, I'm sure you'll find that out—then you let me know. We'll question

150

my staff here. But first . . ." He was still busy organizing when Mike left him.

Once again Mike went by Claire without seeing her. She caught up with him on the sidewalk outside. "Mike, what is it?"

"I have to find her wedding ring."

"But what could have happened to it?"

"I'll find out."

He opened the car trunk. The brown paper bag—name, room number scrawled on it—was there. He stared at it as if seeing it for the first time. It wasn't right. The girl in the Property Office had handed it to him, and he had signed for it. But it wasn't right. There should have been a small white weekend case. It was what she always used to carry her things when she went to the hospital. Her holiday bag, she always called it. Or her maternity bag. Even on that last day, the last trip, watching while he packed for her, she had said, "Now don't forget my talcum powder, Mike. My special toothbrush, and that extra-sexy special bed jacket you bought me. Which I'll wear when those handsome young interns come in to poke and pry, of course."

Instead of the white weekend case, a brown paper bag. He opened it carefully now. He shook out the bed jacket, fingers feeling a tender warmth no longer there. He examined the powder box, the toothbrush, the toothpaste tube. He held her small slippers in his hand. He checked, re-checked, searching with desperate hunger and the expertise of long practice.

The wedding ring was not there.

Also not there was the silver-backed brush which he had had initialled for her on their first wedding anniversary, and the old chrome Mickey Mouse watch that he gave her for hospital use. Going over her things, those few pitiful reminders of the breathing smiling Lori, he realized what else wasn't there. Not a single penny, not a copper cent, though he himself had made sure each night before he left, and on the last one, too, that there was no less than a dollar in change on her night table.

No wedding ring.

No weekend case.

No Mickey Mouse watch.

No silver brush.

No change.

He made the tally once more, standing calmly beside the open trunk, Claire a silent but expanding presence that demanded attention he couldn't give her. He made the tally, his trained mind ticking it off. And he knew.

He saw it as it must have been.

He turned away from the car, from Claire, his long legs suddenly weak, his vision fogged, and found himself wrenchingly ill.

Moments later, heaved out, dry, stony in throat and limb, with Claire murmuring miserably beside him, he set out for Gorman Memorial.

CHAPTER 7

"I just don't know," Miss Dacey said. "I can't think what possibly could have happened."

"Suppose you try," Mike insisted.

"You must understand, Mr. Manning. I'm a registered nurse. I don't handle such things. It's the aides that do such work. I don't have time. I can't be every place at once. So the aides . . ." She looked at Mrs. Meenahan and Mrs. O'Connor. The two of them echoed their colleague, and Miss Dacey went on, "I don't even remember her wedding ring."

"Or a small white traveling case? A silver brush? A Mickey Mouse watch? Not even a handful of change?"

"Mr. Manning, whatever was there, in the night table, the drawers, the closet, all that was there was packed and held for you. You yourself picked it up. I'm sure you did."

"Are you?"

"Of course I'm sure. I told you where the Property Office was. I remember that you asked, and I told you." She gave the two other women an eyes to heaven look, and they nodded commiseration.

"You told me where the Property Office was," Mike

agreed. "You didn't go down there with me. You didn't see me pick it up. You're not sure of anything."

"Just the same, Mr. Manning, I know that everything your wife had with her has been returned to you." Miss Dacey hesitated, then added what to her was the clincher: "And you accepted it, and signed for it, didn't you?"

"I waited a long time. They had trouble finding it. When they pulled out that brown paper bag, I didn't give it a second look." Shame burned Mike's face. "I don't know why. I just didn't look."

"So then . . ."

He remembered that for a little while early in the pink dawn she had tried to be kind to him. He remembered that but it no longer mattered. He gave her a level look. "You're more of a fool than I ever thought. Which is saying a lot." He turned on his heel, went down the hall to the room that had been Lori's until that morning. It was empty still. He wondered if some superstition, or odd good fortune, had kept it that way.

He searched the room carefully, closet, floor, and furniture. It took only a few moments. A few moments that satisfied his suspicion that he was in the wrong place.

Miss Dacey was still at the station. "I know you're upset," she protested. "But we have a routine. There's nothing for you to do here now. You're disturbing the work of the hospital. You're . . . why, Mr. Manning, you're absolutely impossible."

"I'm going to be worse than that," he said. "I'm going to tear this place apart. When I get through there's going to be nothing left of Gorman Memorial but a bunch of crumbling stones and some broken glass. And maybe a few bodies here and there."

She reached for the phone.

He laughed at her. "Call whoever there is to call. Maybe that's just who I want to talk to."

But he didn't wait to find out. He went down to the Property Office. The girl he had dealt with before smiled broadly. "Oh, yes. I remember you," she said.

The other two, sipping soda pop from wet bottles, oozed away toward the corner of the room when he said, "I picked up some stuff that belonged to my wife. Her name was Lori Manning. She was in Room 14402C. She died this morning. You gave me her stuff in a paper bag. It should have been a white traveling case. It should have had in it a wedding ring, a silver-backed brush, an old chrome Mickey Mouse watch, along with some change. I want all those things. I want them now."

The girl's smile faded. She murmured, "I'll check."

"You checked once. Do it right this time. I'll wait."

He leaned on the counter while she went through drawers and cupboards.

At last, with a sigh, she studied the hardcover notebook on her desk. "Really, Mr. Manning, Here it is. See? Your signature. You took the things away with you this morning."

"I've explained. Not all her things."

"You took whatever we received from her room, and you signed for it. Here's your name. See what I mean?"

"Not all her things," he repeated.

"Did you declare them when your wife entered the hospital? If your wife had valuables they should have been checked and listed with the Cashier's Office. If they weren't, then the hospital isn't responsible."

"A wedding ring?"

"Whatever," she said firmly.

He put an elbow on the counter. "You'd better tell me how it goes around here."

"I don't know what you mean."

"Find somebody who does."

"This is the Property Office," she said. "We are in charge."

He didn't answer her.

She took up the phone, dialed, spoke a few words. She watched Mike as if she expected him to go off like a dynamite charge. She was closer to the truth than she actually realized.

He asked in a deceptively gentle voice, "Who should I see now?"

"There's no one to see, Mr. Manning. If you didn't list your wife's things with the Cashiers' Office, then . . ."

He had left Claire to wait in the car. He didn't know how she had tracked him down, but she was suddenly beside him. She made a soft warning sound, and wrapped her fingers around his arm.

But he smiled. "Somewhere in this hospital there are things lost that belonged to my wife. I said lost. I intend to find them. With your help or without it."

The girl made a second phone call. "All right," she said after a moment, "our Mr. Maynor will be right down."

"Who's Mr. Maynor?"

"Our Chief of Public Relations."

"I don't need him," Mike answered. "Who's your security chief?"

"Security?"

"You know what I mean."

"But he doesn't deal with lost and found." She looked

as if she were going to say more but faltered to a stop when Mike grinned. "You put the idea into my head."

Claire said plaintively, "This won't do any good, Mike."

He didn't reply.

Moments later, Ned Maynor appeared. He was a plump little man with a high cheerful voice and a healthy pink color. "Now then," he bubbled, "what can I do for you?"

His bubble died, his color faded, when Mike told him. Thoughtfully, gently, regretfully, he said, "You realize that if these items were not in the hospital safe, not registered through the Cashier's Office, then we are not responsible."

Mike gave him a long slow look. "The hospital is responsible for the belongings of those patients who are not capable of looking after themselves. The dead fall in that category. That much is already settled. But we're not really ready for a discussion of responsibility just yet. Before we are, we'll see if we can trace Lori's things."

"I know you're upset, Mr. Manning. I am too. Such occurrences are unforgivable, of course. Rare as they are, they remain unforgivable. But the fallibility of the human being is what it is. We are both aware of that. We must both try to understand, and to forgive."

"I'm a city cop, Mr. Maynor. Are you telling me about the fallibility of human beings?"

Ned Maynor shrank a little. "You mean a police officer?"

Mike nodded, wide shoulders bunched and ready.

"You mustn't think that this is an everyday affair."

Mike asked pleasantly, "Isn't it?"

"Of course not, Mr. Manning."

Still pleasantly, Mike asked, "How would you like half a dozen of my friends on the burglary squad to go trooping through Gorman, with half a dozen of their newspaper friends one step behind, all carrying cameras?"

Mr. Maynor sighed, turned to the girl behind the counter, "I don't see why you called me," he complained. "Still, you have checked thoroughly, haven't you?" She nodded. "Every possible place?" She nodded again. "Security?" he asked in a whisper. She shook her head. "Then get Benny Myers down here right away."

Mike grinned his relief. Benny Myers was an ex-cop. They would speak the same language, look with the same eyes.

Benny would find out where Lori's things were stashed, dig up the wedding ring, and that would be the end of it.

Mike went to wait for him at the elevator. He didn't notice that Claire, following him, saw a phone booth and disappeared into it.

Once again, she called Joe's office.

This time Bradford was plainly suspicious. "Miss Manning, you say? Again? Didn't you call before? Doctor is with a patient. You know he can't be disturbed for every whim."

"Let me talk to him," Claire retorted, not knowing how much she sounded in that moment like Mike, not caring that Bradford's response was a haughty, considering silence, then a brief, "Yes."

Joe was tired, hurried. "Claire? Something wrong?"

She blurted it out.

"Terrible," he said. "I'm sorry, Claire. What an awful thing to happen."

"What can we do?"

"There's nothing to do, Claire. Just get Mike away from the hospital as fast as you can."

"I can't. And he's driving himself crazy. Something's wrong with him that I don't understand. Not just Lori. More. Much more. You have to help him, Joe."

"Do you really think I know where Lori's things are?" he asked softly. "Am I supposed to keep track of my patients' property, as well as their blood pressure?"

"But what could have happened?"

"I'm afraid I don't know."

She drew a harsh hurting breath. "Nor care, Joe."

"I wish I could help," he told her.

"Thank you very much." She hung up, hurrried to join Mike.

Benny Myers had just stepped out of the elevator. He was a tall, white-haired man, big shouldered and competent looking. He and Mike looked right together as they shook hands.

But when Benny heard what Mike had to tell him, Benny suddenly looked less like a formidable ex-cop and more like a tired, disgusted, discouraged old man. He braced his wide shoulders, but he couldn't brace his facial muscles. He swore softly, and continuously, and studied the tips of his well-polished shoes. Finally, with a slanting glance upward at Mike, he bit out, "Christ, why did it have to happen to you?"

Mike said, "I'm not sure yet *what* has happened."

"Come on." Benny shot a hard look at Mike's face. "You think the stuff is stolen, don't you?"

"Do you?"

"We try, Mike. We sure as hell try to stop it. Christ, we screen them, and check them, and go inside and out. But there's a certain amount of it. Too much, considering the circumstances, I mean. Pilfering, no more than that. Small stuff. But it's there. And Jesus, Jesus, it makes me sick."

"A four dollar wedding ring. That's what it cost me, Benny. A Mickey Mouse watch my father gave me so long ago I don't even remember the birthday. A silver-backed brush, maybe worth seven bucks new, a single buck hocked. A handful of change. A drugstore weekend case." Mike's tone was incredulous.

Benny shot him another look. "Now look, maybe the thing to do is, you go downstairs, get yourself a cup of coffee, and you wait. Let me see what I can do."

"I'll go with you."

"Mike, I can't. I just can't let you put yourself through it. You don't know. You just don't know."

Claire whispered, "Listen, Mike. Listen to him."

Mike looked down at her, wondering where she had come from, and when. He said, "You go down to the car, Claire. You wait for me there. I'll be along when I can."

"No," she said. "I'm staying."

"Now, Claire."

Benny cut in, "We haven't been introduced, but the lady's got more sense than you have."

"My sister," Mike said briefly. And to her, "Now, Claire."

She hesitated. The elevator doors slid open. He touched her shoulder gently. She stepped into it, allowed it to carry her away from him.

"You don't know," Benny said again.

"I'll find out. I'll go with you."

"Listen, I know you're tough. We're all tough. But don't put yourself up against it."

"I've already been up against it, Benny. Nothing worse can happen to me."

Benny studied Mike's face, then shrugged. "Okay. Anybody but you, Mike, and I'd say 'hell no,' and that would be final. But you, you'll be all right. And you'll let me do the talking. You won't say a word. Agreed?" He looked at Mike again. "I want to hear it. Agreed?"

"Yes. But give me a rundown. How does it go?"

Benny winced. "Jesus, what did I need this job for?"

"I have to know," Mike said in his professional voice.

"There's the examination first. They declare it official."

It was as if, by not saying the word, Benny could make the fact unreal.

"After that everything is supposed to be marked, put on a tray, or a cart if necessary. It gets sent to the Property Office. The . . . ah . . . the person is taken down and readied for the p.m."

"Who does it?"

"What?"

"The readying."

"There's a team."

"What do you mean readied?"

"There's often some cleaning up to do, Mike," Benny said hurriedly. "Then the p.m. room. Then——"

"Autopsy. No. Not this time."

"No?" Benny eyed Mike. "No autopsy?"

"They asked. I refused."

161

Benny shrugged. One thing that wasn't his worry. "Then downstairs . . . Christ, Mike . . .!"

"And . . ."

"Preparation for the undertaker."

"What's that?"

"Wrapping . . . and . . . cleaning . . . and . . . oh, you know."

That time Mike was sorry for Benny. He got professional again. "So it could have been any step along the way."

"Yes."

Mike saw Lori in the dim room, small as a child abed for the night; smaller still with love and dreams gone. He forced the image from his mind. He said, "We can skip the undertaker. It happened here at Gorman."

"What makes you say that?"

"The stuff should at least have all gone through the Property Office. Right? It didn't. I got a bed jacket, a gown, a used toothbrush. So it's between here, and there." Benny nodded. "Then let's go."

They went down the hall together.

Miss Dacey was at first impatient, then offended.

She plainly no longer considered Mike an attractive stud, nor remembered that she ever had. She was no help.

Benny finally asked, "When did you send the stuff to the Property Office. Before the team came in, or after?"

She considered for a long time, admitted that she didn't know. And besides, she hadn't sent it. The aides attended to that sort of chore. She had patients to care for.

162

THE DEATH WATCH

"Before or after," Mike demanded, forgetting that he wasn't to speak.

Benny didn't remind him.

"I was busy," she said, and turned appealing eyes to Benny. "Do I have to put up with this, Mr. Myers?"

"We'd like to know."

"They could have done it after. The aides, I mean. After the team came up. I'm just not sure."

"We'll move on," Benny said.

They went downstairs. They saw the first team, then the second. Closed and sullen faces, narrowed listening eyes.

Benny talked.

Mike was silent. He was silent, watchful, and at the same time, he peered in horror at the picture in his mind.

Lori alone, at the mercy of ghouls who, in the first still moments after her death, had handled her body, and touched her loose limbs, and bound her flexed hands, and closed her eyes. Lori alone, rolled into rubber sheets and stared at by ghouls who, seeing that beautiful young body, had maybe lightened the weight of death with ribald jokes, and stolen from her thin finger the wedding ring that had never left it since they'd taken their vows together. Robbing her of the little she had left behind, and laughing together, they had decided how they would split the spoils, and sent her skidding away on a cart, bound, gagged and stripped in death, while they went out to second breakfast, had coffee and doughnuts at their break, ate a hot lunch, and a hot dinner, and screwed the night away in bed.

He lost track of the words and the questions. He stopped listening.

When Benny's job was over, he was empty-handed, hot in the face.

Mike took hold of himself, briefly forgot the images in his mind. He got the teams together. The scar under his ear scarlet, he said, "Okay. You know I'm a cop. You know I can do it if I say I'll do it. And I will. If I don't get the ring back, just the ring, by tomorrow morning, well, then they're all going to be out here. My friends. They'll be sick and sore. They'll be here, the bunch of them. And they'll shake you down, and rattle you, and beat you a little and bang you around. And by Christ, somebody, somewhere, somehow, is going to cough up a little gold wedding ring."

He looked into eight shut and sullen faces. "I know you. So don't kid yourself. Just cough it up. Or else start running." He gave them a last hard look, and walked out.

His mouth and nostrils seemed suddenly full of the thick sweet cloying scent that reminded him of Mary Jensen, and her stuffed animals and satin pillows. A deep wrenching sickness gripped him.

Benny, following, cursed, said, "If only it hadn't been you, Mike," and looked at his watch. "Listen, it's about that time. Come up to the office and have a drink."

"My sister's waiting downstairs for me."

"I'll stand her a drink, too," Benny offered.

"Thanks," Mike told him. "Another time. Maybe tomorrow. Just now I'd better go home."

"I'd better go home," Ellen Stevens was saying.

"You'd better have another drink," Buss Gorman told her, his parchment yellow face earnest with the missionary zeal of a man afraid to be alone with his guilt.

It was not his plea, however, that kept Ellen seated at the bar. Poor Buss, as she always thought of him, could hardly be the agent of her corruption. He was much too far gone in his own. He was, she supposed, an example of what Joe had turned his back on, the teen-age drunk who had become the middle-aged drunk, and now sat with horizons shrunk to the circumference of a martini glass.

"I wish you'd talk to me," Buss complained.

"How long have you been out?"

He grinned wryly, and his parchment skin crumpled into a hundred small canyons. "Since ten o'clock this morning. Would you believe it?"

"Ought you to be here already, Buss?"

He shrugged.

"But is it okay, Buss?"

"Oh, they'll just take me back tomorrow, if they have to. And more shots, more drying out. A very unpleasant procedure." He eyed Ellen, plainly hoping for the sympathy he didn't get. "You don't know what it's like. That's why I'm here right now. Trying to forget about it. I keep telling them at the clinic—Gorman's famous Alcoholic Clinic, I mean, named after me, of course—I keep telling them that if they didn't make it so bad, I wouldn't have to try to forget it. Then maybe I wouldn't be on this three weeks in, three weeks out merry-go-round." Without a change of tone, but with a definite raise in volume, he said, "Jose, get us a couple more drinks."

"His name is Max," Ellen told Buss.

"I call them all Jose. Makes it easier. You don't have to try to remember."

"All bartenders? But why that particularly?"

"All Mexicans," Buss explained with a sidelong look.

"I really ought to go," she said, as if ignoring the explanation would somehow disassociate her from the implications of prejudice, or at least render Max deaf. But she still didn't move.

"Just the one more. How about it, Ellen? Just the one?" Again without a change in tone, but with that increase in volume so unrelated to content that it was like a radio suddenly turned louder, he went on, "Christ, but we used to have fun, didn't we?"

She accepted the drink Max put before her. If Max objected to being called Jose his broad, big-featured face didn't show it. She supposed he had been called that, and worse, many times before.

She looked into the drink as if it were a crystal ball, and the clear icy fluid were shadowy currents in which pictures of past and future floated. She guessed that if she strained, she could see them. She didn't bother.

"We sure as hell did have fun," Buss said reverently, answering his own question, and then lapsed into morose silence.

Ellen was grateful for the silence. Not because she *wanted* to think about the night before, but because she was compelled to, and his indifferent conversation had become an unpleasant counterpoint, much the same as the small reminiscent pain that cross-stitched itself within the confines of her skull at irregular intervals.

The night before. . . . She remembered thinking that maybe Joe knew what he was doing, hoping that he did.

But she remembered, too, that she had been unconvinced. She suspected him to be as bewildered, even frightened, about Gilly as she was herself.

He wouldn't admit it, of course. He wouldn't allow such weakness. Not Joe. Never Joe. He saw himself as sure, self-contained, certain. Joe, with all the answers, a god to whom everyone looked in hope and desperation and love. That was how Joe saw himself. Could it be that way?

She almost wished it were true. And yet . . . yet . . . ? Did she? When, she wondered, had she begun to hate him?

He came down from Gilly's room.

Ellen looked quickly into his face, his eyes. She couldn't tell how it had gone.

She poured the coffee she had made for him. "Well?"

"It's going to be all right."

"But what did she say? Why does she want fifty dollars?"

"Ellen, will you please stop being paranoid. She didn't tell me anything that she refused to tell you. I didn't find out."

"You're carrying professional ethics too far, Joe. I'm Gilly's mother."

He laughed softly.

"I ought to know." Ellen very nearly told him then about the blackmail. Yes, that was the word for it. Gilly's blackmail. It was important as a measure of Gilly's desperation. But Ellen didn't want to dignify it beyond its significance. She resisted the need to pamper her belief in her own honesty. She repeated, "I ought to know."

"I didn't find out what she wants the money for."

"Oh." At least, Ellen thought, she hadn't been left out yet another time. A sort of progress was being made, slowly perhaps, but progress nonetheless.

"And I think it would be good to drop the subject now," Joe went on."

"I couldn't agree more."

They stared at each other for a moment. "If there's nothing I can get you, I'll go to bed," she said, and left him.

She didn't intend to, but when she found herself before Gilly's door, she knocked. "Gilly?"

"Yes?" The impatient affirmative. "What do you want, Mother?"

"Going to sleep now?"

"In a minute."

"May I come in?"

"Yes." Short, curt, angry.

Ellen went in.

Gilly was at the mirror, brush raised to her long hair, face sulky. "What now?"

Ellen remembered the straight bangs, sweet, innocent, over wide open blue eyes. She said, "I just want to know if everything is all right."

"Sure. I got the money. So . . ." Eyes blue still, but opaque. Mouth smiling, malicious.

"I didn't mean that, Gilly. I mean, is everything all right with you?"

That boy at the club. Bud Slater. Blond. Young. How could Gilly think that?

"With you," Ellen repeated, repressing resentment, and at the same time peculiarly shamed that she should still dare hope Gilly would suddenly become her daughter, her child, her love again.

"It's great with me. Now. For the time being," Gilly said.

"Are you going to bed soon? After all, it's rather late."

"Why don't *you* turn in?"

Useless, useless, useless, Ellen chanted to herself, turning away. And, moments later, hearing the car pull out, she nodded. She had been listening, without thinking about it, for confirmation. Gilly dressed, clean jeans and fresh shirt, the wide belt at her waist. Gilly brushing her hair, mouth pink, eyes drawn horribly with black pencil. Gilly on her way out. Where? To do what? With whom?

Ellen had flung herself at the window. It was too late, of course. The headlights flashed on the cottonwood trees at the foot of the drive, arrowed bright beams onto the highway, then faded away. Knowing that Gilly would be going out again, what could Ellen have done to stop her?

She found her gown, robe, feathery mules. She ran a warm bath, added scented bubble oil.

She undressed and slipped into the warm water, and lay soaking, her tense muscles finally relaxing. The faint ache at her temples eased and faded away. Gilly forgotten at last but something of her still there, lingering, so that suddenly, without willing it or wanting to, Ellen was remembering when she herself was seventeen. Seventeen, instead of forty-three.

The war that Gilly now called history had turned the sleepy southwestern town into a city ringed with air bases and training fields. Great linked fences closed off miles of red mesa, and new factories poured spirals of smoke into the wide blue sky.

169

Everywhere new faces, new hustle, new ideas that even touched the isolated backwater of Ellen's group, the select families, friends for generations, married and intermarried until they were more than friends and business associates; they who were the leading element, the rich, the strong, the tidy-living, whose voices in politics and taste had created the town in the first place. Into that group even, came the new faces, new ideas, at the club, in the homes. Ellen, too, was swept up in it, her horizons widening for the first time beyond the small circle she had always known, the circle that included the Stevens's.

Joe was in college then. Ellen waited breathlessly for him to come home that spring. She was sure that when he saw her grown, her auburn hair now great masses of curls piled in a high pompadour and sweeping to her shoulders in thick waves, why, she was sure that he would remember how they had kissed just before he went away.

When he returned, there was a big party for him at the club. She went with her parents. He came late, spread perfunctory greetings around, and left early.

Ellen stumbled outside to weep. Her mother found her, said, coolly, "Come inside. It doesn't look right." And Ellen returned to the party. Someone asked her to dance. One of those new faces, an Army face; all she ever recalled of him was his very deep voice and straight dark brows. They danced, he holding her so tightly that she felt his blouse buttons at her breasts.

When her parents left, her mother smiled at her. No one must ever know that Ellen had crept outside to weep and returned to laugh. The new face offered to take her home. A ride first; a brief stop to look at the stars, the town.

She hardly listened while he spoke of the lights going out, the war, his transfer overseas. She was intent on the deep internal melting that she felt, his voice Joe's in her ears, until she forgot finally that Joe hadn't noticed that she had become a woman. In the car, with the lights of town spread out below, and the deep male voice whispering around her, with a touch and a stroke, she allowed the melting warmth to enfold her, and finally leaned against him to put a long hard kiss against his white smile. And in a little while, she whispered, "Please don't make me," because his hand was where no man's hand had ever been before, and she loved it and didn't want him to stop.

"Make you?" he'd said. "What do you think I am? You have to want it, and want it bad, too. Otherwise it's no good."

"Oh, please," she repeated, telling herself that he would make her, he must make her, even if she didn't want to.

Having made her obeisance to the submerged voices of her parents, having nodded to her conscience, she spread her legs and arms, and rose to meet his lunge. They had sex, a quick passionless scramble amid cotton skirt and belt buckle.

She never saw him again.

For days afterwards, she waited, wan and anxious, for pregnancy, or disease, and wept for her lost innocence, and breathlessly re-examined those moments which were her burden and her joy. And now, twenty-six years later, she wondered what all the fuss had been about.

She had been raised to believe that sex was the deepest expression of love. Her first doubts had begun that night when she was seventeen. Now that she had stopped believing in love, nothing but sex remained. Nothing but sex.

She lay in the tub, and sighed, and stroked her body, soaping the small roundness of her stomach, the curve of her thighs. The warm bubbly water lapped at her nipples and they rose up, responding as if tongue-touched, and at the same time, a knot of hunger thickened in her groin, and began to pulse hotly. She found herself thinking of Bud Slater as she stepped out of the tub to powder and perfume herself. Without conscious thought, she put aside the night clothes she had chosen earlier, and took out a new gown, tissue-paper-thin blue lace. She brushed her hair long and loose so that it fell in waves to her perfumed shoulders.

She turned off all but one small bedside lamp, and lay down so that its pale glow fell on her barely hidden breasts.

Where once she had listened to a man's slow voice talk about the war, and thought of Joe, now she waited for Joe and thought about Bud Slater.

Finally, Joe was there. He came in yawning, a hand raised to his shirt buttons. "Not sleeping yet, Ellen?"

"I was waiting for you."

"Sorry. I didn't mean to keep you up. I didn't realize the time."

"I didn't mind."

She stretched, long legs reaching, the curve of thigh visible through the thin blue mesh. She took a deep breath, her high breasts lifting in the glow of the lamp. Somewhere in the back of her mind the proud thought

172

flickered that she wasn't too bad for a woman of forty-three; she knew that Bud Slater had noticed her, just as she had noticed him. But the proud thought flickered out as Joe prepared for bed, moving around with carefully averted face.

She knew that it wasn't going to be any good. The hard knot of desire in her groin began to shrink and wither. She tried to remember what signals they had once used, how they had told each other, without needing words, that they wanted to be together that night. When they had slept in the same bed it was easy. She had snuggled close to him, or he had drawn her close. But now it was different, and the signals had had to be different, too. Surely in the ten years since they had begun to sleep separately they had somehow reached across the space between. She tried to think of the last time they had slept together, how it had happened. She panicked when she couldn't remember the last time. Was it six months? Was it even longer?

"Joe?" She didn't intend to put it into words, but somehow, she couldn't stop herself. "Joe, what's wrong? Why don't you want me anymore?"

"Want you?" he asked, obvious caution lacing the question.

"You know what I mean, Joe."

"Ellen, that's an odd thing to ask."

"I don't see why."

"It just is. After all, we've been married eighteen years. I'm forty-five years old. I've had a hard day. It seems to me that———"

"Are you trying to say that you just plain can't get it up any more, Joe?"

Caution became, disgust. "What an extraordinary remark."

"Is it true?"

He didn't answer her. He went into the bathroom. She lay there fuming while he showered. She lay still, and the knot of desire melted into a knot of pain that cramped her and sent long echoes arrowing upward to strike beneath the delicate shield of her skull, exploding there like red rockets in the quickening current of her pulse.

Just as he came back, she switched off the bedside lamp. She lay wrapped in sheets of pain, listening as he padded softly across the room to his bed. She said into the darkness, "Or is it just me, Joe?"

"What do you mean?"

"I'm sorry I offended your sense of gentility. Sometimes there's only one way to say things, and that's bluntly."

He laughed softly. "Never mind."

"And you still haven't answered me. What's wrong with us, Joe? What's wrong with me?"

"Nothing. That's why I can't understand what this is all about. We're a perfectly normal married couple."

"And I'm a perfectly normal forty-three-year-old."

He laughed softly again. "I should hope so."

"Then?"

"I might add, Ellen, that I think I'm perfectly normal, too."

She imagined him looking into the dark, his blue eyes wide open, intent and interested, while he thought of ten different things, none of which concerned her.

There was always one available weapon to use. She used it without a qualm. "Gilly went out, Joe."

"Yes. I know."

"Why didn't you stop her?"

"I thought it best not to."

"But where would she go now so late? How do you know it isn't the same as before?"

"We have to trust her, Ellen."

She heard him moving again, and suddenly he was beside her. He touched her shoulder, smoothing the silken skin with warm fingertips. He lay down beside her.

"Let's not talk about Gilly now, Ellen."

She gasped as the sheets of pain tightened, but she clung to him, making pain seem passion, hurrying him with small anxious movements of her hips.

He kissed her throat and her throbbing temples, and made that small wordless gesture that meant it was time for her to take off her gown. Instead, while he got out of his pajamas, she simply slid the blue mesh up. When he returned to her she didn't seem to notice that she had left it bunched around her shoulders. His body seemed very young and lean, hard-muscled against hers. She opened her thighs, and he went between them, and then in, in deep. But all she felt was a swift stab of pain in her head. Her whole body contracted with it, resisting the rhythm of his thrusting weight. He didn't seem to notice that either.

She cupped his cheeks in her hands and drew his face down to hers, reaching for his mouth, moving her lips against his until they opened to her tongue. She tasted him, heat and antiseptic sweetness; clinical observation that had no place in desire. But his short-cropped hair against her fingers made her think of a slim, sun-touched form. And when she slid her hands down to clutch

175

Joe's hard buttocks, the slim, sun-touched form had a name. She said it silently, and aloud gasped, "Oh, Joe . . ."

When he left her, she fumbled blindly in the bedside table drawer.

"What is it?" he asked. "What are you looking for?"

"Pill."

"Headache?"

"I'm afriad so."

"I'll get it for you."

"It's all right."

But he was up. He brought her a glass of water and handed her a capsule.

"Sorry," she whispered.

"But why didn't you tell me?"

"I don't know," she gasped.

"Try to fall asleep right away."

"Thanks."

"Okay now?"

"In a few minutes." She turned her face into the pillow, waiting for the capsule to work, hoping it would work, but knowing that she had waited too long. She would fight the night through, struggling within the tightening strait jacket of pain, retreating into the shadow world of migraine to get from him the sympathy, the love, he gave so freely to everyone else.

"Ellen," he said gently, "it's all so needless. Don't you know?"

"Yes."

"The whole thing tonight . . . that ridiculous scene . . ."

She agreed dryly, "Ridiculous, yes. A wife trying to

seduce her husband, and finally talking him into making love to her . . ."

"Oh, no. I mean your doubts."

". . . and then shaming him into making love to her, and at the last driving him to it by making him want to change the subject. That was what worked. You didn't want to talk about Gilly."

"Ellen . . ."

She stared painfully into the dark, watching zigzags of lightning, the visual echoes of the arrows at her temples. "More ridiculous than can be imagined, especially when it's obvious he doesn't want his wife, that he is only performing the required function like a stallion servicing a mare."

"Your headache is running away with you."

"You didn't want to kiss me. You didn't kiss me. Not until I made you."

He laughed softly. "Wild, wild insights. That was only cafregot that I gave you, wasn't it, and not some fantasy-producer?"

"Stop it," she gasped.

"Then sleep now and let the capsule work."

"I will."

"Good night, then."

She sighed, thinking dimly that in the morning she would be ashamed to face him, to face herself. She would have to apologize. She would tell him she was sorry, that she didn't know what was wrong with her. She had everything, everything a woman could want. It was childish to want, demand, what he didn't have to give her. As she fell suddenly into sleep, she thought of blond Bud Slater. She decided that she simply wouldn't go to the country club.

But she did go, of course.

She awakened with a headache hangover, and Gilly still wasn't home, and Joe said, "Never mind, she'll turn up some time today," and went to the office, as unruffled and untouched as if nothing at all had happened. Ellen was glad that she hadn't apologized.

Without thinking about it, she dressed more carefully even than usual. She wore a square-necked orange dress, unfashionably narrow at the waist, that made her feel very young. She brushed her long auburn hair and let it hang on her shoulders. She darkened her thick brown eyelashes, batting them seductively at her pleased reflection.

Tula grinned, "You're looking pretty good, Mrs. Stevens. Where you off to this morning?"

"I'll be at the club," Ellen told her, hearing the words with some surprise and a great deal of satisfaction.

She was greeted with sophisticated unconcern by Joe's parents, fragile wisps lit by the sparkle of alcoholic flame. She wandered around outside for a while, and since she remembered some signals, although she had apparently forgotten others, she made a date with Bud Slater. Now, although thinking that she ought to forget the date and go home, she was waiting for him.

Buss Gorman joggled her elbow, complaining, "Jesus, Ellen, you're the slowest drinker in the world. Jose, get us a couple more, will you?" he yelled and promptly fell backwards off the bar stool.

CHAPTER 8

The sun made golden patterns on the ceiling.

Ellen examined them with anxious eyes.

She had been armored with the conscious awareness of her own sophistication while she sat with Buss in the country club bar, and said aloud that it was time to go home, yet waited with increasing doubts for Bud Slater to appear.

He appeared at exactly the right moment. He helped Max to raise Buss to his feet, and carefully led him into the parking lot, with Ellen following discreetly. He handed Buss over to the mercies of the attendant there, saying, "I don't give a good goddam what you do with him, but do something. Only remember: he's a Gorman."

The attendant raised hopeless eyes to heaven.

Bud grinned at Ellen. "Let's you and me cut out."

Some time, within those few minutes, he had seized the initiative from her, and she had found her crisp smiling sophistication decaying into a seventeen-year-old's naivete, so that now, waiting for Bud to come back from the kitchen, she felt very much like that seventeen-year-old who had waited for Joe to notice her new curves and long hair. But he hadn't noticed, and she had taught herself that she must not weep. He went back to school. By the time he came home for good, she was twenty-five, and she didn't know how she felt about him any more. She had had a few experiences since that first time with the young soldier. She had refused several proposals, though her parents considered her willful and predicted a lonely spinsterhood, particularly when she rejected Buss Gorman with a mixture of pity and horror.

Then she had a chance meeting with Joe in the lobby of the old hospital where she was doing her weekly nurses' aide stint, part of the busywork her mother had programmed for her, although Ellen hated the hospital smell and atmosphere, and the sick, and had to force herself to put in her six-hour day twice a week.

She looked good in her uniform, however, and apparently Joe noticed, for after the chance meeting, there were planned ones. Since they had known each other all their lives, a long courtship wasn't necessary. They were married a few months later in an elaborate wedding, witnessed by approving families and friends, and much photographed for the newspapers. They were waved away in showers of rice for a month-long honeymoon in Acapulco. She had been a glowing, eager, expectant bride. She was a disappointed, cold, frightened wife. Because Joe still carried Belena's picture in his wallet, and Ellen knew that made her second best.

Oddly, the knowledge only intensified her own hunger. She loved him; she wanted him to love her. A year later, Gilly had come. Joe was delighted, a fatuous father, first spoiling the baby, then spoiling the growing child.

Ellen, watching, was still deprived, and still hungered.

With Gilly's coming, she had been rendered sterile, so it was just the three of them. An odd triangle, it soon seemed to Ellen: father, daughter, and mother. The first few years set the pattern that never changed. Belena, Gilly, Joe's patients, they all stood between Joe and Ellen. She knew that she had never had a chance. He had drawn an invisible line between them the first night of their marriage, and she had never been able to breach it. He was simply the man he was. And she still loved him . . . and hated him.

Now Bud Slater came back from the kitchen. He passed before the window, and the blocks and angles of sun and shadow shifted along the ceiling.

Ellen's dress slid fluidlike across her knees as she swung her long legs gracefully to the floor and leaned back against the sofa cushions.

"All set," he said. "The comforts of home." He jiggled the ice bucket.

"I like your place," she told him.

He had a well-shaped head, his blond hair cut into smooth waves. His eyes were a pale translucent blue, set almost too close together under heavily ridged brows. His nose was short, broad; his mouth heavy-looking and sensual. He had a bronze tan, his arms covered with springy sun-bleached hair. He stood, moved, even smiled, with a certain aggressive animalism that she had always found exciting, and now more so.

Now he shot her a quick look over the half pint of gin that he had produced earlier with such an air of experience that she had been taken aback. "What makes you think it's my place?" he demanded.

She was taken aback again. "It's obviously somebody's, so I thought . . ."

"It belongs to a friend of mine. Which means it's a helluva lot better than a motel."

She managed to hide her disapproval. She would not let herself ask him about the possibility of someone walking in on them.

Bud said, "And safer, too. You noticed the long ride we took getting here? Plenty far out, and I played around some. Just in case we were followed."

She stopped herself from telling him there was nothing to worry about on that score.

He brought her a glass of what seemed to be half gin and half ice cubes, and bent over her, grinning, to touch her glass with his. "To us."

It was the right thing for a cliché situation, she thought. She was there because she had decided that she might as well be hung for a sheep as a goat. Because when you give a dog a bad name he earns one. Because . . .

She drank without answering, and choked, and felt her cheeks burn and her eyes fill.

He seemed to think that was funny. He laughed as he quickly refilled her glass, and she caught him, then, giving his watch a surreptitious glance.

"Are you in a hurry?" she asked.

"Not me. You?"

She shook her head. She was definitely not in a hurry. If she went home now, it would only be to wonder about Gilly, to pace the floor, listening for the sound of the convertible in the drive, and to wish that Tula would not scatter cigarette ashes on the freshly washed kitchen tile.

"You don't have much to say for yourself," Bud told her, settling himself on the sofa beside her.

"I was thinking the same about you."

"What's to say?"

"Do you like your job at the club?"

"Sure. It pays me for what I like to do."

"And you can get along on that?"

"I don't need much." He grinned. "At least not much money."

"And that's what you're going to do? Pro at the club?"

"Why not, as long as I can?" He emptied his glass, refilled it without checking to see if she were ready for another. "And I've still got some good mileage to me."

She didn't know how to answer that, and when he moved closer, she was glad; it was the necessary distraction from talking. But when he smoothed her dress back from her knees, said, "You have pretty good legs," she was confounded again. She didn't know whether to hand him a compliment in return, or whether to simply smile, or whether to put her arms around him. She temporized by ducking her head in a silent thanks. It seemed to suffice.

He put his glass aside, then continued to smooth her dress back from her knees until it was up around her hips.

She felt nothing but a faint embarrassment.

The sofa groaned when he took her into his arms and positioned her. She had to restrain a giggle at the seriousness with which he went about his athletics.

But then her hands were clutching his narrow hips, and she said Joe's name in her mind, and something began to happen inside her. Whispered urgencies rose to her lips, and while she was still breathing them, clutching Bud, he grunted one last time and collapsed over her, and immediately got up and disappeared into the bathroom.

In a very little while, they were ready to leave.

Bud said, "Oh, yeah, I almost forgot," and reached into his pocket, and drew out a handful of change. Then he shrugged and searched his wallet. "I guess I don't have it," he said finally.

"Have what?"

"Oh, usually I leave my friend twenty-five bucks. You know, kind of courtesy for his trouble."

"Do you?" she asked.

"I figure he deserves it," Bud told her, grinning. "I mean, it being his place and all." He gave her a wry look. "Or maybe you think it's too much?"

She took out two tens, five singles. "This will do it, I suppose."

He carefully arranged the bills on the coffee table. "There now. He'll find it without any trouble."

"Oh, I'm sure he will," Ellen agreed.

She supposed, driving home, after Bud had taken her back to the club, that twenty-five dollars wasn't really too much. Most probably he collected the same fee from all the women he took from the club to his "friend's" apartment. He was quite safe. They would never mention that part of it. They would be too embarrassed even to remember it. Or, perhaps, as Bud had implied, they considered him worth it.

But, as far as she was concerned, it had been like a certain kind of tennis game. A good hard punishing promising serve, with no recovery at all, and no rally to speak of. With that thought, she experienced a return of her earlier sophistication, and she found herself smiling.

But her smile faded when she reached the house, and

saw Joe's long gray car parked there, but not Gilly's convertible.

She wished, for once, that Joe hadn't decided to come home.

Joe thought much the same thing. It had been an impulse of the moment. He had spent his usual four Friday afternoon hours at the clinic, a chore to which he never looked forward, but always managed to accomplish with aplomb, although he found it difficult to talk to the poor, and was never certain, no matter how careful he was, that what he said was fully understood. It was impatience, rather than cruelty, that fueled his curtness, and he was always, after every Friday session, faintly ashamed.

He was disdainful of some of the medics he knew who devoted themselves to poverty cases, meanwhile boasting about having starved through school. They were too wary about their accomplishments, and too greedy for money, he thought. He, having never lacked it, had no greed about money at all. Yet his fees were the same as every internist in town, and he spent exactly the same amount of time on charity patients.

He was not the man to have an impulse without explaining it. He told Ellen now, "I was wondering if Gilly were home. I came to see."

"I gather she's not."

"And now you're saying 'I told you so,' as hard as you can." He managed to soften it with a faint smile.

"I'm not saying anything, Joe."

"You're looking it." He smiled faintly again. "And I can't say I don't deserve it."

"We knew we were taking a chance."

"We knew *I* was taking a chance, Ellen." He paced restlessly, while she sank into the sofa.

Friday night was his regular night with Claire. But now he just didn't know. If she were not with Mike, if Mike didn't need her, then logically . . .

Ellen said softly, "She still might come home. After she's spent the money."

"What?" Joe was startled, confused.

"Gilly," Ellen told him.

"Oh, yes. Sure. It's not time to start worrying yet."

"But perhaps you should call Dr. Richards."

"No. Not yet."

There was plainly a shadow of reproach on Ellen's face. She was still thinking of the night before, Joe supposed. But what did she want of him—reassurance that she wasn't aging? Of course she was. So was he. Reassurance that he still loved her? He did. It was ridiculous to think otherwise. This thing with Claire was simply a bypath. It had nothing to do with Ellen. If he had known the right way to tell her, he would, at that moment, have sat down to explain.

But he didn't know the right way, and she put her hands to her tmeples and squeezed her head, and the signal of the coming headache was suddenly too much for him.

He said, "I have to get down to the hospital, Ellen. I'll call you about Gilly later, if I can't get home."

"I'll be here," she told him.

He supposed he should ask if she were all right. There was an odd look on her face. She seemed drawn, haggard. He was about to offer her a cafregot when he heard the car stop in front of the house.

"Gilly," he said.

She sagged back, nodding, her face veiled suddenly by her auburn hair.

"I have to go, Ellen." He grinned: "See? It's okay."

He went out, not waiting for a reply, to meet Gilly. He couldn't help but smile at her.

She came bounding up the steps, her long hair flying, her legs scissoring, "Hi."

"Hi yourself. And where the heck have you been?"

"Here and there. I even came home before. But nobody else was, so I lit out again."

"I'll talk to you later, Gilly. About last night."

"I'll be around."

"I mean it, Gilly. Don't take off. Promise?"

"I promise. I swear. I give my word. Cross my heart and all that crap." She laughed when he winced, and threw a kiss at him and went inside.

As he went down the steps he heard Ellen ask, "Where have you been, Gilly? I want to know. I have to know."

"Out," Gilly retorted.

"Doing what?"

"Nothing."

"But out where? Any why didn't you come home last night?"

Gilly snapped, "I was at the club today. Isn't that good enough for you?"

Joe sighed and got into his car. There ought to be a way to handle the tension between Ellen and Gilly. But he didn't know how.

By the time he reached the hospital, it was twilight. He parked in the back lot, and went in.

He received several versions of Mike's morning visit

187

while making rounds. The grapevine whisperers had added their own embellishments, he was sure. It was difficult to know what had actually happened.

Joe had a moment's unease when, out of habit, he walked down the corridor toward Lori's door, and halfway there, realized she was gone. He swung back to the nurses' station. Miss Dacey, Mrs. Meenahan, and Mrs. O'Connor gathered to regard him with anxious eyes.

"I suppose you've heard," Miss Dacey said, spokeswoman for the group, as always.

"I've heard a lot of things," Joe grinned. "What 'specially do you have on your mind?"

"Mr. Manning. He accused us—can you imagine it—accused us of stealing his wife's wedding ring."

Joe said gently, "You know he didn't mean it."

"But really, Doctor, we're professional people. And he came in here like a one man gestapo . . ."

It was easy for Joe to imagine how it must have been. Mike was, after all, a physical type, the brute male. All muscle and jaw, and head lowered to charge. Joe had always somehow pictured him in creaking leather, Sam Browne belt, holstered gun at his hip, shin high boots, although Mike was a plainclothesman, and had been for a long time. Joe chided, "You mustn't take these small incidents seriously, you know."

"It didn't seem small at the moment." Miss Dacey looked at the other nurses. "We were actually scared of him."

There were some physicians who played general to the nurses' private, demanding and exacting instant obedience in all things large and small. There were some who played lover, earning absolute loyalty.

Joe kept to a role somewhere in between. Now he said,

"But it's all over, so forget it," and turned his back on their pleasurable excitement, and at the same time he decided that he had to see Claire. He had to talk to her.

He finished his rounds quickly, his last stop Mrs. Taylor. She smiled at him sadly, "Doctor, do you really think I'll ever be well again?"

He told her that she just about was, and her wan smile brightened.

He gave her a few moments in which to talk about the good days when she was young, his wide open eyes interested and concerned, while he thought of Claire.

As he left the hospital, Al Kelly limped hurriedly to open the door. "Hi yah, Dr. Stevens. How you doing tonight?"

Joe gave him an all-encompassing nod, and stepped out into the sudden darkness. The door slowly eased shut behind him.

Bess Bradford rose up from the depths of a chair, flounced on red stiletto sandals across the tile, and blinked a shy acknowledgment as Al Kelly held the door open for her, too. She hurried after Joe, feet hurting and breath shortened by a too-tight girdle.

It had been a terribly long and wearing day. Joe had been in the office for only a few hours, then departed for the clinic.

She supposed he had to do it, and that her father would sardonically approve, but she loathed the idea. It was four hours he gave away, took from her, to waste on those lazy, feckless, undeserving welfare people who, she was certain, could never appreciate a man like Joe Stevens.

She saw him pass under a light. He seemed tired, walking slowly, his head bent.

She wished that she dared catch up with him and ask, "What's wrong, Joe? What can I do?"

But she imagined that he would just stare at her, his wide open blue eyes assessing her, hardly knowing that she, Bess, after all their years together, surely had the right to speak to him, offer her help.

He got into his car, sat there for a long silent moment before the motor went on, the lights flared.

She wondered what he was thinking about as she hurriedly backed her car out, circled, then, without planning to, followed him out of the lot, away from the pale glow of the hospital, down the empty highway, and into the bright glow of the city.

There had been some small difference in him for some time now, and it troubled her greatly. She had known it without being able to define it. Following him, hardly aware of what she was doing, watching the shape of his head in the occasional flash of lights, she tried to pinpoint the change in him. But it didn't come clear, and she suddenly forgot to think about it as she began to wonder where he was going.

He was winding slowly but surely into Old Town, the car rocking on the potholed streets. His twin lights were a white tunnel into the shadows. She dropped back, following still, but cautiously, until quite suddenly, somewhere just off Rojas Lane, his lights disappeared, and there was nothing but the cold white glow of the moon, and a scatter of low dark buildings, and a myriad of dusty lanes. She didn't dare drive in lest the car become trapped between two close-leaning buildings and keep her there forever.

She drifted to a stop, peering into the shadows, until finally, she backed out, turned, and set her sights for home.

An uncomfortable cramp bit deep in her belly.

Friday done.

The office hours. The clinic. The hospital rounds.

Where could he have gone?

She mulled that over. It occurred to her that he must have had an emergency call. True, she couldn't think of a patient for whom he would make a house visit; still, there might be someone. But Joe's patients didn't live in Old Town. Well, maybe some of his clinic people did . . .

She slid smoothly into fantasy then, and the car moved faster, and she murmured, "Gosh, Joe, you really let those people take advantage of you. If you don't watch out, you're going to end up just like my father: an exhausted old man, with nothing to show for all your effort and love but gnarled hands and an empty bank account."

After a pause, she went on, smiling sweetly at the empty seat beside her, "I know how you feel. It's your duty. But you mustn't drive yourself so."

She turned, finally, into her street. She parked carefully. "I know what you need," she said archly. "A relaxing martini, ever so cold, and a good steak dinner, and a few hours of real rest, Joe. And that's what you're going to get."

She got out of the car, smiling brilliantly, and tripped on a small stone. She turned her ankle, and swore. "Oh, it's all right. It's nothing," she cried, and limped into the apartment house.

The stairs seemed an amplifier of raucous music and harsh laughter.

She jerked her chin. "You know these places, Joe. They take all kinds. But we'll be quite comfortable, and alone."

She had her key out and ready, and when she reached her door, it took only a quick movement of a plump wrist to have it open and shut behind her. With a laugh, she said, "Let's have some light on the subject, honey."

She switched on the lamps, and did a small graceless dance which felt good to her. A spin and shift and jiggle of thick hips. Her silvered hair fell in her eyes. Her red skirt popped open at its too-tight waist. She reached out to embrace empty air. "Come on, Joe, let's have something to drink, and talk a little. Get comfortable and I'll rustle up the martinis and put the steak on and cut the salad, and we'll have our evening together."

Still talking, she slipped out of her skirt and blouse, and hung them away. "Our evening, Joe. How I wish they were all our evenings. But I know. Oh, please darling, don't look at me like that. I *know*. I didn't mean to reproach you." Her voice became husky, "And we're so lucky we have this much."

Wearing her bra and girdle, swaying on her spike heels, she paused in the kitchen doorway. "I'll only be a minute, Joe."

She hurriedly mixed the drinks, set up the tray, the two martini glasses. She was out of peanuts, but made a fast mix of curried tuna, and spread it on crumbly crackers. The salad lettuce was brown-edged and wilted, but she spruced it up in ice water, and shook up a garlic dressing, and thrust a tray of frozen muffins into the cold oven before she trimmed the steak and set it under the unlit broiler.

"All set now," she crooned. "I'll just put on something more comfortable, and we'll have our drinks and talk."

In the bedroom, she re-did her face, thick black eyelashes pasted on and stroked with mascara, a great greasy red cupid bow mouth, a showering squirt of Shalimar. Then she took off bra and girdle, sighing and rubbing the dented flesh for a moment before she donned a red lace gown, whispering, "Red for Friday night, Joe."

Back in the living room, carrying the tray with its pitcher of martinis and two glasses, and the curried tuna, she smiled at the sofa.

"And here we are darling, Now you pour for me, and I'll pour for you."

She snuggled down into the cushions, and filled first Joe's glass and then hers. She clicked the two rims in the usual toast, whispering, "To us, always."

She was silent for a little while, taking small quick sips of her drink, and smiling, and finally, she said, "Oh, Joe, dear, I didn't mean to suggest any such thing. Of course I'm happy with the way things are."

And then "It's like there's nobody else in the world. Just the two of us, Joe."

And later still, "But you mustn't feel that way. I'm not giving up anything for you, Joe. I'm getting as much from you as you get from me. Oh, but I do, Joe. The others? They mean nothing. I don't care what my father says, or those crazy brothers of mine. I only have one life to live. One ride on the merry-go-round.

I have to take it, hold it, love it. And you're that life, Joe."

And even later, "I know you feel that way, too. It doesn't have to be put into words. We're so close, so entwined with each other, we don't have to spell out our emotions. Oh, Joe . . ."

She fell back on the sofa, writhing in her own embrace, her face crushed into the pillows, her head twisting from side to side. "Oh, Joe, the steak . . . your dinner?"

A soft laugh. "Oh yes, yes, yes. Hold me, Joe . . . here and now . . . just hold me . . ."

The martini pitcher toppled soundlessly to the floor, the liquid blotted into the braided rug, leaving a dark wet ring.

The light glowed and faded in swift rainbow rings. Her breath came harder, harder. "Oh yes, Joe. That way, and more, more. Love me, kiss me, squeeze me. Ah . . ."

Her back arched and quivered. Gooseflesh puckered on her round bare thighs. Her legs trembled. "Oh Joe. yes . . ." She moaned, and collapsed with her ears ringing and her eyes blinded by sudden mist.

CHAPTER 9

There had been an unusual early morning rain, and now the cemetery grass was a fresh and painful green.

The sky was a sharp eye-burning blue above the tops of the cottonwoods, and the mountain peaks, jagged and black as bat wings, reached for high wispy clouds.

Mike stood at the edge of the new turf that covered the hard red clay of Lori's fresh grave. His hands were jammed in his pockets. His wide shoulders were bowed.

A few steps behind him, Claire and Miguelito waited. All the others had gone.

The words said, the prayers spoken, Lori consigned to hereafter and heaven, Mike knew only the grave at his feet. Now that his heart was buried there with Lori, he learned that the automaton he had been for these bitter months had become the man. The sallow emptiness of the moment was permanent reality.

She had been dressed in aquamarine, a quick bright color that would have matched her closed eyes, had they been open and alive. She had chosen it herself, in those days, which seemed long gone, when she still cared enough to choose.

Her thin, childlike hands had been folded on her breasts, folded gently against the silk, and on her left hand was her gold wedding band.

Mike had twice given it to her: once on the day they were married, again on the day she was buried. Both times he had experienced overwhelming satisfaction, different but equally strong.

He had been sitting over coffee, sleepless and remembering, in the pale hours before dawn. He heard a sound at the door. When he jerked it open, the hall was still and empty. But an envelope lay at his feet, and within it, the ring. He breathed silent curses on a frightened ghoul. And that was how the ring came to be on Lori's finger.

"It's over," Claire breathed, standing behind him. "Miguelito, can't we get him to leave now?"

Mike heard, agreed, and promptly forgot. He listened to the remembered sound of Lori's voice, saying, "Six months wasted. Doubting myself, doubting you. Love, time wasted. And there was so little time."

He had denied it. "Lori, no." He had refused to think of that part of it then. It was for later.

Later had come. It was now.

He dared remember now what they had had between then. Her hot glowing body in his arms—no part of him her lips hadn't touched with fluttering butterfly kisses, no part of him her hands hadn't caressed and known. The others, fooled by her fragile wrists and slim legs, had called her his child bride. Only he had known her strength. He thought of that time, early in their marriage when he had lain on her, and she had said, "Get your weight off your elbows, Mike. I want to feel all of you." When he had tried, but cautiously, she made a small fist and clubbed him low on the spine, clubbed him so hard that the blow sent him into an uncontrollable spasm, the two of them rocking with it in glory, and she gasped amid laughter and cupped his cheeks and licked the surprising tears from his face.

Now, daring to remember, he remembered the rest, that she had whispered tiredly, "Oh, Mike, why did I let it go bad? Why did I start doubting myself and you? Why didn't I have the faith to know?"

"You didn't let it go bad, Lori. It didn't. I swear . . . I swear . . ."

He had sworn truly. It had not been Lori. That was his guilt.

"Oh Mike," she had said, when it was too late to change it, "Mike, if only it hadn't seemed so dirty and puny and petty. As if I were trying to punish you by being sick. As if I were trying to get out of sex with you. I could take anything but having us messed up so. I could even take what's going to happen. But this way, Mike, oh God . . ."

His was the burden, his the guilt. He had allowed Joe to corrupt him. He had allowed himself to betray Lori.

He had believed Joe only because what Joe said, without ever putting it into words, was what he himself already believed. That first morning, when he realized that she was ill, he had thought that it must be his fault. He was asking too much of her, too much of her small, fragile body. He made up his mind then that it would be different. He would hold himself back, no matter what it took. He would give her a chance to be herself again. He was sure he could handle it.

He could tell from small things Lori let drop after her first few visits to the doctor that Joe had decided much the same thing.

"Vitamins," she had said. "Vitamins. And rest, rest, rest." She grinned, "He also mentioned that there can be too much of a good thing. He meant sex, Mike."

Mike had set out to help cure her.

It hadn't been easy. Not for him, nor for her. She would reach for him, and when he achingly pretended to be asleep, she would sigh. She began to watch him, her dark-encircled eyes growing bigger and bigger as her face thinned down.

Finally she had said, "You're carrying this crazy idea of Joe's too far, Mike." She said, "Maybe you just don't like skinny women, Mike." She said, "Mike, damn you, don't turn away from me tonight." That time, mercifully, he hadn't.

And then, suddenly, they both knew it was no longer a matter of helping her adjust to marriage. That had never been the problem. They knew they were fighting for her life. And what they could have had together for that short time had been lost, and was gone forever.

"I shouldn't have let it happen, Lori," Mike said softly. "God forgive me, Lori, and you forgive me. I let guilt ride me instead of faith in you."

Behind him, Claire whispered, "Miguelito, please. Please, I can't stand it. Let's get him away from here now," and Miguelito shook his head.

"We have to," she pleaded.

"He's got to get it all over with, Claire."

"Not this way." She surged forward, caught Mike's arm. "Please, Mickey. Come on now. That's enough. You can come back. You can visit again. But for now, come home with me."

"Home," he said.

"Yes, Mickey. Please."

He raised his head finally. The scar on his neck was dark red. "No, Claire. I'm going to work."

"You can't."

"I have to."

"Not today. You need some rest."

"It's all over," he said gently. "I've got plenty of time to rest. Don't you see? I can think about it now. I have to think about it."

"No Mickey."

"I don't expect you to understand."

"I don't. I can't," she cried.

Miguelito intervened. "It *is* time to leave, Mike."

Mike blinked hard and turned away, walking so swiftly that Claire, hurrying to catch up with him, had to run, and Miguelito caught her arm to steady her when she tripped.

Miguelito took the wheel. Mike put Claire in the middle, and settled down beside her, sighing. He was too big for the narrow space, but too preoccupied to notice.

Pressed by him, Claire leaned against Miguelito. She covertly studied Mike's face, looking for a clue to what made him seem a stranger. Unable to find it, she remained unable to understand her uneasiness.

Mike sensed her glance, said "Don't worry. I'm okay. You know I've been expecting this for a long time."

"I know, Mickey." Then. "It was nice that Joe was able to come."

Mike was still, considering what problem she couldn't guess, and she suddenly wished she hadn't mentioned Joe. She wished she didn't feel the urge to think of him, speak of him.

The night before, aching for him, she had been surprised when he knocked at her door.

She let him in, and he must have read the look on her face. He said, "It *is* Friday night, Claire."

"So it is," she agreed, bitter in spite of her joy that he had come. "We mustn't let anything, not anything, interrupt our little routine, must we? But how did you know I'd be alone? That Mike wouldn't be here with me?"

"Mike is the kind of man who goes off to lick his wounds in private, Claire. Besides, I just had to see you."

"Even though today is the day Lori died?"

"I just had to see you," he repeated.

"That's all I've been thinking of all day, Joe. Ever since I heard . . ."

"I wouldn't have known that."

"I'm sorry, Joe." She curled up in a corner of the sofa, her hands folded in her lap.

He studied her, his wide blue eyes expressionless.

"Please," she burst out. "Please don't look at me that way!"

"I don't know what you mean." There was a faint edge of impatience to his voice, and he moved his long legs as if he were about to rise.

"Clinically," she said. "As if I'm a patient, and you're wondering, very impersonally, of course, just what the hell is wrong with me."

He laughed softly. "Well, in a way you're right. I'm not feeling very impersonal toward you, but I *am* wondering what the hell's wrong."

"You don't know? You can't imagine?"

"Claire . . ."

"All right," she said. "I'll tell you. I feel a very deep embarrassment that you should be here now. I feel a very unhappy guilt that I want you to be."

200

"I see. But why? Why do you?"

"Because of Lori, I guess."

"I don't follow you."

"She's dead. Dead, Joe. Mike's heartbroken. So how can we sit here and talk to each other? And maybe, in a little while, we'll adjourn to the bedroom and stop talking to each other. How can we pretend that nothing's happened when it has?"

"Death happens every day, Claire," Joe told her gently.

She ignored that. "And . . . and there's something quite wrong with Mike. You ought to see him, talk to him. Maybe you can help him."

"I can't now, Claire. Of course there's something wrong with him. He's been deeply hurt. He'll get over it."

"You're sure?" she said wonderingly.

"I know. It's my business."

"Death?"

"Claire!"

"Oh God," She sobbed, dropping her head into her hands, "oh God, will we ever be the same again?"

"We are the same. Now. Right now," he said, and took her into his arms.

Aching for him still, she remembered their time together. The slow drying of her tears, their limbs entwining, her mouth searching his for surcease from the memory of loss and the weight of fear. She wouldn't allow herself to say his name again, even though she wanted to.

Miguelito drove slowly through the Saturday morning traffic, brushing her arm occasionally, murmuring an apology. Once, turning, his forearm brushed along her breast. He didn't apologize that time, though she was sure that he was as much aware of that brief touch as she.

"I'll drop you off," Miguelito told her finally. "Say where."

"Home. Unless Mike wants me."

"I don't," Mike said. "Get busy doing something, the way I'm going to."

"I can't," she cried. "It's not just another day."

Mike glanced at her sideways, a strange dark look.

She lapsed into shamed silence. She had no right, she knew, to imply that to him the day of Lori's burial was just another day. No right and no reason. She knew better. But she wanted to see him weep. She wanted his hard face to break, and his gravelly voice to sob. She wanted him to complain and curse. That would be normal. Once done, hurt aired and loss bewailed, he could begin to be whole again. She had known him all her life. Now she didn't understand, and she was frightened.

She made one last try as Miguelito turned into Rojas Lane and stopped before her house.

"What about it, Mickey? Change your mind and stay with me?"

"You'll be okay," he said.

"Mickey, please. Not me. You."

"I'll be okay too."

Miguelito said, "Take it easy, Claire," with a reassuring smile.

Mike got out, held the door open for her.

She slid out. She put her hand on his arm, and suddenly, she had to say Joe's name, to hear it aloud and watch Mike's face, his eyes, when he heard it. "Mike," she said, "Mike, you ought to talk to Joe. If you won't talk to me, then try him, please try him. He'll help you, Mike."

Even as she spoke, she heard the words ring false. A sour bell tolling. She felt the queer catch in her breath. Had Joe been able to help her? What had he given in answer to her questions, her fears?

Mike said bleakly, "Joe's already done all he could do to me."

More shrilly than she intended, she cried, "What are you talking about?"

Mike, watching her as intently as she was watching him, noticed the pallor in her pixie face, and the terror in her amber eyes. He said softly, "Joe spoiled it, Claire. For Lori and me. What was between us, he muddied with his crazy ideas and crazy questions." Mike let his breath out in a long tired sigh. "And I let him do it, Claire. That's what's even worse."

"Oh Mike, no! You can't blame Joe!"

The scar on Mike's neck became a raw scarlet ribbon. He got back into the car without saying anything to her. "Come on, Miguelito, let's go to work."

They were men much like himself. They weren't really surprised to see Mike come to the precinct from the cemetery, just as most of them had done within the last hour.

Mike was sure that before he had arrived, there had been a few squad room jokes about that Saturday morning being a good day for the city's criminal population, with a large part of the force off to say good-bye to Lori. But there were no jokes in his presence, only the quick condolences offered as freely as the blood given before.

And in that atmosphere Mike began to ask himself the questions he had refused to face for a long while. *What about Claire and Joe?* Since it was the time for questions, it was also the time for answers.

Mike didn't wait. He told Miguelito he had changed his mind and was leaving.

Miguelito, whose facility for knowing made him suspicious, asked, "How come, amigo?" and unsatisfied with the reply, which was a shrug, managed to move an adamant and resisting Mike from the precinct to the bar down the street.

There, over drinks, he asked, "Mike, what's eating at you? And I don't mean Lori. I'm talking about Claire. You were pushing her. Why? What are you driving at with her?"

Mike eyed his partner over the glass rim, drank deeply, and considered. He supposed it could be explained in the most simple of terms. Joe and Lori. Lori had been despoiled before she died. Joe and Claire. What would he do to her? Mike himself the third point of the triangle. Through him Joe had met the other two. Very simple to explain. He said, "Why don't you mind your own business, amigo?"

Miguelito smiled faintly. "If it concerns Claire, I'd like to make it my business. If *you* don't mind."

"I don't mind," Mike said flatly, and pushed back his chair, and told Miguelito he was on his way.

"Yeah, sure," Miguelito answered, and handed over the car keys. "See you tomorrow. And take it easy,

Mike." He added gently, as Mike turned away, "I suggest you leave the drink behind."

Mike realized, then, that he still held the half-full glass, and he emptied it and set it down.

As he walked away, he heard Miguelito say, "Remember what I said about Claire."

She stood before the house with plumes of dust rising and falling around her, hearing the raw sound of Mike's voice and listening to his words again. She shivered with sudden cold in the heat of the August noon.

She heard her name spoken, once, twice, before she turned and saw David coming toward her. "I came over because I thought I could do something for you, maybe," he said.

She shook her head. "No, no, thank you."

She hurried inside to wander aimlessly from room to room, trying not to think nor feel, but somehow helplessly afraid.

She thought, when she heard the knock at the door, that David had returned. She called out, "Not now, David. I'm busy. Some other time, okay?"

Mike came in, stood there looking at her, dark head lowered, dark eyes hard.

She knew then that she had been expecting him, waiting for him. He hadn't quite finished what he had been saying earlier, out on the lane, about Joe. And Mike was not a man to leave a task undone. She knew that, and she knew she didn't want to listen.

He stood there, big, silent, shoulders hunched in the baggy jacket, hands rammed in his pockets. She felt as if the hot humming world outside had disappeared, and she was alone, his prisoner in some small gray room from which there was no escape.

She tried to look away from him.

She tried to speak.

She waited.

The room was absolutely still.

He asked quietly, "What's between you and Joe Stevens, Claire?"

Just as quietly, she asked in turn, "Why do you want to know?"

"You know why."

She shook her head, her short dark curls dancing in emphatic denial.

"It's been in the back of my mind for a long time, I guess," he told her reflectively.

"I'm not going to talk about it, Mike."

"You will," he said gently. "I want to know."

She took a deep breath, more like a sob. She turned her back on him, and went to the sofa, and curled up in a corner. She didn't realize how much she looked like some small trapped animal at bay before a poised hunter. She said finally, "I'm a big girl, Mike. I've lived my life on my terms for a long time now. I don't answer to you or to anyone."

"What about to yourself?"

"That's my concern," she told him, still quietly. But his question had cut deep. She knew she had been trying to answer to herself during Joe's unexpected visit Thursday, and again on Friday, and even that morning, while Lori was being buried, Claire remembered how she had peered cautiously at his set face, and asked herself what what was going to happen.

Mike said, "You're not telling me that I'm wrong, Claire."

"I don't want to talk about it," she told him. "You're just my brother, Mike. Not my judge."

He said dryly, "I'm neither at the moment. For want of a better word, I have to call myself your saviour." His sudden grin was bitter. "For want of a better word."

"I don't want you to save me, Mike."

He said savagely, "I'm not giving you the choice."

She gave him a quick look, then glanced around the room. Her eyes on him again, she asked, "Why do you hate Joe?"

"You know why. Maybe you couldn't have known before. But I told you, I explained it to you."

"It doesn't make sense to me, Mike. I think you just *want* to hate him. And you mustn't, you mustn't!"

She shrank back as he bent over her, but she couldn't evade his reaching hands. He drew her to her feet, moved her to the window. He put a thumb under her chin, and turned her face up to the brilliant sun. "Tell me the truth," he said.

He was no longer the brother, as he had told her before. He was the ruthless inquisitor.

"We're lovers," she whispered. "You knew it. Why make me say it? But all right. We're lovers. Are you satisfied?"

There was some subtle alteration in his face: a slight flattening of his dark straight brows, a narrowing of his lips.

"Don't look at me like that," she cried.

He let go of her, turned away. His wide shoulders blocked the light, so that suddenly she stood in shadow.

It was a release from pain. She said, quietly again, "It has nothing to do with you, Mike."

"Of course not." But he turned back to her. "When did it begin?"

She touched the red scar that climbed out of his collar. "As far as I was concerned, with this. But nothing happened until later. Do you remember the night I introduced you to Lori?" Her voice shook, saying the name. She went on, "I left you both. It was to meet Joe."

"That long ago." Mike's voice, thoughtful, gave no hint of what was to come. "When is he going to divorce his wife and marry you?"

She gasped.

"Never?"

"I don't know," she said. "It doesn't matter."

"You're willing to settle for being his unpaid whore, for as long as that lasts?"

"Mike . . ."

"Is he all that good in bed?"

"Stop it!"

"You don't even know what it should be like, could be like. You don't know what you're throwing away for a man that takes, but doesn't give. A man who can't give his whole heart to anyone."

"People do fall in love, Mike," she said hesitantly. "You don't always plan how it can be."

"We're not talking about love. And we're not talking about your morals, Claire."

"I never expected it to be like this," she cried.

Mike grinned, and it was ugly.

She winced under its impact.

"What did you expect?" he demanded.

"Please leave me alone," she pleaded.

"Why don't you ask him when he's going to marry you?"

"Stop it, Mike."

"Okay," he said. "I'll stop. It's up to you."

"Yes. Up to me. So leave Joe out of it. Don't hate him, Mike. You mustn't hate him."

"Not even for what he's going to do to you?" With that, Mike laughed softly, and walked out.

Claire stood shivering.

CHAPTER 10

As the stretcher was lifted to the ground, the blanket-wrapped figure began to struggle.

"Should have stuck a jacket on him," the attendant grumbled.

"On a Gorman?" the other jeered.

Joe, passing stopped and leaned over the stretcher. He grinned, "Hey, Buss, quit making trouble for the staff."

Buss squinted red eyes. "Joe? That you, Joe? Oh, she's a pretty girl. If she were mine, though, I wouldn't let her hang around that bar. Pretty, pretty, and if she were mine . . ." The words trailed off.

The attendants winked at Joe, and rolled the stretcher away.

He forgot Buss Gorman as he pulled out of the parking lot, unaware that Bess Bradford, in a car he had never seen, dressed in a yellow outfit bought especially to please him, was following close behind.

He was thinking about Claire, the messages she had left with the Medical Service, the messages she had left with the hospital switchboard. It wasn't like her to have been so indiscreet. Still, the last few days had been difficult ones.

He supposed her insistence had something to do with

her concern over Mike. He had looked close to a breakdown that morning at the funeral. Under rigid control, of course, the brutal face rock hard, but with tremors in the clenched muscles of the heavy jaw that told Joe Mike was going through the same pain that every human being suffers at one time or another. A pain for which there was no remedy but time. It was Mike's turn now.

So he was no longer the tough cop who had sat in Joe's living room and said bluntly, "You'd better face it, Dr. Stevens. Your daughter's a thief. I don't know why. I don't know for sure what you can do about it. I *do* know you'd better face it. Because if you don't, there'll be a next time. And next time I won't be able to do what I did tonight."

Joe couldn't imagine his small Gilly, her face frightened under her bangs, her wide blue eyes bewildered, in a police station. He couldn't imagine her in the hands of a man like Mike Manning. He was grateful enough, however, that Mike had tried to help, so that he listened, resenting, even as he did, Mike's callous description of what Gilly had done, and how she had been. A man like Mike couldn't possibly understand a child like Gilly. He had been forced to accept it, with some unvoiced reservations, so that Gilly had begun her sessions with Dr. Richards. She had stayed out of the hands of the police thereafter; the battleground had shifted.

Joe hadn't seen tough Mike Manning again until he brought his young wife into his office, and said, "I guess you remember me, Dr. Stevens," and waited for Joe to work a miracle that couldn't be worked. By then, of course, there had been Claire . . .

Joe cut off the highway, into Old Town. It had been a

hectic Saturday evening at the hospital. It was a hectic Saturday evening on the streets. He was annoyed that he had to slow down.

The many messages, the indiscretion of leaving them, meant that Claire was anxious. It would take time to reassure her; he wasn't even certain that he could. She didn't understand, of course. She assumed, as did everyone, that Joe Stevens had every answer.

It took longer than it should have, longer than it would have if she had been reasonable and let him set her up in one of those pleasant condominiums across town. But finally he parked in the shadows of Rojas Lane, took his bag, locked the car, and hurried to her door.

It opened immediately at his knock.

Claire lifted her arms to him, outlined against the dim light from within. "Oh, Joe, Joe, I'm so glad you came."

He was too conscious of the lane at his back to kiss her there. He touched her lightly, moving her away, and went inside.

With the door closed against the night, he put his bag down, hugged her briefly. Then he asked, "Now, what's all the urgency about?"

" 'Now what seems to be the trouble?' " she mocked him.

He grinned. "Okay. Whatever the patient prefers."

She backed away from him to sink into the chair at her desk. Pale lamp light touched her face before she pushed the light away. Her eyes were feverishly bright and swollen, the pixie look washed away by tears. She wore the same black shirt and skirt that she had had on for Lori's funeral.

THE DEATH WATCH

"Is it about Mike?" Joe asked, trying to get her started, because she looked, as some of his patients looked, as if she didn't know where to begin.

"Mike?" she answered. "Yes, in a way. And no. No. Not really I just had to talk to you."

Joe knew then that he had made a mistake. It would have been better to have ignored the urgency of her calls and given her time to calm down. In the morning he could have skipped his usual Sunday golf game with Sam Upson, and seen her instead.

Her voice was a pale whisper. "We can't. You and me, we can't go on like this."

"I don't understand."

"Then you don't want to."

"I'm sorry, Claire . . ."

He had had a long day. Lori's funeral first. The office hours. The hospital rounds. And there was Gilly. He knew that he'd have to talk to Gilly when he got home. He wasn't up to coping with Claire, yet plainly he would have to. He said gently, "Claire, dear, this is not a good time for discussing big things. You're upset with the fact of death. Perhaps you're frightened suddenly by the thought of your own mortality. Anyway, let's just leave it alone for now."

"But it has to be now, Joe."

"All right," he said. "Tell me."

She was watching him, he saw, waiting, asking something of him. He wanted very much to reach out for her. He ached to hold her; he felt the beginning of a dull sensation in his groin. He could imagine himself pulling her into his arms, carrying her to the king-sized bed, and stripping her mourning clothes away. He could imagine himself falling on her slim body . . .

213

But she was waiting for him to speak, to say more than "all right," but there was nothing for him to say.

At last, she spoke. "Joe, are you ever going to divorce Ellen and marry me?"

The silence that fell between them vibrated in rhythm to the quivering within him.

"No," she whispered, answering herself. "Of course not. No. Then what?"

"We've been fine, Claire. Just as we were."

"You've been fine, Joe. Not me. I've ached, and cried, and hungered. I've even prayed. Does that tell you anything?"

"It was understood from the beginning. You knew how things were," he said defensively.

"No one ever really knows how things are, or accepts them. We always think we'll get what we want."

"I'm sorry, Claire."

"What for?"

"Sorry if I've made you unhappy, if you think I led you to believe we could be anything more to each other than what we've been."

"You made me believe that by loving me, Joe."

"We're both adults. We entered into this out of free choice. I thought you understood."

"You don't know much about people, Joe. You never did, I guess. You were wrong about Mike. Even wronger about Lori."

"Claire," he said stiffly, "Claire, don't blame me for Lori's death."

"But Mike told me, you see. You were wrong about her at first. And then there was no time left."

"There's always a need to blame. The doctor is handy.

He ends up the patsy. Mike will get over thinking that. And it has nothing to do with us."

"But you were just as wrong about me."

There was nothing left for him to say. He picked up his bag.

"All that love now hate," she whispered hoarsely. "Because you've made me feel ashamed."

Until the door was firmly closed behind him, he expected her to call him back and hurl her soft body into his arms. He expected it.

When he was outside in the still night, crossing the patio, he began to understand that it had happened: love had indeed gone to hate. She hadn't called him back.

There was sudden grief, quick, hot and hurting. He noted it clinically, and informed himself that it would pass.

There was relief, too, and he informed himself that it would grow until soon, sometime within a foreseeable future, the grief would be completely gone. It had been that way with Belena; it would be that way with Claire.

And he would be certain, then, that he had been right—sensible and wise. He could not muddle his life, the neat planned structure of his life, with a divorce that he didn't want, that he had never wanted.

As he got into the car, a tall slim form passed him, familiar somehow in outline, but the face shadowed and unrecognizable even when it turned back to look, and look again.

As Joe drove away, David moved quickly onto the patio and up to Claire's door.

THE DEATH WATCH

It had to be. There was no other way.

That morning, he had seen Claire get out of the car and been sorry for her, thinking of how it had been with him when Paul died, and he followed after her, saying, "If there's anything I can do . . ." But when the door had closed, and he stood alone, he wished that she had remembered about the job, and knew that she hadn't, and he was feeling ashamed, that he was thinking about the job when he knew how she felt.

But Tuesday was coming fast, and Gilly had spent so much of the fifty dollars she had gotten. He had discovered that he needed a ten-dollar entry fee, or the statue wouldn't even be admitted for judging. And meanwhile, he needed something to eat on, and to keep her happy on, too.

He had known he had to figure out something, so he set his shoulders and went back to his room, feeling whipped and worn, but refusing to admit that even to himself. Soon, back at work, going tap tap tap at the small stone Gilly that was his love and pride, breathing on her, whispering sweet words to her, he forgot time and trouble, and whistled joyfully because Gilly was coming out and she was going to be something. Oh, something so beautiful that to think about it scared him a little, made him jealous of the hands that were making her, conscious of the terrible mystery of their talent.

Silence. The tap tap tap of the small mallet. His tuneless whistle. The hum of the bees at the window. Time easing by.

And then, then the squeal of brakes in the lane, the slam of a car door. Rattle and bang. Gilly came dancing in, Gilly, in the flesh, laughing.

He looked up. "Hey, Gilly, you promised me you were going to go home. You know if you don't go home they'll call the police, and then we're in trouble. But if we play it right, we do just what we want."

Her long mouth twisted maliciously. "See. There you go. You don't trust me, and you're bossing me. And I don't like it."

"Well, then . . ." he breathed gently on the small statue, stood back to study it lovingly.

"All you care about is that," she said sullenly.

"It's you, Gilly. That's why I care about it. And it's going to make us our fortunes. So if you'd just be patient . . ."

"I am patient," she cried. She flung herself on the bed, all elbows and angles and sweet girl body. "The trouble with you, David, is that you don't have any imagination."

"Imagination?"

"That's what I said," she crowed. "Because if you did, you'd have figured it out. I did go home. Just like you told me to."

He left the table, went to her. "Did you? Really? No lies now."

"Just like you told me."

"What happened?"

She grinned. "'Where you been? What did you do last night?' Etc. etc. etc. And I said, 'Nothing,' and 'Nothing' again. So it was, 'But Gilly; why?' and some more of that. And I got myself cleaned up a little." Blue eyes begged for approval. "Just for you, David, and now I'm back. And you didn't even notice. You didn't even look. You're all the same. You just talk, but you don't give a good goddam."

217

"Of course I noticed, Gill. You look great." But at the same time, he glanced sideways at the small stone statue.

"And don't look at *her,* dammit!"

"I have to get it finished, Gilly." But now he was looking at her, and hard. All that cursing meant something; she knew he didn't like it.

She was charged up, burning inside. Maybe his mistake had been to send her home. But that had been necessary. They couldn't take any chances.

She shook her head slowly from side to side. Her long chestnut hair swung in shining ripples, sweet soft waves, beautiful and clean. So of course she had been telling the truth. She'd washed it, just as she'd promised. And she'd changed clothes, too. Her blue jeans were clean and pressed, and her white shirt was starched. The heavy conch belt around her narrow waist gleamed as if it had had a rubdown. He was a little ashamed of himself for doubting her, but worried, too.

He didn't like the way her head went back and forth, and the way her eyes peered up at him, wide open but somehow sly and defiant.

He grew more worried when she pulled a red rubber band from her shirt pocket and jerked her hair back and fastened it in a messy pony tail.

"No," she said finally. "No, David."

"No what?"

"You don't have to finish the goddam statue."

"Why not? What do you mean?"

"I want to play and have fun."

He said patiently, "But you know it's for you and me. So we can be together."

"Hah!"

218

"It is," he insisted. "And it's Saturday night, and by Tuesday——"

She laughed suddenly. "Oh, go on. I'm just kidding. I love to see you go all serious, David. Work, work. I'll sit here and be quiet as a mouse. I won't say a word to you. Work, man. Make me real."

"You're the realest thing I know," he told her, but he turned back to the table and took up the mallet. He breathed gently, prayed silently, and let his hands do the job that was theirs to do.

"Tap, tap, tap," she said, rolling over to curl up on her side. "Why don't you make a nice rhythm of it, David? Try some rock. Try some soul."

"I'd be afraid to," he grinned. "You might get up and start dancing, and then where'd I be?"

"I want to see it, David."

"Hey, Gilly. You know. Pretty soon now."

"Did she get you a job?"

He thought of seeing Claire earlier, and the look on her face, and how he had turned away, ashamed. He said, "I told you, didn't I? How her sister-in-law died?"

"That's just an excuse, I'll bet. If she cared, she'd have gotten you something."

"She has too much on her mind now, Gilly."

"What, for instance?"

"I told you, Gill. The death in her family."

"Death," Gilly retorted, "death doesn't matter. It's nothing but night. And it didn't happen to her."

"But this does matter to her, Gilly," David answered, thinking of his brother Paul lying in the narrow coffin, face rouged and plumped out, and the agony painted away.

"All right then. What are we going to do?"

He squinted at her over the table. "Do you have any of that money left?"

"Nope. And I'm not going to tell you where it went either."

"Oh, come on. You can tell me. What did you buy, Gill?" But he was hardly listening now, hands busy, breath careful, eyes anxiously fixed on the small Gilly under his tender fingers.

"You can ask, but I won't answer. It's a surprise." She giggled and shook her head back and forth so that her pony tail whipped across her face.

"We need that money. Every little bit helps."

"Too late, David. But I know you'll approve."

"And when do I get this surprise?"

"When I decide. Maybe tonight. Maybe tomorrow."

"Okay. I'll wait," he said, thinking hopefully that maybe the surprise was really the money, and that she'd saved it for what would be to her the right time. He went on working, looking up once in a while to smile at her intent face, wondering suddenly why she had become so still.

Finally, she asked, "Let me see it, huh, David?"

"Pretty soon," he told her. "It won't be long now."

She got up, pacing aimlessly, closer and closer.

He sneaked a look at her wide open eyes. They seemed aglow with malice. He made himself grin. "You're getting ready to pull a fast one on me, aren't you?"

"I'm getting ready to explode, David."

"Oh, come on. You're okay. We're doing fine."

"I want to do something good and sweet. I want to feel like I'm alive. I want to be me, David."

"You're always you," he said soberly.

"Oh, David, does this go on forever?"

"You know it doesn't. I get the statue done. It goes into the show. Maybe somebody'll buy it. Maybe not. But either way, I'm started, right? And I'll get a job. And you'll turn eighteen. And we can get married, and go back to Taos."

"I don't want to get married, David."

"It'll be just how you want. I promise you, Gill."

"Then why don't you get a job and start making it how I want?"

"I'm trying."

"She could get you a job. If you asked her."

"You know I asked her once. And the way things are, I'd better not ask again now."

". . . . Or she could give you some money."

"No," he said quickly.

"Why not? If we had money we could have some fun tonight, David. I want to have fun."

"If you hadn't spent what you——"

"But I did!" she yelled. "And I'm saving it for a surprise."

"Okay then." He decided regretfully that the surprise wasn't the money.

"And I'm hungry," she said plaintively.

"Why didn't you eat at home?"

"I didn't want to."

"Well, then . . ."

"I'm still hungry, David." She threw herself on the bed. "Oh, hell, I hate it the way it is."

"Hey Gill, Gilly . . ." He carefully placed the small mallet on the table, and took up the old shirt and threw it over the figure. He went to her, his arms outstretched.

She was still, looking up at him.

221

He could feel her body trembling. He said softly, "Look, are you really hungry?"

She nodded.

"We've got some cereal," he offered, "and some of the milk you brought yesterday, and maybe we can rustle up——"

"I want steak, David. Good strong red meat." She grinned at him. "Protein's the gas I go on, and protein's what the doctor ordered, you know what doctor, and I always go by what the doctor says, so . . ."

"Steak!" he groaned. "Ye gods, Gilly!"

"I got the money a day before yesterday. Remember? I went home and got it. Okay. So today it's your turn. You get the money today."

"But where? How?"

"From her. From Claire Manning."

He began to shake his head. But there was a glint in her eyes that stopped him. He hesitated, thought, fought himself, then, "Yeah, okay," he agreed. "That's what I'll do. I'll go borrow back that five dollars I returned to her the other day."

"You do that," Gilly said sweetly. "I'll wait right here. And then we'll have steak. And maybe then," she went on, "maybe then we'll have my surprise."

So he went with no enthusiasm, and a good deal of shame, down the street once more. He saw Joe leaving Claire's house, and the shame was gone. Hardened and stern and judging, because Lori Manning was dead and buried, and Dr. Joe Stevens couldn't possibly be needed at Claire's any more except for another reason, David was able to do what he hadn't been able to think of doing before.

Claire let him in. "Something wrong, David?"

Which was just what he had been about to ask her. Because once he saw her face, he forgot to be stern and judging and just got scared.

She kept looking at him, waiting.

He said, "Listen, do you still have that five bucks I brought back the other night? Because if you do, I sure could use it."

She kept looking at him blankly, not understanding, or not caring.

"I guess I should have come before." He paused deliberately, took a long slow aching breath. "I should have come when Dr. Stevens was still here. Maybe he'd have had five bucks on him he could spare me."

A crimson flush spread up her throat, dyed her haggard cheeks and brow.

She turned silently and took up her big black purse. She rummaged inside, found her wallet and pulled it out. She took a handful of bills and thrust them at David.

Her voice was rusty and tired-sounding: "You must need it very much, David."

"I do." He cleared his throat, repeated, "I really do, Claire," and closed his fingers around the money, not knowing how much was there, and not daring to count it.

He mumbled his shamed thanks, and turned to the door.

"You could make a lot of trouble, I guess," she said softly, "if you wanted to. But it would all be for nothing now, David."

"No," he whispered hoarsely. "I didn't mean it like

that." He couldn't look at her. "I really didn't. But you know how it is. I've just got to manage some way until Tuesday. I wouldn't, I won't . . ."

He had to stop trying to explain. He had to get out of there, and fast. He was crying, and he didn't want her to know.

As he fled, he heard the ring of the phone, heard Claire say, "Hello? Hello? Who is it? Why don't you answer me? Who is it?"

CHAPTER 11

Bess Bradford listened, nodded, smiled, and set the receiver back in its cradle.

Claire Manning.

Of course.

It was perfectly clear now.

"Oh, Joe," Bess whispered, "how could you? How could you do it to me?"

"Tim's the name, baby. Just call me Tim," said the man beside her lounging against the wall.

"Oh, Joe, I don't know what to do," she mumbled, glazed eyes awash with tears.

"Let's have another drink," Tim suggested, ducking his head to nuzzle her plump bare shoulder. "We'll have another drink, baby. And I'll tell you my name again. How about that, huh?"

Bess frowned at the phone, then brightened. "Now that's a good idea," she cried. "That's just what I need."

Tim draped a thick hairy arm around her shoulders. They weaved their way back to the bar.

She had waited in the lobby, dressed in her beautiful new yellow outfit, a halter-top affair under which her full breasts danced invitingly. She was made up, her hair brushed to a silver halo. She breathed Shalimar mist. She had waited for such a long time because she had been sure Joe would make his rounds, no matter what he and Ellen had on for the night, no matter how long a day it had been. And besides, Bess had thought he might need her. The Manning funeral had been that morning. Joe had felt he had to go. She told him she didn't see why; it would be too hard on him. But he'd said simply that he wanted to. That was how he was. Nobody really understood how difficult it was for a physician to lose a patient. Each time it happened, a part of him died too. Oh, *she* knew. *She* understood. So she thought he might need her that night.

Waiting, peering anxiously from behind the column where she hid, she had seen them bring in Buss Gorman, and suddenly, Joe was there, too, leaning over to say a few words to the struggling blanket-wrapped figure. Poor Buss instantly went still. Joe headed for the parking area, and Bess scurried after him.

She managed to be right behind him when he cut into the highway, and to stay with him when he turned suddenly. She had to brake, to lurch on ahead of another car. He was driving faster than he usually did, and she had been so sure he was going straight home that she almost went that way automatically.

It was Saturday night, after all. And Joe and Ellen were probably going out. They were very popular, much in demand, and Bess didn't imagine them sitting at home, playing two-handed gin or watching television.

But Joe's sudden swift turn through the heavy traffic —the same one, she realized, that he had made for the past few nights—proved that he wasn't going home.

Not that it mattered to her where he went. She was just following him to see him for one last time, another moment or two, before the emptiness of the night and Sunday closed in.

The long gray Cadillac turned again, leaving the bright lights of the highway behind. She let herself follow. From two blocks away, she saw his red blinker signal right, and the headlights arch up against adobe walls then disappear. Old Town. Slummy, hippy, run-down Old Town. He *couldn't* have a patient there. She knew everything about him; after fifteen years, and as close as they'd been, she was bound to know everything about him, including his patients' addresses. Besides, he didn't make house calls.

She coasted to the corner, braked, and got out. Very cautiously she crept to the edge of the adobe wall, and peered around it. The long gray Cadillac was parked before one of those sagging compounds that housed Bess couldn't imagine *what* sorts of people. Who could Joe know there?

She walked gingerly up the dusty lane, anxiously eying the moonlit shadows, then hurriedly stepping into them, when Joe left his car, carrying his bag. She crept on. At the opening in the wall, at the broken gate, she paused.

Joe was standing at a door.

It opened as she watched.

The woman was no more than a shapely silhouette in the pale light from behind her. A silhouette with arms lifted to embrace Joe Stevens.

"Oh, Joe, Joe, I'm so glad you came."

The door suddenly closed, blotting out all light.

Bess crept back to her car, sick and cold. She tried to

tell herself that Joe was stopping by to see an old friend, maybe; maybe a cousin that Bess had just never happened to hear of.

She was being ridiculously suspicious for no reason. But, she told herself, there *was* a reason. Something had been different about Joe for some time, and she'd sensed it. Shivering as if the pale stars above were bombarding her with chips of ice, she managed to get the car started. She found her way back to the main road through the winding streets, sure she could never do it again. She turned into the freeway heading home. She couldn't really believe it even though she had seen it with her own eyes. No . . . Joe was so straight. He couldn't be engaged in some sly, ugly, dirty, horrible love affair. He couldn't be jeopardizing everything he stood for: his good name, his standing in the community. His marriage.

Bess blinked against tears, and her eyes burned with a sudden tide of dissolving mascara. It was because Joe was married, because of Ellen and Gilly, that he had never looked at Bess, never spoken to her with the lover's voice she could so easily imagine. It was because he was married that she and Joe could never be more to each other than what they were now.

All those years given freely, with love. She couldn't stand it . . .

"Oh, Joe," she whispered aloud. "How could you do this to me?"

She found herself suddenly on her own street. She parked, and stumbled out of the car.

A neighbor muttered at her near the lobby mailbox. She shook her head violently and hurried on.

Door open. Slammed. Locked. Chained. Lights.

THE DEATH WATCH

She stood in the middle of the room, waiting for something to happen, moaning, "Oh Joe, Joe, Joe . . ."

Silence.

She whimpered, and stumbled into the kitchen. She found her bottle, and took two quick drinks, the fire spreading through her body in liquid waves. She carried the bottle into the living room, and lay down on the sofa.

"Joe," she said. "Joe, please, please . . ."

She stared at the ceiling, taking one fast gulp after another, the gin spilling from the corners of her mouth and staining the yellow halter at her breasts. Images formed and broke and re-formed before her wide staring eyes.

Joe and that woman.

Obscenely attached.

Obscenely throbbing.

Hands, mouths, thighs.

A slim silhouette with arms raised . . .

The bottle was suddenly cold, dry, against Bess' lips. She flung it away and got up.

She had promised herself she would never go back to Tony's, never again be embarrassed waiting for the invitations she knew she would have to refuse. It was one thing to listen to the juke box, to have a few friendly drinks; it was something else again to have to put up with the stares, the tentative approaches. She thought that because everybody at Tony's knew her, it ought to be all right. They should understand that she wasn't the kind of a woman who picked up men in bars. But there were always some strangers around. And after that last time, months before, when that beefy truck driver had lurched over her, laughing. . . . "Listen, melt, will you? You're giving me the willies. This is supposed to be a good time place. So how about it, sister?" When she said, "Go away please," he'd answered, "God save us from your kind. What're you taking up bar space for?" Everybody had laughed at her. She heard them as she went out, kept hearing them all the way down the dark block. So she'd promised herself that she'd never go back. And besides, she knew she'd never find Joe in Tony's. It wasn't his kind of place.

But she had to go somewhere. She had to do something. She locked the door behind her, and went downstairs.

The night air felt good on her hot cheeks. She decided she'd walk the four blocks.

Tony's loomed up, a flicker of red and blue neon. She went inside. Not the way she used to, closing the door quietly and creeping in, timid and a little scared. No. She let the door slam, and marched in, and walked hard and flat-footed to the bar. She climbed on the stool with a flourish of fat legs and a jiggling of breasts. "Hello, Sam," she said breathlessly, "I'll have a bourbon and water and light on the water."

Sam got her drink, pushed pretzels and ashtray closer, and said, "How you been? Ain't seen you for a while." Then he moved on to chat with somebody else.

She didn't intend to knock the drink back. But suddenly her glass was empty. She frowned at it, fingering her silvered hair, re-crossing her pudgy legs. One plump thigh brushed the hip of the man sitting beside her. She apologized quickly.

"You're excused," he said, grinning. "Hey Sam, how about some service down here? The lady wants another." He winked at her. "You do, don't you?"

"I do," she told him, her breathless voice rusty.

"I'm Tim Jordan. I just came to town a while ago, and I need some talk to make myself feel like I'm still on this earth. Know what I mean?"

He was thick-shouldered, tanned dark, with thinning sandy hair, pale gray eyes, and a deep slow voice.

She gave him a quick absent look, acknowledged she knew exactly what he meant, and then concentrated on her new drink.

Tim talked to her, leaning close, and kept the drinks coming, and suddenly, blinking into the smoky haze, she remembered that Joe had been standing in the doorway of a crummy adobe house on Rojas Lane, and that a woman had waited for him, slender arms open and hungry to hold him.

Oh Joe, Joe, I'm so glad you came.

Let me talk to Dr. Stevens. Let me talk to Dr. Stevens.

And it was patients' hours. He was busy. But he went into his office and closed the door, so that all Bess heard was the mumble of his words, and not the substance of them, because she hadn't dared hold the extension line open and listen. Though she had wanted to. Yes. Yes, she'd wanted to stoop that low. Because she'd known, oh God, yes. Joe. Joe, I knew even then, I *did* know. I must have known . . .

"Baby," Tim said, lounging over her, a shoulder nudging her breast, "baby, listen, I'm a stranger in this town. What's there to do for fun?"

She barely glanced at him. "I have to make a phone call. Where's the phone?"

He shrugged his shoulders.

She wavered off the stool, headed for the door.

He touched her arm, guided her toward the back. "Here's your phone, baby. Hanging right on the wall. Hope you're not planning on privacy. It's the best I can do for you."

She gave him a blank look. "I need a book. I don't know the number."

"Don't see a book, baby. Try information."

"I need a dime."

He grinned, put a dime in her hand.

"Thanks, Joe," she said absently.

"Tim's the name," he chuckled, "just call me Tim."

She dialed information, and got the number. Her dime didn't come back. She waited helplessly, wondering what to do.

"Must be an awful important call," Tim said, and put another dime in her hand.

She dialed again, and heard the two rings, and then the voice of Claire Manning came on. She listened for a moment, then she hung up.

"Wrong number?" Tim asked.

She shook her head.

Claire Manning. Yes. Yes. Claire.

"I have to make a phone call," Bess said.

Tim searched his pockets, gave her another dime. "You need information this time too?"

She didn't answer. She dialed, waited. It was the right thing to do, of course. Ellen ought to know about it. It was Ellen's right. Joe couldn't do that to her.

Bess and Ellen shared him between them, and Bess saw more of him than Ellen ever did. True that they lived together, slept in each other's arms, and wakened to smile at each other, Joe and Ellen. But Joe and Bess . . .

"Dr. Stevens' residence," Ellen said suddenly. "This is Mrs. Stevens."

Bess blinked at the phone.

"Yes? Hello?"

Sounds of tinkling glasses, subdued music, a burst of deep masculine laughter.

Bess hung up wordlessly.

Tim leaned over her, squinting through the smoky haze. "Wrong number again? Maybe you better give up and have a drink. How about that, baby? What do you say we settle down and have ourselves a ball?"

"That's a wonderful idea," she said breathlessly, smiling at him. "Let's do that, Joe."

Ellen shrugged, and replaced the phone. She gave the silver cocktail shaker she held an extra jiggle and danced down the hall in the direction of the living room where her guests were gathered.

With the laughter rippling out toward her, she heard the car in the driveway outside.

Joe.

It didn't occur to her, as she stopped and waited, that it might be Gilly. Gilly's convertible had its own sound; Gilly's approach was unique. A spray of gravel, a roar, a squeal. But the slow purr, the decisive clamp of brake, the muted door slam could be no one but Joe.

She passed the shaker from hand to hand, unconsciously shifting her weight from hip to hip. Her floor-length dress floated in clouds of green chiffon around her feet.

Its sequinned top molded her full breasts as she took a deep breath.

Joe was late. But she wouldn't reproach him.

Why should she? She felt too good to worry about being second best. She knew that she looked well—auburn hair aglow, with every wave in place; thick dark brown lashes accentuating her eyes; lips scarlet, and faintly knowing. Her mirror had told her so. Her friends had told her so, too. She had accepted their compliments with confident amusement. The same confident amusement that she had been cherishing since the day before. There was, after all, young Bud Slater to think about.

It didn't matter that she still had a faint ache in her neck from the athletics he seemed to so enjoy. Nor that she had had to hold back giggles of embarrassment at his so proudly employed technique. Remarkably, nor even that he had conned her out of twenty-five dollars. She had discovered that sex was a series of mechanics; all it required was two bodies, properly equipped. Useful information for a woman who was second best.

Joe came in slowly. He closed the door behind him, then stopped, surprise on his face.

She nearly laughed. He looked unusually off-balance. His hair was ruffled, his tie askew. Even his usually shining shoes seemed dusty.

"What's going on?" he asked, plainly bewildered.

It would be ridiculous to reproach him. She said, "It's been on your calendar, both here and at the office, for weeks. We're having six couples for drinks, and then we're going out to the club for dinner and dancing. And if you don't hurry, we're going to need all your medical skill to keep our friends from total collapse.

They were on time, and they've been going strong since they got here."

"I'm sorry, Ellen. I got tied up."

She smiled brilliantly. "We all realize that."

He straightened his shoulders, grinned. "I'll just be a minute."

"Of course." But she stood there, squeezing the shaker and looking at him. Something was not quite right. There was a tension in his tall, lean body. His shoulders were too rigid, jerking his coat awry. And, more than enything, instead of hurrying off to shower and shave and change, he remained where he was, looking back at her.

At last he said, "I'd better get started."

She nodded. She continued to the living room to announce Joe's arrival, and to offer one more round before they departed en masse for the club.

Later, she wished that she had had a little less to drink, had been a little less gay. She wished that she had had senses somewhat less blunted with which to enjoy Joe's attentiveness.

It was a good evening, and they came home laughing. But when he poured a nightcap for her and himself, he said, "Thank God that's over. I didn't think I'd make it." Then he collapsed down on the big sofa.

"What are you talking about?" she demanded, angry because he was making her joy seem false. "I thought you were having fun."

"Oh, I was, Ellen." He sighed, grinned, shrugged. "But maybe I'm getting too old for that kind of fun."

She thought of them toasting each other across the candlelit table, and rising to dance, her body soft and warm against his. Across the room, past his shoulder, she could see Bud Slater smiling down at a new partner. She had laughed to herself, and snuggled closer to Joe.

But it had all been an illusion. She didn't feel good any more. The amused confidence was gone. She said coldly, "Maybe you're getting old."

"But you're not?" he asked, still grinning, his wide eyes alert, interested.

Which, of course, didn't fool her, though she knew it did fool most people. He could be thinking of anything, *anything*, and still look like that.

She was suddenly conscious of her frown lines, and under them, deep inside, a tightening band at her temples. She studied him thoughtfully. Now that they were home again, home and alone, she saw it: something *had* happened.

"But you're still a damn fine-looking woman," he told her.

She didn't respond.

"What is it?" he asked.

"That's what I was wondering, Joe."

She saw his face tighten, close, mask itself.

"Wondering?"

"You know."

"I don't understand, Ellen."

But she could see that his mind was elsewhere, considering—remembering? The tightening band at her temples cut deeper. She knew it would soon be too late for the capsule to work, but she lingered, captive of the need to probe. She said lightly, "Well anyway, tired or not, old or not, it was still a good evening. And I wish we could do it more often."

236

"All right, we will. If you really like that sort of thing."

"Why shouldn't I?"

"No reason. I didn't mean that, Ellen."

"Then what did you mean?"

"I guess I don't really know. It was quite a day."

"Yes."

"Oh, by the way, they had to bring Buss Gorman in this evening."

"I knew that was going to happen. I saw him at the club yesterday, and he looked terrible."

"So that's what he meant," Joe said.

"Buss?" Ellen grimaced. "Did he tell you that he fell off the bar stool? I thought he'd fractured his skull at least, but he seemed all right when I left him."

"No, poor Buss didn't mention that. He was saying something about a pretty girl. I couldn't follow him, didn't much try to. He hardly ever makes sense any more, permanently pickled as he is. One of these days he'll go out, suddenly, twenty years before his time. And everyone will wonder why."

"Do you know why?" she demanded.

"No. I can't say that I do."

"He's unhappy, Joe.

"Who isn't?"

"That doesn't mean anything."

"Nor does what Buss is doing to himself."

It was useless to try to explain to Joe what he was constitutionally unfit to understand: he simply could not understand weakness. And that, she decided suddenly, was a quality that she disliked.

She got to her feet. "Gilly's not home yet, Joe."

"I surmised as much."

"But why didn't you ask?"

"We had guests. We went to the club. We came home and spoke of other things."

"I've told you now."

"What do you want me to do about it?" he asked.

"You could think about it, Joe."

"I'm doing that. But I repeat, what do you want me to do?"

"Maybe she's gone again."

"You've no real reason to suppose that."

"But maybe she is."

"Do you want her to be?"

Ellen winced, flared, "What do you think?"

"I think we oughtn't to start this now," Joe took off his black tie, dropped it on the sofa.

She had never seen him do that before. Not precise and careful Joe. It was as if a stranger sat in his place. But she wouldn't allow herself to be distracted. She asked, "When should we start it?"

"Some other time, Ellen."

"But now is when she's not home. And now is when I'm scared."

"There's no need for that."

"How do you know?"

"Ellen, please . . ."

" 'Please.' " she repeated. "I don't know what that means. I don't know what you're asking of me."

"Only that you not upset yourself. We've had a pleasant evening. Why don't we leave it that way?"

"Because the evening wasn't pleasant, Joe. At least not for you. And I think it's time you understood: I am not upsetting myself. It's Gilly. She's upsetting me."

"No, Ellen."

"But that's the truth. If it weren't for Gilly . . ."

"If it weren't for Gilly what?"

Ellen shrank back, confused. "Oh, nothing, nothing. What's the use?"

"She'll be along soon."

"And then . . .?"

"She'll be all right, Ellen. You'll see."

"So sure, Joe?"

"Of course I'm sure."

"She'll be along, and she'll be all right. This time. What about next time?"

"There won't be one."

"And how do you know?"

"Because she's just out having a big Saturday night the way girls her age do. Pretty soon now, she'll come breezing in."

"I'm glad to hear it. And I hope you're right." Ellen rose, walked slowly across the room swinging her hips, the green chiffon fluttering around her long legs. She was suddenly conscious of his gaze on her. It lingered appreciatively, and she decided to forget about Gilly, and to think about herself. "Will you be along soon?" she asked.

"Just a couple of minutes," he told her.

"It *was* a nice evening, Joe, And there will be more of them," she said, thinking ahead now to the bedroom, the dark, to his body beside her, and feeling a sweet warm excitement begin to build in her.

"Yes," he agreed. "And Buss was right."

"Buss?"

"You are a pretty woman. Very pretty, Ellen."

She thought, as she readied herself for bed, that she

should not have used Gilly as a weapon this time. Ellen knew she had done it only because Joe's perfection had driven her to it, and Gilly always worked. She, herself, never worked. Or hardly ever, she decided, remembering how he had looked at her when she left to prepare for bed. She perfumed her aching temples, and imagined the touch of Joe's mouth on hers. Ready, with the bitter memory of Gilly exorcised, she waited for him.

She was surprised when he lay down in his bed. She asked, "Not reading tonight, Joe?"

"Too tired," he told her, and sighed, and switched off the lamp.

Waiting still, with the memory of his eyes following her, and the imagined touch of his lips on hers, she heard him settle himself, and the distance between the two beds seemed to widen in the dark.

A long time later, she found herself asking, "Joe, are you sleeping?"

He mumbled a wordless response.

"Because, if you are, then you'd better wake up. I want to talk to you."

"We've talked, Ellen."

"Listen to me." She went on, conversationally, "Do you think you're the only man in the world?"

"Are you sick, Ellen?"

"You're the doctor."

"Jesus, will you try to make sense?"

"I won't live like this any more. I'm not a nun. If you don't want me, I'll find a man who does."

He chuckled, "Why Ellen, is that a threat?"

"A fact," she exploded, knowing that all along she had intended to tell him.

"I think you should go to sleep," he said dryly.

"Don't you want to know?" she shrilled.

"Not really."

"You don't care?"

"Let's skip it for now."

She felt the hot blush surge through her body, then recede, leaving the skin icy cold, while a film of sleet seemed to settle, melting through the flesh and bone so that even her heart was invaded with the chill.

"But I have to be honest with you, Joe. I can't bear not being honest with you."

"Spare me."

But that was what she wouldn't do. She said softly, "You see, Joe, yesterday . . ." She stopped because she was choking on sweet wild laughter that she knew would soon echo in the dark and become sour sobs.

"Yesterday?" And there was a new note in his voice.

She had his complete attention at last. She savored the moment. "Yesterday. I expect that's what Buss Gorman was trying to tell you in his drunken stupor. That your wife was getting ready to take off with another man, and did."

There was a shift of bedsprings, then silence.

"And did," she repeated. Then, "Oh God, don't you understand? I slept with Bud Slater. It was in his friend's apartment. We got drunk together on straight gin, and did it on the sofa. He thought I was pretty damn good."

"Congratulations," Joe said. "I hope you were discreet. I'd rather that you not be discussed by every member of the club."

"Is that all you care about?"

"Not all, Ellen. But I *do* care about that, too."

"You don't believe me, do you?"

241

"Does it matter?"

"You think it couldn't happen to you. Don't you know that the double standard went out with seersucker suits? You're just operating on an old routine, Doctor."

"Am I?" he asked gently.

"No," she whispered, "no. Not you, Joe. Me. I'm working on an old routine. I was so proud of myself, flirting with Bud Slater, and getting down to it with him. He's so young, Joe, and there he was panting over *me*. I was so, so proud of myself, and gleeful, making it with him and thinking of you. Yes, of you, Joe. And now . . ." Her voice broke. She made herself go on, "Now I'm so ashamed. I'm sorry. And I'm ashamed."

"You'll get over it," he said, and turned on his side, willing his mind blank and his muscles loose.

"He made me give him twenty-five dollars, Joe. For his friend . . . the use of the apartment. But you know what it really was."

Joe didn't respond.

Her voice dropped to a rasping whisper. Finally, after fumbling in the night table, moaning as she took her capsule, she settled into exhausted silence.

It was then that the muscles he had willed into looseness suddenly began to quiver, that the habitual control of which he had always been so proud crumbled. His heart began to beat against his ribs, and his pajamas were soaked with a foul sweat, and his eyes stared, burning and hot, into the dark.

He was thinking that the Joe Stevenses of this world knew how to handle the Bud Slaters, and he would. Then, quite suddenly, he fell into the cave of sleep, and wandered there, restless and afraid in misty nightmares.

CHAPTER 12

She was wan in the morning light. Her pink robe hung around her, limp and too large, as she moved heavily from stove to counter top. She said, "Tula's late again. Of course, it's Sunday morning, and we both know that Tula, after a big Saturday night . . ."

"Not just Tula," Joe said. "What about us?"

She blinked bloodshot eyes. "I've made you some coffee."

"Thanks. But perhaps you should have stayed in bed, Ellen."

"I couldn't. I don't know what to say . . . how to act . . . I just . . ."

"It's all right. Will you pour for me?"

She filled a big pink mug. "Are you playing golf with Sam Upson as usual?"

"I'd planned to. Why?"

"It's a beautiful day for it."

He agreed. It would be a beautiful day for golf. And he needn't be troubled by seeing Bud Slater when he and Sam arrived at the club. By then, Bud would be gone. Moments earlier, Joe had made a quiet phone call from his study, making use of one of the prerogatives of Dr. Stevens: he had used such words as insolent, shifty-eyed, and paranoid; The club manager had immediately said he'd been wondering about Bud Slater himself. By the time Joe was ready to tee off, Bud would be gone for good.

Ellen sat next to him at the counter. "Listen, Joe, about last night . . ."

"There's no need to talk about it."

"But there is, Joe. We have to get it settled. I can't bear not knowing what you think, what you feel. What's going to happen."

"But you do know. Everything will be all right." He gave her a straight took out of reassuring blue eyes. He considered telling her that she would never have to see Bud again, but decided not to bring up his name.

She whispered, "Oh, Joe, it wasn't some fantasy I made up just to hurt you."

"I know."

"And I'm truly, deeply sorry. It was the first time, and the last. I promise you that." She smiled faintly. "To be perfectly honest, it wasn't any good anyway. Never mind what I told you last night. Bud's a bit kinky in his way. And it all turned out really rather awful. I just felt like a terrible fool. I still do."

"Never mind." He sipped scalding coffee, glancing at his watch.

"It frightens me, Joe. You're so calm about it. You sit there, getting ready to go off with Sam, as if nothing has happened."

"Don't think it's because I don't care what you do. I always have, always will. But you mustn't expect me to break down into hysterics about this, Ellen. Such behavior isn't in me. Besides . . ."

Later, but very briefly, he wondered what had happened to him in that moment. Why, then, in the Sunday sunlight, the safety of his stone walls and perfect kitchen, at the coffee counter with the pink mug in his hand, next to his wife, why, set in the world he knew and loved and had made for himself, he had suddenly felt it necessary to destroy it all in one quick sentence. But that was later, and very briefly, and he never had time to learn the answer.

Ellen was watching him, so still that she seemed to be holding her breath.

"Besides," he said silkily, "two people can play at your game. I am not hypocrite enough to act the outraged husband and to let you cover yourself with guilt when you had ample provocation for what you did."

Her straight back wilted. Her pink robe hung open, exposing her white breasts. He could almost see her heart pounding beneath them.

"What are you talking about, Joe?" she whispered finally. "I don't know what you're talking about."

"You mentioned the double standard to me last night, remember? Well, truthfully, I thought you knew then. It surprised me that you didn't say it straight out. But I was quite sure that you knew, Ellen."

"Knew what?"

"About Claire Manning and me." He thought of her pixie face, and anguished amber eyes, and the way her small curved body had fit to his. It had been good while it lasted; he wouldn't regret it. But it was over now.

Ellen gasped, "Claire? Claire Manning and you?"

"Of course. I told you, I thought that was what it was really all about. You mean you really didn't know?"

"No." She shook her head so violently that her auburn hair whipped back and forth across her wan face. "No, of course I didn't know. Isn't the wife always the last to hear about it?" Her pale lips twisted bitterly. "And you let me apologize to you, Joe!"

"Not really, Ellen."

She said hoarsely, "First Belena. Then Gilly. Then all your patients. And then Claire. Where does that leave me, Joe?"

"Where you've always been, Ellen. You're my wife."

She was silent, considering. Then she said bitterly, "Thanks very much, Joe."

"Try not to feel too put upon. Just as I don't feel prepared to be outraged, so you oughtn't to either." He was proud of his quiet voice, his professional tone. Proud, too, that he could, after what she had told him the night before, still be concerned about her. "We've both learned that adultery isn't a total disaster. It's behind us. We can forget it."

"You and Claire Manning had an affair? You and that overage hippie?" Ellen said wonderingly. "You never had time enough for me. But you found time for her. And how long did your great romance go on, I'd like to know?"

He hesitated. He had the feeling that no good would come from further discussion. But he knew, somehow, that Ellen couldn't be stopped. He answered, "Something like a year, I guess."

"You don't know? You couldn't keep track? Not even of her?"

"It's over now. It doesn't matter. It's finished. It was finished last night, Ellen."

"But it happened. You slept with her."

"As you slept with Bud."

"That was a minor rebellion," she cried. "A bit of childish play. Empty and meaningless. And there was no real disloyalty in it to you. You know that. You know it, Joe. But you . . ." She rocked her head back and forth, auburn hair flying. "You . . . what you did . . . a relationship, a real one. Long term, solid. With dates, and promises, and lies lies lies to me. Oh, God, Joe!" Her face suddenly sparkled with flooding tears. "That's betrayal true and complete. That was killing me, Joe."

"Oh no," he protested. "Oh no, there's no difference, Ellen."

"Yes. There is. There is."

"I didn't mean to hurt you. I didn't mean for you ever to know."

"I wish I didn't. I wish you hadn't told me."

"I can see that you might feel that way. But it's better for us now to start with the air cleared between us. Your Bud out of the way. My Claire . . ."

"Why did you tell me?"

"I had to," he said.

"Had to? Joe Stevens never has to do *anything*! And your Claire . . . why did you need her? What could she do for you that I couldn't? What could she mean to you that I couldn't mean?"

"Let's not go into that," he said coolly.

It was not to be discussed. The lost Belena, and Claire. The Claire who had seemed free, and feckless, and undemanding, had been manufactured in his own mind. The clandestine meetings to which he had looked forward with excitement had been meetings she looked forward to with dread. What he had thought of as perfect, she had plotted and prayed to change.

"I have the right to know!" Ellen cried. "Joe, answer me!"

"There's nothing to answer. It's pointless." He glanced at his watch.

"Sam Upson will have to wait," she commanded. "Unless you want me to think I'm second best to him, too."

Joe finished his coffee.

When he put down his mug, she demanded, "Tell me about her, Joe. Is she good in bed? You congratulated me, said you hoped I enjoyed it. Was she good? Does she know things I never learned?" Ellen's voice quavered, "I can learn them. I'm not cold, and I'm not a stick. I can do anything, Joe."

"Please stop it," he sighed.

"But why?"

"Why you and that cheap bum at the club? The bum you ended up paying for?"

"I didn't know before. Now I do." She smiled faintly. "Thank yourself, Joe. I knew. I sensed it. I felt the change in you. Whatever I did is all your fault."

"Perhaps."

"Why couldn't you be honest with me, come to tell me what was happening," she sobbed. "Why couldn't you just say you wanted a divorce, that you wanted——"

He cut in firmly, "Because I didn't. So there was nothing to tell you. Don't you see? It had nothing to do with you."

"Nothing to do with me?"

"Of course not."

"Taking from me what's rightfully mine, Joe? That has nothing to do with me?"

"But nothing was taken from you, Ellen."

"You screwed her, didn't you? And came home too tired for me. You made me feel less than a woman and made her feel more than me. You gave her your body and sweat, and when you did, you gave her what was mine."

He didn't answer.

"Or are you going to tell me there was plenty to go around?" Ellen jeered.

"Don't be disgusting," he said angrily.

"You're the one who's disgusting."

He carefully used the pink napkin to pat away the perspiration on his upper lip.

"And my pride," she whispered. "Just by being with her you made me nothing."

He gave her a long steady look. "I think you should lie down."

Ellen ignored that. "Her breasts," she demanded, "Claire's breasts, Joe. Are they more beautiful than mine? Does her skin taste sweeter?"

"Stop it, Ellen. Remember who you are."

"I'm nobody. And that's why I hate you!" She flung her head back. Her face was bloodless, lips, even eyes, seemed drained, dead.

"That's enough," he told her. "If you must weep for your pride, at least think of it now."

"I hate you for what you've done to me, to my whole life. For ignoring my love when I was seventeen. For tolerating it after that. For making me second best. And then for sitting there, your weight on your elbows, relaxed and listening, and looking at me as if you were somehow God, all-wise, all-good, all-understanding. And at the same time———"

He swung off the bar stool. "I'm sorry. But Sam Upson's going to be waiting for me."

"Then I'm second best to him, too!" she screamed. And the door suddenly opened.

Gilly stood there, legs apart, her wide open eyes assessing and curious and, at the same time, peculiarly opaque.

Joe's first reaction was overwhelming, almost dizzying relief. She was home, and her presence would force Ellen to pull herself together. Later, quietly, he would make her see that nothing irrevocable had happened. They had a past on which to build, and a future to live together. Love does not become hate. He glanced at her sideways. Her twisted lips, her narrowed eyes made the words in his mind a lie.

"I could hear you halfway down the block," Gilly said.

Concentrating on her, then, his first relief was tempered by sudden caution.

Her hair, pulled back into the careless pony tail that he detested, was wisping around her face. There was shadows, like great blue thumb prints, under her eyes and on her cheeks.

She seemed thin as wire, vibrating with electric tension. Her clothes were dusty and rumpled, a rip in her jeans, another in her shirt just over her silver conch belt.

Ellen said coolly, "I'm not surprised you could hear us, Gilly."

He noted that she was herself, drawn up, the pink robe belted, prepared to deal with Gilly. He said quickly, managing a slight smile, "I'm afraid we were having a fight, Gill."

"That so?" Gilly's cloudy gaze shifted from Joe to Ellen. "What about?"

"That concerns us," he answered.

Ellen said, "But it wasn't about you."

"Of course not," Gilly grinned. "Why should you fight about me?"

Joe remembered the car then. Still smiling slightly, he said, "Maybe because we were shouting, I couldn't hear the car. Did you drive up?"

"Drive?"

"The convertible, Gilly."

"Oh."

"Where is it?"

She shrugged. "Somewhere I guess. I don't know."

And that gave him the excuse to ask, "Where have you been?"

"Listen," she said, "don't you two want to go on with your fight?"

"We've finished," Joe said.

Ellen slid off the counter stool, braced on her long legs, very straight and determined. "Finished or not, that can wait. I want to know where you've been."

"Around."

"That's no answer to me, Gilly."

"It's going to have to be."

She grinned again, wide, bright, empty, and then, suddenly, as Joe watched, her face broke. It became a gaunt map of deep dark lines, eroded by time, worn by hard usage, acid-etched with fear. Her long mobile mouth narrowed with malice. Her wide open eyes narrowed and rolled up, the cloudy irises no more than waning crescents.

"We're spinning," she said hoarsely. "Spinning through the void. Bits and pieces of melting nothing."

"What are you talking about?" Ellen cried. "Make sense, Gilly."

251

"Us." Gilly tipped her head down. The chestnut pony tail slid across her face and away. "Why can't you understand? We're nothing, melting nothing."

Joe made a dismissing gesture as Ellen whispered under her breath, "Oh God, oh my God," and shivered.

He told Gilly, "All right. If that's what you need to believe now. . . . But tell me where you've been."

"Why?"

"I want to know, Gilly."

She giggled. "Yes. Of course. You always have to know, don't you? God must always know. God always does know."

"I'm not God. I'm your father. Please try to control yourself."

She threw her head back and laughed.

It was an ugly sound, and it shook him, and listening to the raucous coughing laughter, he forgot to be Father, and became Physician.

Ellen whimpered, "Oh no, oh no, Gill. . . ."

He wanted most urgently to go to her, to take Gilly into his arms and hold and console her. But caution held him still. He didn't know what she might do if he touched her wire-thin, vibrating body. He was afraid to find out.

He made his voice steady, demanded, "Gilly, what are you on? What did you take? Where did you get it? Where have you been?"

"I've been everywhere, and I've taken everything. Like all my life. Nothing."

"Hophead," Ellen cried. "Dope fiend! You're crazy with it. You've always had everything. That's what's wrong with you. Your father wouldn't believe me . . ."

"How could he believe you?" Gilly demanded, spreading her arms wide and sweeping off to her left to swing wildly around the end of the counter. She crashed into the refrigerator. Leaning her narrow shoulders against it, she peered at Joe through her wisping hair.

He saw that her grubby hands were clenched. She held something, held it so tightly that her fingers were trembling. He didn't know what it was, but he thought it might give him a clue to what she had taken.

He asked gently, "What's that you're holding?"

"Nothing. That's what I am. Nothing."

"But what is that?"

"Me." She gave him a beatific smile. "It's me, Daddy, You want to see?"

He nodded, began moving toward her slowly.

She pressed against the refrigerator, watching him out of the narrow crescents of her eyes, the cloudy look becoming a light blinking on and off, a warning signal that he recognized but didn't understand.

In front of her, close enough to touch but not touching, he stopped. "Listen, Gilly, what's this all about?"

"In snow," she said. "Cold, white, beautiful. And all the graves . . ."

Ellen whispered, "Call Dr. Richards, Joe."

Gilly heard. She chuckled. "Call Dr. Richards, and Dr. Kildare, and Dr. Casey, and Dr. Stevens."

"That's enough," Joe said firmly.

"But I don't need a doctor, Doctor. I need a father."

Joe said gently, "I'm here. Why don't you listen? I'm waiting to help you. I want to help you."

"Oh no," she cried. "You're not my father. You're the monster." Her eyes widened, seen but unseeing. "Oh no," she moaned, waving her clenched right hand.

"That monster that's all arms, slimy, sucking, sick, dirty. . . . Oh no, oh God no . . ."

Ellen retched against her fingers.

Joe said softly, "Gilly, I'm your father. You're my little girl, my beloved child. My flesh, my blood. I love you, Gilly." Slowly, speaking softly still, he reached out to her, kneeling to where she crouched now at the refrigerator. His fingers just barely touched her clenched right hand.

She spun away from him, rolled across the tile, legs and arms flying, then flashed to her feet. She hit the door blindly, and tore it open. Then she was out, running in the calm sunlight, running aimlessly into the shadow of the pink and black umbrella over the wrought iron table, and from there to the angle made by aster-filled window boxes.

He cornered her with the backdrop of flowers behind her, and she sank down, whimpering, "Oh no, you're destroying me."

He had to know what she was holding so tightly. It could help him help her. He put a gentle hand on her thin shoulder, and smiled confidently. "Gilly? It'll be okay now." At the same time, he opened her resisting fingers and took from her the small carved figure. He knew instantly what it was. But he asked, needlessly, revulsion choking him, "What's this supposed to be?"

"Me," she told him. "Can't you tell? Somebody loves me. Loves mean, bad, mad Gilly. And he made me. And here I am. The way I am. Me. Gilly Stevens. Myself. Real. Damn you! Can't you tell that I'm real? I'm not you. You screwed and begat and said you'd made me, your power made me. That's what you think. But *this* is me. David made me, damn you!"

THE DEATH WATCH

It had come too quickly for Joe to assimilate. There were things she said which he would want to ponder, but he had no time then. He looked at the small figure carefully. He looked at the small slim body, the widespread arms, the tilted head, hair flying behind. He felt the coolness of stone and the warmth of flesh. His thumbs touching the tiny pointed breasts, forefingers curled around the long slim thighs, he brought the figure close to his face, to his disbelieving eyes, visualizing her nude, posing for some hunched and panting animal . . .

Ellen was a pink blur in the calm sunlight. She screamed, "Joe! Don't!"

He didn't hear her.

"So that's what you've been doing!" he yelled, and turning, hurled the small figure against the terrace wall.

It hit with an explosive crack, and shattered. Small white and gray flakes and chips rattled on the terrace stone.

Gilly's breath hissed like a whiplash in the sudden silence. She crumpled, as if her bones and flesh had shattered too.

But when he bent over her, she was all heat and storm, screaming, "You've killed me, damn you! You've killed me. That was me, and you've finally done what you always wanted to do. You've destroyed me. That was what you wanted. You've destroyed me, and I hate you!"

"Stop it," he told her. "Gilly, please, no more. Hang on to yourself, hang on tight and don't let go. Listen to me, hang on, because if you don't . . ."

But she was past listening, past understanding. Finally, not wanting to, he slapped her, slapped her hard, telling himself that it was the necessary therapy at the moment. But he noticed that he got satisfaction, even pleasure from it, and, hating himself, he slapped her once again. Ellen was screaming, "Stop it, Joe. Stop it!"

He ignored her. He managed to haul Gilly to her feet, half drag, half carry her past the pink blur that was Ellen, and into the kitchen again.

She, following, begged, "Call Dr. Richards, Joe. You have to call him."

"Not yet." Joe didn't take his eyes from Gilly's scream-contorted face. "Get my bag, Ellen, and cancel the date with Sam Upson. Hurry."

Gilly sagged in his hands, but the screams poured from her taut throat. She tore wildly at her hair, great thick strands of chestnut floating around her.

Joe knelt beside her, whispering, "Gilly, listen, baby, listen, get hold of yourself. Tell me, tell me, what did you take?"

Her screams continued.

Ellen put the bag in his hand. He fumbled in it, found the right vial. He loaded the hypodermic needle with tranquilizer. Fingers steady, though his heart beat wildly and sweat poured into his eyes, he captured a flailing arm and shot the drug into her.

Holding her writhing, rocking body, trying to blank out the sound of her screams, he suddenly looked up.

Tula stared at him balefully. "Listen," she said, "listen, what's going on here? You want me to get to the kitchen or not? That's all I want to know. I been waiting and waiting. How do I get to the kitchen with everybody laying around on the floor?"

CHAPTER 13

Bess moved and something hurt.

Something hurt, and there was a strange brassy taste in her mouth. She tried to lick her lips, but her tongue was thick and dry and swollen.

She turned her head and felt pain in her temple. She rolled on her hip and felt pain in her ribs. She held her breath, hoping to be able to retreat into sleep and forgetfulness. But sleep was gone, and returning memory created its own pain.

She swung to her feet, and peered cautiously at the reeling room.

The three-wing dressing table mirror reflected three horrified faces at her. Bruised staring eyes, a swollen lip. Her nude body was thumb-printed at hip and thigh and breast.

She backed away from the multiple reflection, and hit the edge of the bed, and fell into it, burying her head beneath the pillows in search of an impossible escape.

"Oh, Joe," she whimpered. "Joe, how could you do it to me?"

She remembered now, faintly, the big man in the bar, and tanned, thinning sandy hair, and drinking with him, and leaving with him. The four blocks back to her apartment were a moving river, with currents tugging her this way and that, while she leaned against his steadying arm and laughed at his jokes without understanding them. Tim. Yes, drawling Tim. The two of them on the stairs, her apartment door open at last. He said, "Hey, this is a pretty nice place you've got here. Gives a man ideas. Like he ought to make himself at home."

"It is your home, Joe," she'd said then, and smiled, and patted the sofa cushions. "Now you just sit right here."

"How about you call me Tim," he'd told her.

And she'd laughed, agreed, "All right, Joe. I'll call you Tim if that's what you want. Anything you want, Joe. You know that. You've always known that."

But in the kitchen, mixing drinks—martinis, of course, because that's what Joe liked—she suddenly remembered Claire, and how Joe had gone to her, moving into the lover's arms raised to him. How he had betrayed Ellen, and Bess who had always loved him, betrayed them both for Claire Manning.

Bess remembered, and shivered, and bit her lip. But when she went back to Joe, she was smiling again.

"High-class martinis, huh?" he said. "Say, don't you maybe just have a can of low-down beer?"

"But you always want martinis."

"I do?" he grinned. "Okay then." His big hand took the slender-stemmed glass, and he drained it.

"Our toast, Joe," she said quickly but too late.

"Okay," he told her. "Here's to you."

She made herself smile again. "To you."

"I'll buy that, too." He looked at the frosted pitcher. "Want me to help myself?"

"Of course. Please. Whatever you want, Joe."

He grinned. "Whatever I want? Just like that?"

"Of course, Joe. Always. It's always been like that, hasn't it?"

"Beats me. But okay. If that's what you say, then that's how it is."

"I don't know what you mean, Joe."

He leaned forward, filled his glass, drained it again. "I could get used to this stuff, I guess."

"You *are* used to it. We both are."

He reached out to put the glass down, but missed the table by a foot. He didn't seem to notice when it fell from his fingers and bounced on the rug at his feet, leaving a small trail of drops that spread into the colorful braid.

She smiled forgivingly, which was something else he didn't seem to notice.

And suddenly she remembered. She saw him leaning toward Claire's arms, face bent to hers, speaking in a lover's voice. She suddenly remembered.

She sipped her drink, looking at him, wondering how to say it, how to tell him that she knew, that he wasn't fooling her any more.

Finally, she said gently, "We have to talk, Joe."

"Sure. You name it, I'll carry on."

"About what's happened, Joe."

"What's happened?" he grinned. "Nothing's happened yet. And I don't mind telling you, this act can go pretty sour pretty damn fast."

"Act, Joe? Don't you realize what you've done? Don't you care?"

"I haven't done anything yet," he answered.

His smug assurance hurt. She leaned forward tensely, breasts jiggling within the stained yellow halter. She said, "Oh, Joe, Joe, after all these years. Why lie? I think you owe me some honesty. I think you owe me that much after what I've been to you. Asking for nothing. For nothing, Joe. Except for the chance to love you. And now . . ."

"You've got the chance, baby. Why don't you shut up and use it. I'll bet you don't get many of them so you shouldn't throw nothing away."

"Ben, all the others, they never meant anything to me. They knew how I felt about you. That's why I'm alone now. And I was willing, happy even, to settle for that. I didn't care. Because of you."

"Real sweet," he said, putting a thick hand on her bare shoulder. "You think you could shut up for a minute? I'm getting tired of this. Besides, my name is Tim."

"Excuses don't matter, Joe. I don't understand."

"Woman, knock it off, will you? Who do you think you're kidding?"

"Oh, I'm dead serious. You better believe me, Joe. I won't let you do this to me, to yourself either."

"I'm not about to do it to myself," he growled. "What do you think I'm sitting here and listening to all this stuff for?"

"It just doesn't make sense," she answered.

"It sure as hell don't." He thrust his face against hers. "Come on, baby, knock it off." His arms closed around her.

She struggled, but just a little, protesting, "Oh, not now, Joe." Then, she said archly, "Later, maybe later, after we've talked, and after you've made me understand."

"Ain't going to be no later, woman," he growled.

"I've played along, Now I want what I'm here for."

"A woman has her pride, Joe."

"Shove that. I got something else on my mind."

"I don't know what you mean," she told him.

Clinging to her cool dignity was difficult in her position: half over him, her pudgy hip pressed between his thighs.

"Oh Joe," she whimpered, "please, Joe, love me, kiss me . . . oh Joe, please . . ."

But he was no longer listening, nor bothering to pretend that he was.

He seized her, and as his red bloodshot eyes and red grizzled cheeks and red wet mouth pushed down toward her, she cried, "Hey, what do you think you're doing, mister? Get off me!" Remembering that his name was Tim, and she'd met him at Tony's bar and brought him home with her, she struggled, outraged, shouting, "Who do you think you are?"

He hit her twice, hard, savagely, and slammed his hips down, butting and thrusting and ripping.

She went limp, suffering the invasion in wondering surprise.

Even in her early teen years, then through the long desert of hunger and expectation, through the dreams and the hopes, she had never imagined her flesh as so vulnerable.

Pommeled, invaded, and suddenly abandoned, she stared wide-eyed at the ceiling, and whimpered, "Oh Joe, why did you have to hurt me?"

A shadow moved over her. A door opened and closed.

A long time later she dragged herself up, stumbled into the bedroom, cast aside her torn clothes, and collapsed into bed.

THE DEATH WATCH

Head buried in the pillows, faintly remembering the big man she'd met in Tony's bar, and her phone call to Claire, then to Ellen, Bess trembled, fighting nausea, and struggled with dry tears. Finally, squinting into the hot sunlight through swollen eyes, she roused herself, and bathed, soaking away the dried blood on her thighs, scrubbing away the smell of the big hands on her hips; big hands that seemed now, in retrospect, long and slim and immaculately clean as always, though the night before they had been neither long nor slim nor immaculately clean.

She dressed carefully in a simple white shirtwaist dress, dismissing the irony of symbolic innocence. She did and re-did her face: foundation cream and foundation eraser, powder, rouge, lashes, mascara, shadow.

Painted, blotted, painted, and blotted, her face remained blotched and puffy and marked. But it was the best she could do.

Ready then, with bag packed and purse at hand, she went to the phone. It took a long while to reach the small mountain town. The phone rang and rang before the receiver was lifted and she heard her father's gruff voice. "This is Dr. Bradford. Yes? Yes?

"It's me," she said in a hoarse whisper.

"Bessie?"

"Yes, Papa."

"What's wrong?"

She swallowed hard. "What do you mean? I just called to say hello."

"What's wrong, Bessie?"

"I told you."

"Ha. Expect me to believe that? You're in trouble, aren't you?"

"No, Papa."

"Sure you are. Always knew you'd get into trouble one of these days. Always knew it. Ever since you left home. I knew, and your brothers knew. That's why you left. So you could get yourself into trouble."

"Papa . . "

"Well, what do you want?"

"Nothing. Really, Papa. Nothing."

"If it's nothing, then what do you want? Why did you call?"

"I don't know."

"It's time for me to go to church, Bessie. On Sunday morning good Christians go to church. Why aren't you in church yourself, Bessie?"

"I don't know, Papa."

"You see? I always said you'd get into trouble. I got to hang up now."

"Good-bye," she said. "Good-bye, Papa."

The sky was a bright scalding blue.

She got into the car, and set out with no destination in mind. But when she found herself in Rojas Lane, she wasn't surprised.

It was empty there, still, under the brooding black ridges of the mountains.

She parked behind the only other car on the block, and got out.

Just as she reached the broken gate, a convertible backed wildly out of an adjoining compound, and spun in the center of the narrow lane, throwing up a cloud of red dust.

Belatedly, she turned for a second look, wondering because it seemed a car she knew. But then, with a shrug, she went into the patio, and it was like stepping from day into night, from reality into a dream.

Her lips moved, producing a frantic whisper, "Oh Joe, why did you do it to me? Why did you hurt me so? Didn't you care how much I love you?"

A man stood at the door, hand raised as if he had just knocked.

The door opened and Claire was there, head tilted back, smiling.

Bess backed away, her breath a sibilant whisper. "Damn your soul forever, Joe!"

Mike, turning, saw her tripping away in her high-heeled white sandals, her plump hips jiggling, her silvered head bent between her drooping shoulders.

The white dress, the ironic symbol of innocence, clued him. He asked, "Wasn't that Joe's nurse, Claire?" and then went inside, instantly forgetting her.

Claire answered, "I don't know. I didn't notice."

Mike didn't know what she was talking about, and stared at her in obvious bewilderment.

She understood. "Never mind, Mike. I'm glad you came over."

"I wanted to be sure you're okay."

"I am," she said. She smoothed her very short white shorts over her narrow hips, and then touched the pencil pencil stuck behind her ear. "I've been working. Want some coffee?"

He nodded his dark head, sank into the sofa.

But she hesitated. "Were you at the cemetery this morning?"

"Yes. Do you think I shouldn't have gone? Is that it?"

"Not shouldn't, Mike. But it would be better if you gave yourself more time."

"I have all the time that I'll ever need, and more."

She nodded, and went into the kitchen.

The room seemed emptier with her gone, and he suddenly understood why he had come. It was not to see if what he had said to her the day before had made them permanent enemies. It was not to see if she had finally stopped shivering. It was not for her, but for him.

He had been at Lori's graveside, waiting for something to happen, for the stone within him to melt, the steel cables of his nerves to shred. Finally, still bound within that thing which was himself, within the automaton become man, he had driven to Claire's in search of comfort.

She brought him coffee, and when he glanced up to thank her, he caught the look of desolation on her face. Offering comfort instead of taking it, he said, "It's going to be all right."

"Yes," she answered. "I saw Joe last night. I had to, after what you said. And you're entitled to one brotherly 'I told you so.' "

Mike understood the desolation now. He stretched out his long legs, watching her from under lowered lids.

She sat quietly, her hands folded in her lap, her dark head bent.

For the first time in years, he saw the something that showed they were brother and sister. The something that lay not in coloring or form, but in the set of the head, the angle of the jaw.

Because he saw that something, he knew what she was thinking. "Forget it," he said gently. "Forget him, too."

265

"Of course I will. . . . But when I woke up this morning, I wondered how I could feel this way. How could I, if I ever really loved him?"

Mike didn't answer her.

They looked at each other, deciding simultaneously that there was nothing more to be said.

He got to his feet, put down the emptied coffee cup, then paced restlessly. "I wonder what Bradford was doing in Rojas Lane."

Claire watched him uneasily, suspicious of the comfort of shared hate.

It was Miguelito who interrupted the silence. He came with food in bags under his arms, and a white smile, and no apology.

"The two of you got to eat. And I figured you wouldn't. So here it is. You, Claire, trot out into the kitchen and show me what you can do about heating up enchiladas and tamales and refritos. Mike, you see if she's got some beer to go with it. If not, I'll get some."

"Thanks, amigo," Mike said softly.

"For nothing."

"Beer," Claire called from the kitchen.

"She's my business," Miguelito told him.

"Good," Mike answered, knowing that Lori would have been pleased.

And Miguelito, knowing, said, "Don't think about it now, Mike."

"I'll think about her every minute, every second, until the day that Joe Stevens dies."

"But what are you going to do?" Ellen asked. "You can't keep her here like that, drugged and asleep, forever."

"I don't intend to," Joe said.

"Why don't you call Dr. Richards?"

"Because I can handle this myself, Ellen."

"But, suppose, when she wakes up . . ."

"She'll be all right when she wakes up."

"You're taking too much of a chance, Joe."

"I know what I'm doing."

"I'm not sure."

She was dressed now, the pink robe put aside for a black dress. He wished she had chosen something other than that ominous color, and chided himself for permitting the weakness of superstition. He said, "I'm sorry that you feel you can't trust me, Ellen, but I promise you, if there's any reason, any reason at all, I'll call Richards."

"May I see her for a minute?"

"I'd rather you didn't."

"I won't disturb her."

"She needs rest."

"But I said I won't bother her . . ."

"Ellen, please . . ."

"Oh why, why did you have to do it? That was the worst, the last straw . . ."

"It was the only way to quiet her down," he said dully.

"You're deliberately misunderstanding me. Why did you break the figure, Joe?"

"Do we have to keep talking?"

"How can we not?" She studied him through swollen eyes, patiently awaiting the answer that did not come. At last, she demanded, "What's wrong with you? Don't you feel anything?"

He moved his head and looked at her. She saw the white ridges around his lips, and the twitching muscles in his jaw. She supposed that he did care, and those were the signs, but it seemed inordinately important then that he should talk to her.

After a while, he got up, moving slowly now as if suddenly aged, and went down the hall.

Ellen strained, listening.

Nothing. Nothing.

Soon he was back.

She looked her anxious question.

"No. Not yet, Ellen."

"But shouldn't we be doing something, Joe?"

"I am."

"It's been hours and hours." She shook her head back and forth, back and forth, and her auburn hair whipped across her haggered face. "We ought to call Richards. Or take her to the hospital."

Joe winced.

"You don't want to. Dr. Richards, the hospital . . . it means a report, doesn't it? And the police?"

"Yes. And if we can avoid that, for her we will. If it's necessary, I'll call Richards. I'll take her in myself."

"It would be safer, Joe."

He shook his head. "Ellen, will you please stop it?"

"Listen to me. Just this once. Gilly's my daughter. I don't want you taking chances with her. I don't care about anything but her. We've already taken too many chances, and now look what it's come to."

He began an answer to her, but there was a shrill awful sound from the room beyond.

Ellen leaped to her feet.

Joe beat her to the door. "No, no. Stay here."

She wilted, unable to oppose him, afraid even to try,

afraid to follow him lest what she find be more than she could bear.

The shrill awful sound faded away slowly, leaving long echoes that beat like pulses in Ellen's head and became icy slivers of pain needling into her temples.

She gasped, and clung to the wall.

Joe was gone for what seemed a long time.

When he came back, she asked, "What happened?"

"She's dreaming, Ellen."

"Maybe it's more," Ellen whispered. "Maybe it's a forever dream and she won't wake up, and she'll never be Gilly again."

"Stop it."

"If anything happens to Gilly," she cried. "If anything happens, Joe . . ."

He wondered what time it was. It was very dark outside, and he supposed it had been dark for many hours. All he had to do was lift his wrist, glance at the illuminated dial of his watch, and he would know. But the effort required hardly seemed justified by idle curiosity. The time didn't really matter.

Ellen, sprawled on the sofa in crumpled black, seemed finally to have fallen asleep.

It was a relief to him that he had temporarily escaped from the burden of her emotionalism. He had found it more difficult than he would ever have imagined to listen to her, and utterly impossible to know what to say.

Down the hall, Gilly was sleeping, too, sleep so profound now that he had begun to wonder uneasily if the tranquilizer he gave her hours before had been too strong to mix with whatever she had taken earlier. That she had taken something, he was certain.

Later, when Gilly wakened, he would find out what it was. He would know what to do. For now, there was nothing to do but wait.

Ellen didn't understand waiting.

She, too, believed in miracles, She too turned to him with tearful hoping eyes, expecting that he could do God's work and resurrect the dead, reverse the course of nature, re-stitch the broken mind, re-build the shattered self.

And like all the others, when he failed, her hope would become hate in the syndrome of the disappointed believer. It was the doctor's cross, as well as the minister's.

Joe shrugged. He told himself that Gilly would be all right. She would awaken soon, smiling and rested, and they would sit down together, the two of them, alone, and discuss what had happened and what they must do. They would decide it between them, and she would accept the decision they came to, because it would be her decision, too.

They wouldn't find it necessary to talk about the small figure that still lay in shattered flakes and chips on the terrace.

Ellen's body rippled in a small movement, and she clenched her jaws and audibly ground her teeth. Her slim hands raised to her temples and pressed there.

He leaned forward, ready to reassure her, but she was still again, and he dropped back. He wondered if she were pretending sleep, but watching him, studying him in the dark, as she did so often.

Having moved once, he made the further effort to check his watch. It was eleven o'clock. The seemingly endless day was almost over. Soon now. Soon.

There was a faint, faraway sound.

He listened, and watched Ellen. She was still.

It was Gilly then, turning in her sleep.

A whisper again. A murmur of movement. A muted grate of wood on wood.

He rose.

"What is it?" Ellen asked.

He had time, in that instant, to think that she had been pretending sleep as he suspected, and to accept the familiarity of her question that had come with every nighttime call he'd had since they were married. He had time for that in that instant, and then he recognized the sound he had been listening to, and ran for Gilly's room.

A muted grate of wood on wood . . .

He thrust open the door he had left ajar, and knew he had been right.

A flash of long bare leg at the window, a bare foot. The scurry of a panicked squirrel on the grass outside.

He leaned out, yelled, "Gilly! Gilly, come back here!" and saw a slender white shadow flash away across the lawn.

Behind him, Ellen screamed, "What's wrong, Joe?"

He threw a leg over the sill, dropped into the feathery juniper, and ran as he had never run before.

So fleet of foot, his graceful beautiful Gilly. So quick and strong, dancing away through the dark under the thin sliver of a silver moon. So beautiful, the Gilly that he had made.

Across the lawn, through the carefully tended gardens, down to the street she raced.

He, calling, strident urgency muted to a whisper lest the neighbors hear and know and come out to frighten her, tracked behind her as fast as he could.

But he knew that he would never have caught her if she hadn't stopped at the tree line, the single street light on her face and nude body; if she hadn't stopped and turned at bay, eyes wild and lip lifted in a snarl.

"Gilly," he panted. "What in the hell do you think you're doing? Come inside with me right now."

And she growled, growled and spit and launched herself at him. He staggered under the weight of the onslaught, but managed to keep his feet and grab for her clawing hands. He felt her teeth rake his jaw, while one hand, freeing itself, stabbed for his eyes.

He tried to enfold her, but she was like a small quick cat in rage, sleek and sinewy, and scratching with toe and finger and teeth.

He finally brought her down, and rolled on top of her.

She was still, glaring up at him, and then she began to struggle, her body heaving under his in a mockery of sex while her bared teeth went for his throat.

There was only one way to bring her under control.

He managed to get a handful of hair and jerk her head back and away. He hit her as hard as he could. This time there was no satisfaction in the blow. This time there was only terror.

She gasped. Her glaring eyes rolled up and slowly closed. She went limp and still.

CHAPTER 14

"Leave me alone," David moaned into the dark. "Jesus Christ, please, leave me alone."

But the faces came spinning in, Paul's plump and pleading and painted, his mother's and father's. . . . They came spinning from misty corners, twisting and swelling, shrinking and stretching. Grotesque, taunting, hating faces. They jeered and chortled, and cursed, and laughed.

"Stop it," David pleaded, and folded his arms over his blond head, and burrowed into the angle between day bed and wall, the blankets enwrapping him in a cocoon, one frayed edged at his lips. It was good for a moment. But then he thought of womb and tomb and began to choke for breath as the air became no-air, and his breath sparkled, shot through with arrows of light that exploded into music, shrill never-twanging music that became pain as the faces slowly receded into the distance of mist-filled corners.

Moments later, he tasted musty lint on his tongue, and spat it out, and raised his head. "Jesus," he said aloud, "what's going on here anyhow?"

He got to his feet slowly, and fumbled his way to a lamp. When he touched the switch, light exploded like shooting stars, red, gold, silver, Roman candles arching across a sky that wasn't there.

He stared, wincing, shivering. He asked, "What's that?" and finally the light settled and muted, and he could see the boundaries of the room.

He saw them safe and steady, and sighed. "That's good. Yes. That's right." And then the hairline cracks in the adobe grew and darkened and swelled. He watched them, his eyes widening, bulging out under his brows. He watched, and the cracks spread, and became rents in the earth at his feet, great faults from which steam and flame spewed up to claim him.

"Oh God, please," he moaned, singeing, charring, burning.

"Oh God, please."

He listened, unable to tell the difference between his speech and thought.

"Help me."

"Help me."

He clutched the frayed blanket to his mouth, and swayed in steam and flame, and lurched back, back and away from the great fault in the earth.

He stumbled into the table edge, and the blow at his back was a flash of red thunder overlaying distant whimperings. Clinging to the table with both hands, the blanket a tangle at his feet, he waited.

Slowly the cracks in the adobe wall sealed. The steam and flame died away. The red thunder was still.

He peered carefully into the corners, beneath the bed, Only the whimpering remained.

He peered carefully into the corners, beneath the bed, behind the chest, even into the open suitcase. He sought the small lost animal that must be making that terrible sound.

And, at last, feeling the constriction in his throat, the vibration in his chest, he knew that he was the small animal. He was lost.

Lost.

David was lost.

He clutched the table with numb fingers, trying to concentrate.

David.

David?

No. Gilly. Gilly was lost.

And with that, he remembered. He remembered but didn't believe.

He turned very slowly.

He leaned close, brushing blond hair from his eyes, to study the top of the table.

A mallet, a chisel, chips, flakes, dust.

He forced his right hand to reach out.

Gilly was gone. The small stone Gilly . . .

On the floor at his feet was the tangle of blanket, and near it, the old torn shirt that he had used to cover the small figure.

It was gone.

Now he not only remembered, but he believed.

He had come back from Claire's, twelve dollars in his sweating fist. Gilly was waiting.

"Well? Did you, David?"

"Yeah." But he thought quickly enough to separate two from the ten. "She gave me a couple of bucks."

"A couple of bucks! That's not enough for steak, David."

"We'll have hamburgers." He tried to grin, but his

275

face ached. He told himself to quit thinking about Claire. It was Gilly that mattered.

He was glad that she was still thinking so hard on steak that she didn't notice that he actually had more than two bills in his hand. He was very careful and casual about tucking the ten away.

"Hamburgers!" Gilly muttered. She flung herself back on the bed, making a sound of vomiting.

"Lovely for the appetite."

"What?"

"That noise, Gill."

"So what? Since we don't have enough to take care of an appetite anyway."

"She didn't have any more, Gill."

"I'll bet."

He didn't answer. He thought momentarily of admitting to the extra ten bucks, and then thought of Tuesday and what it could mean to both of them. He knew what he had to do. He said, "I'll tell you what. We'll skip the hamburgers. You can get a pretty big pile of french fries for two dollars, and we'll soak them in catsup, and we'll gorge. What about that?"

She considered, then grinned.

So he knew that was okay, and he went back to the table, moved the weights off the shirt, and looked down at the small statue.

"When are you going to let me look, David?"

"Pretty soon now, Gill. Maybe tomorrow."

"That's not soon enough."

He carefully covered the statue, wishing that he could work on it but knowing that Gilly had to have his attention.

"You could have taken a peek," he said, "while I was at Claire's."

"Oh, I wouldn't do that."

"But you could have."

"You'd have known, wouldn't you?"

"I'm sure I would, Gilly."

"That's why I didn't," she admitted. "You trusted me with it, and left me here, and the moment you looked, you'd have known and been mad, so I didn't let myself do it."

"You're my good Gill," he grinned.

"But I wanted to. And I thought of it."

"Thinking isn't the same as doing, though."

"Sometimes it is."

He shook his head. "Listen, should we go out and get the fries now, or wait, or what?"

She snapped the rubber band that held her pony tail, and swung her long hair over her face, peering at him through the chestnut veil. "Do you like me like this, David?"

"Every way there is, and maybe some ways I don't even yet know about."

"There's a lot of ways you don't know about."

"I'll find them out, Gill. We've got lots of time ahead together. You and me. We're going to know everything about each other."

"Huh," she chortled. "That's what you think. A woman needs to have her little mysteries, David. You can't know everything."

"Maybe I need my little mysteries, too. So we'll be even."

"No. I won't let you have them. Just me."

"You call that fair?"

"Who has to be fair?"

He said solemnly, "We do. To each other."

She brushed the veil of hair aside, re-tied it behind her head. She was no longer smiling. "I know. I know."

"Remember how it was in Taos? The two of us, Gilly? Our little place. The sun. The sky. Remember the mountains, Gill? And the stars at night?"

"All ancient history, David."

"Oh no. Not history. It's ahead of us, not behind. It's the future, Gill."

"History." She rolled to the edge of the bed, bounced to her feet. She stretched tall, her thin body pulled out and lean, then folded at the waist and swung low in fluid grace. "Oh, I wish we could do something good. Oh, I wish we could get out."

"Out?"

She straightened, put her hands on her hips. "Out of ourselves, David."

"Why?" He smiled, though he didn't feel like smiling. He needed her answer, though he knew he mustn't press her. "Why out of ourselves, Gill?"

"Because we're trapped inside cages we never made for ourselves. Trapped! Inside, inside. And I want out!"

"In Taos," he said. "Soon."

"It doesn't matter where you are."

"Then you don't care about Taos," he told her before he could stop himself, "not the way I do."

And she looked at him sideways, a cold, withdrawn look out of wide open and blank blue eyes, and then suddenly she smiled, and spun toward him, arms wide and reaching. "Oh, David, I do. I do. I can't wait until we get back to Taos. It'll all be different there. You. Me. We'll both be different, won't we?"

"Not too different, I hope," he laughed, holding her tight. "I don't want to start over again as strangers. I want us to be as we are."

TO BE AS WE ARE . . .

He heard the words again as if they had been screamed aloud in that very moment. He clung hard to the table, while the concrete floor rippled in small slimy waves at his feet, clung hard, fighting his out-of-control senses, and waiting. Soon the floor was flat and smooth again.

He remembered that he wanted to work on the small Gilly, but the larger Gilly was restless.

They had gone out for a ride. They had two dollars' worth of fries, and licked their fingers, and went back to his place with catsup-red lips.

"I'm hot," Gilly said, and stripped off her shirt, and grinned at him.

"That's what I like," he told her. "A shy woman. A woman with wiles."

He noticed the silver gleam of her belt against the bare flesh, and though he'd seen it he didn't know how many times before, he suddenly realized that it was worth a lot of money. Indian, made a long time ago, and pawned. . . . If they did the same, he and Gilly, they'd have all the money they needed and more. But she would never think of it. She hadn't traveled as far as he had. She didn't know about hock shops. And he would never never suggest it. No matter what happened. Briefly, then, he thought of Claire, and what he had done to her, and winced.

279

But Gilly cried, "That's me. A woman with wiles," and giggled and wrestled him down to the bed.

They played bear, hugging each other as hard as they could, hugging each other until their ribs ached, she tiring first and wriggling away to tickle him out of his clothes. He, clued in, tickled her out of her jeans, and then they played people. They played people the three ways they knew—the ways they had learned together, he liked to pretend to himself, although he knew it wasn't true. Sated for a little while, they rested. Then she reached for him, and with the untiring strength of seventeen and nineteen, they played people again.

He remembered that he fell asleep holding her, with the tip of her pony tail in his ear, and her cheek warm on his shoulder, and her sleeping breath just as gentle as his when he blew on the small stone Gilly to clean it, mold it, to make it alive.

He had awakened suddenly to find her standing beside the bed, peering down at him.

"Hi," he smiled. "Where you going?"

"I've been."

He sat up. "Did you go out like that?"

She was wearing nothing but jeans, and he had a sudden awful picture of her wandering around in Rojas Lane, nude on the top, and her father stepping out of Claire's house and seeing her that way.

"Just to the car," she shrugged. "What's wrong? You shook?"

"I guess not. It's dark outside, isn't it? Nobody saw you?"

"Dark enough. And if they had, so what?"

"But what were you doing, anyhow?"

"I told you. I went to the car." She giggled then. "It was for the surprise."

"And that is. . . . ?"

"Get up. Now is the time, David. Now."

He pulled on trousers, a yellow sleeveless T-shirt. He stepped into cracked moccasins, and brushed his hair, and washed his face to remove the small catsup stains spread by her kisses.

She waited, rocking back and forth on her fare feet. Finally she said, "You make such a thing about things." She brought her hands from behind her. Each held half a slice of pear. "The surprise," she said. "I bought it yesterday. I've been saving it in the car glove compartment. Maybe it got a little mushy in the heat, but it ought to be good."

He studied the slice in her right hand, the slice in her left. "Is it a game? Do I choose?"

"Try and find out."

"Hey, Gilly, what are you up to?"

"I thought you'd be pleased. Something sweet, David, for a sweet David."

"Okay," he said hastily, and chose the slice in her right hand. "If you've stuffed it with chile, I'm going to pound on you a little."

"No chile," she giggled, and bit into her half, grinning at him.

And then . . .

Now David clung to the table, shivering.

There was suddenly snow in the room. Great shifting white drifts of it, swirling and spinning. His teeth chattered. His jaws ached. The inside of his mouth burned with the acid of bitter frost.

They finished the pear, and talked, and Gilly said, "Tell me again about Taos, David."

"We'll go there . . ."

"Not that way. I mean from the beginning."

"Tuesday I'm going to take the figure in, and enter it." He stopped because she was watching him, sly-eyed and waiting to pounce. He saw the trap too late.

"How can you enter it? You need ten dollars, David."

"I have it," he confessed, and hurried on. See, Claire gave me twelve, but I knew we'd spend it if I didn't put the ten away, so I did, and we got rid of the two, and it was swell, wasn't it? We had a good time, didn't we? And I still have the ten for the show."

"Only we didn't have steaks," she observed.

"I'm sorry I lied to you, Gill. But it's for Taos. So I enter the figure. You, Gilly. You. And . . ." He stopped again, reached for her, because suddenly she seemed to have thinned, lost her solidity, become a form without substance. "Gilly?" he asked.

"What's the matter, David?"

"Is something the matter?"

"That's what I asked you."

"I'm sorry I lied to you, Gill."

"That's okay. It was for Taos."

He squinted at her. "Gilly?"

She laughed softly, and he winced and covered his ears. To him the soft laugh was the painful squeal of a high-speed drill.

When he could bear it, he dropped his hands, and got up slowly. "Gilly, wait a minute. Tell me. What's wrong with me."

"Nothing, David."

"I feel funny."

"I don't."

282

THE DEATH WATCH

"Gilly . . ."

She tipped sideways, spread her slender arms wide, and gave a great prancing swoop at him. "Did you know I can fly? We can all fly. If we want to."

He ducked back, and seemed to fall through space into a white snow storm. There was dead silence until suddenly he heard the howling of arctic winds, of hungry wolves, and somehow he knew it to be the sound of her laughter.

Slowly, slowly, he fell forward, and he was back in the room, and he saw her curled on the floor, sleeping, with her thumb in her mouth.

He saw the faces swell in the corner, his mother's lips snarling, his father's bloodied, Paul's pitiful face done in clown colors. He whimpered and moaned, and at last the faces receded. When they were gone, he wept.

Then Gilly uncurled herself. She threw back the blanket and cried, "David, you're so beautiful! I never knew how beautiful you are. Truly, I never knew. You have hair sculptured of antiqued gold strands, and eyes carved of the bluest marble."

He said, "Gilly, tell me. What did you do?"

"I bought it," she whispered. "I told you I wanted something exciting to happen. Well, it's happening, isn't it?"

"But what did you do, Gill?"

"I bought it the other day. Don't you remember? I got fifty dollars from my mother by hinting that she was screwing Bud Slater, and you should have seen her squirm at that. But it was really my father that gave it to me. And he squirmed, too. I don't remember what I did to make him squirm. But he did, and he gave it to me. And then I got the LSD. And I brought you

283

some groceries—remember the melon?—and some five dollars, or something, and then——"

"Gilly!"

She held her head. "Sometimes it gets big and sometimes it gets small. I don't think I like the way that feels."

"Both of us?" he demanded. "Did we both take it?"

She giggled, "On the pear halves. Sprinkled like sugar. And you didn't know, didn't guess. I told you: a surprise."

He was terribly afraid, without quite knowing why. He said, "We have to stay together. We have to take care of each other, Gill. Promise me? Promise you'll stay right here with me?"

"Sure, David. Why not?"

"You'll stay right here?"

"Right here, David," she crooned. "And we'll take care of each other."

He didn't remember all of it. There were moments when he was gone, gone into some strange place from which he had to fight his way back. There were moments when her face was obscured by the faces that came out of the corners, when her voice was drowned by their voices.

He remembered that she had been a baby for a little while, curled up under the blanket again, sucking her thumb and wetting her pants. He had tried to get her to change to a pair of his, but she wouldn't.

He remembered that she had suddenly become old, old, and crouched in the corner, staring blankly at a wall, saying prayers that mixed obscenities with promises.

He remembered that he had turned the light on and heard music, and turned the light off and heard screams.

Finally he slept. At least he thought he had slept. When he wakened, she was gone.

Gilly was gone.

He searched the room, once, twice, three times.

He stumbled, and fumbled, and whispered to himself. He stopped, and rested, and searched again.

Gilly was gone.

Gone. Wet pants and no shirt. Oh God, oh Gilly . . .

He searched once again, daring the light and the music, and that time, the last time, he knew there was no shirt, and breathed easier. He straightened up, breathing easier. She would be all right.

And then he saw that the small stone Gilly was gone too.

The cover shirt was on the floor near the tangle of blankets. The table was bare except for dust and chips and mallet and chisel.

He had staggered outside, seen the car glowing in the sunlight. He got into it. The keys were in the ignition, where Gilly always left them although he had begged her not to. He imagined her wandering lost and alone somewhere in Old Town. He had to find her.

He didn't know where he'd been, or what he'd done. He knew only that he hadn't found Gilly, and that he must have come back. Because he was there now, in the room, staring at the table, and clinging to it, and remembering.

But that wasn't enough.

He had to find Gilly.

He pushed himself away from the table, and felt the snow begin to fall around him.

He grabbed up the blanket, and wrapped himself in it, and raced out to where the car was waiting in the dark.

CHAPTER 15

Ellen heard the roar of the convertible spinning into the driveway and screaming to a halt.

She gave a quick automatic sigh of relief, of annoyance. Gilly was home at last, but why did she have to drive like that?

And then Ellen remembered. It wasn't Gilly. It couldn't be.

She ran to the door, flung it open.

By then, David was at the threshold, the blanket pressed to his cheek and cascading down his side.

"Gilly?" he gasped. "Is she home?"

"No," Ellen told him, thin-voiced. "No. And where did you come from? What are you doing here? What do you want?"

"Gilly," he whispered, staring at Ellen.

Her hair and eyes were wild. Her face was gaunt, old, pitted and scarred. She was no longer the woman who had walked, sleek and assured, into the garden of Eden, into the small adobe, and found Gilly and him together, and looked down, red mouth curling in disgust, and torn Gilly away from him, away from Taos.

Gaunt, old, pitted, scarred. And dressed in black.

In black.

He whimpered, and shook, and edged toward the car. Cold metal burned his fingers.

He leaned there, clutching the blanket to him, and crying, "Oh no, please, no, stop it. No . . . no . . . no . . ."

Joe turned at the door, paused for one last look.

Gilly lay still, but within the restraints that might prove necessary at any time. Now she was small, limp, and totally mild.

It was hard to believe that so short a time before, she had bared her teeth in a taste for blood, and clawed at him, leaving burning red trails on his jaw.

"She'll be all right, Doctor," the nurse said comfortingly. "I'll keep my eye on her."

"Of course," he agreed.

He had subdued her finally, his weight on hers, his strength against hers, until he could hit her carefully enough to make her lose consciousness.

Somehow he managed to get to his feet. She was as light as a child in his arms.

When he got back to the house, Ellen screamed, "What happened, Joe? Why is she naked?"

"Call Dr. Richards," Joe told her quietly.

Quickly then, he got his bag, prepared a light sedative. He gave it to Gilly, and even in his haste, he studied her arms for telltale marks. There were none. Not heroin then. He sighed in relief.

Ellen cried, "Richards is away. Can you imagine? Away for the weekend. Whoever is covering him . . ."

"No. It doesn't matter." Joe knew what he had to do. "Help me," he said.

Ellen ran for blankets, but he insisted on a dress.

They got it on her, and carried her out to the car.

Ellen made as if to get in.

"No," Joe told her. "Stay here."

"She's my daughter. I won't . . . I won't . . ."

"Don't be a bigger fool than you have to be. The less obvious we are, the better. For Gilly. The two of us, Gilly and I, going into the hospital together late at night . . . well, maybe if I can just get her on her feet, maybe then we can get away with it."

She began an angry protest.

Joe said coolly, "Ellen, we don't know where she's been. We don't know what she's done. Or what may happen. Stay here and wait. I'll call you."

Ellen clung to him, weeping, but he thrust her aside, and settled Gilly in the front seat.

He supposed, in the part of his mind that troubled to think of Ellen, that she thought he was punishing her now for Bud Slater. But what she thought didn't matter any more than what she did.

He drove away.

They were nearing the hospital when Gilly stirred, mumbled.

"It's okay," he told her quietly. "Take it easy. We're almost there."

She subsided, and he speeded up, swung into the parking lot, cut the motor and lights, and went around to her side.

She raised her head, stared at him blank-eyed. "Where's this?"

"The hospital. We have to make a stop for just a minute. Can you walk?"

"Sure," she said drowsily. "Sure I can walk. Why not?"

He helped her out of the car.

She crumpled against him, and grinned. "I feel funny. It must be all the star dust."

"Oh, Gilly, Gilly, why did you do it?"

"You gave me bad genes, I guess. That must be what it is, Daddy. You gave me bad genes."

He had called the arrangements in before leaving the house. He knew they would be waiting for him, ready, upstairs.

Leaning on him, she went with him quietly through the lobby, and into the elevator.

The moment the doors closed, she exploded into a pale fury that spewed foul language and terrible screams into the antiseptic air. He held her writhing body until the doors slid open again, and the attendants took her away, leaving his arms and his heart empty, nothing in his mind but her curses.

The procedures he had always before considered rational and routine and right were suddenly exacerbating. The questions to be answered, the forms to be signed. . . . He sickened over them.

"She's Dr. Richards' patient?" the Chief Resident asked.

Joe nodded. "But he's out of town. He'll be in first thing tomorrow. I left word for him."

"But somebody must be covering. And it would be——"

"There's nothing else I can do, you know. And a stranger now . . . well, Doctor . . ."

It was patently out of the ordinary, and very probably not acceptable, since she certainly ought to have gone through emergency and Dr. Harner first. But here she was. Knowing that he might end up on the carpet for it the next day, but reminded of the facts of life and status by Joe's very cool tone, and by the faintly overstressed "Doctor," the Chief Resident nodded, and sighed, and signed Gilly in.

Now, with a last despairing look, Joe told the nurse at his side, If there's any change at all . . ."

"We'll call you."

He heard the familiar words, the light, reassuring, empty words he had used so many times before. The sickness was in his throat, and he hurried away.

The lobby was quiet, a usual Sunday night. He crossed the black and white tile, and pushed open the glass doors.

As they swung heavily shut behind him, he remembered that he had promised to call Ellen. He didn't know any longer how much time had passed. He decided he wanted to sit down with her, to talk to her face to face, not over impersonal wires. He must be with her. And it would only take him a little while to get home.

The car was parked crookedly, angled across several slots. It hardly seemed to matter, except that another one had pulled in beside it. It had pulled in too close, angled, too, so that moving would be difficult. He was in no mood to waste time. It was important to get back to Ellen quickly.

Swearing softly, he looked and then looked again.

He recognized Gilly's convertible.

He made the identification at the same time that he saw the boy clinging to the car, a blanket clutched in his arms.

Joe strode toward him.

The demand for an explanation died on Joe's lips as he made the second identification.

Claire's friend.

The sleeveless yellow pullover . . . the blond head . . . the too-tight pants and cracked moccasins . . .

Claire's friend.

With Gilly's car?

Confused, he peered into the boy's face.

And then he knew that this was the boy Ellen had told him about, the boy with Gilly in Taos. This was the boy whose name Gilly had never mentioned.

David spoke first, a hoarse painful whisper. "Gilly?" He saw Gilly's wide open eyes, her long mobile mouth twisted with malice. He saw her slim shoulders leaning toward him.

"What did you do to her?" Joe demanded. "What did you give her, damn you!"

"*To* her *To* her?" David flung the blanket away, balled his fists.

Gilly's face was gone. He was looking at her father. "To her? It's what you did. You!"

"Tell me what happened," Joe said.

"Where is she? I have to see her. I have to find her."

"Inside. She's sick. After what you've done, she's so very sick that I don't know if she'll ever be well."

"You," David said again.

Joe said again, calmly but insistently, "Tell me what happened."

"What happened?" David stared into the shadowed face before him. "I don't know. What do you mean?"

"The way she came home."

"LSD," David whispered. "Don't you know? Didn't she say?"

"No."

"On halves of pear. One for her, one for me."

"And you let her!"

"I didn't know," David moaned.

Joe turned on his heel, swung away.

David stumbled after him. "Wait. Where is she? How can I find her?"

"You'll never see her again," Joe said, and slid into the car.

David hung on the door, weeping. "No, listen, please. What have you done to Gilly? I need her. I have to find her."

Joe thrust the door wide open. It flung David away.

He tripped, and fell. Rising again, he felt burning air streak his cheeks, saw pale parabolas of sound become flaming arrows across his vision.

A single face floated in the hot black mist.

The small stone Gilly, distorted and damaged, but he could fix her. There was still time. He could fix her. He could save her.

He leaped on Joe.

The chisel was in his hand, his delicate fingers knowing what they must do, and doing it, while he panted, "But I can fix her. Yes. Yes. She'll be just as good as new."

The chisel struck, smoothed, angled.

Joe screamed once, and was still.

David murmured, and blew gently on his handiwork, let his hands do the work they had been made to do.

And then the hot black mist cleared.

The stone under his hands was wet and dark around the gleam of bone, the gaping mouth, the glaring eyes.

He dropped the chisel and fled.

They were just about through for that Sunday night.

Mike was ready, and more than ready. The long hours of dismal routine had left him limp and weary and disgusted. Another shift off, and then another, wouldn't have made any difference. He had known that he might as well go in, begin again the life that was no life without Lori.

"I've got a date with Claire," Miguelito said. "To-morrow." he paused. "It might work out, but it might take some time."

"You can always write 'Dear Abby' about it. Or you can keep trying."

"I come from a very formal people," Miguelito grinned. "It was a matter of a brother's permission. Now that I judge myself to have it . . ." he shrugged.

Mike gave him a quick, startled look, felt heat in the scar on his neck, then considered. At last, he asked, "Listen, did you really think I mightn't like the idea of you and Claire?"

"It occurred to me."

"Little Mike," Mike said. "Little Mike. Jesus, what's wrong with you?"

"Nada, I theenk," Miguelito retorted, giving it the hard rising inflection to make absolutely certain that Mike followed him.

"Maybe I'll have to withdraw the permission," Mike told him. "I don't want my sister tied up with a man that's got rocks in his head."

"Better in his head than in his heart, Mike."

Mike turned, looked at him. "What does that mean?"

"Consider what a small town this is. I saw her with Joe Stevens exactly twice. And twice was enough. How many times did you see Claire and Joe Stevens together, Mike? How many times? And what did you see?"

It was sweet and stubborn truth. He had no answer for it except that, in Lori's name and memory, he must try to give the automaton he had become a more knowing heart.

The radio reported a stolen car, a baby-blue convertible. It gave a license number. It suggested a special alert for all units near Gorman Memorial Hospital.

At the intersection just ahead, a baby-blue convertible rocketed by.

Miguelito muttered, "It's not really ours, but he better get stopped before he kills somebody," and he rammed his foot on the gas.

The convertible flew through a black snow storm.

Guiding it, David's hands were numb, frozen.

He heard the wail of the siren behind him as a great burst of red rockets, heard the drum of his burning tires as pink and awful pain.

The culvert leaped at him suddenly from the further side of a curve. He saw its retaining wall as a great white hand rising up to slap at him.

The car slammed into it at a hundred miles an hour and straddled it, the undercarriage ripping away. It sped half a dozen yards before its nose flipped down and its rear end rose.

David was thrown out and over, sailing through the dark air like a four-legged bird that did not quite know how to fly. He landed on his back, slid a long way along the macadam leaving a wet trail behind him.

Mike crouched beside him.

THE DEATH WATCH

David opened his eyes wide, raised blood-covered hands. "He destroyed them. Both of them."

An ambulance whined nearby.

The red dome of a scout car blinked on and off.

"Gilly," David said, and was still.

Mike got to his feet. Gilly? Gilly Stevens?

Miguelito motioned to him. "We've got to go, Mike. There's some trouble out at Gorman."

EPILOGUE

"It was an exceptional turnout," Al Kelly said. "That's what it was, Daisy. An exceptional turnout for an exceptional man. That was him: Doctor Joe Stevens. Like the minister told us, it'll be a long long time before we see the likes of him again. A man well-loved, Daisy. That's what the minister said." Al Kelly sighed and peered into his nearly empty coffee cup. It was almost time for him to start his rounds. But he was already tired, and his gimpy leg ached, and somehow he didn't look forward to stepping outside into the dark.

"Want another cup?" Daisy Trunnel asked. "Think you can stand it?"

He nodded, accepted the refill gratefully. It was a pretty quiet Tuesday night, and he would get started soon.

"And if it gives you the heartburn," Daisy told him, "then come back. Because I've got something for that, too."

It was something, he had told her, that he just had to do. Out of respect. Because, after all, he had known Joe Stevens a long time. So Al had been there that morning at eleven.

He had watched the mourners gather, eyes darting

busily to gather the details, planning how he would tell
Daisy about it. As an old cop, he was aware of the value
of specifics, and proud of himself for still being able to
retain them.

Now he went on, "Everybody was there; the Mayor
himself, the whole of the City Council. Why, they
even got poor old Buss Gorman pumped full of stuff
and up on his feet so he could go."

"I wouldn't have thought they could do that," Daisy
observed. "Not the way he was."

"Well, they couldn't with her. With the girl. The
doctor's girl, Gilly. No, she's upstairs, poor thing. Likely
to be there for a long long time." Al's meager shoulders
moved uncomfortably in his uniform. "Who'd have
thought, when he walked her in here Sunday . . ."

"You never can tell," Daisy said.

"And just like that . . . out of the blue . . . some
crazy wild kid from nowhere. It was God's providence
and punishment that boy died the way he did."

"And so it goes," Daisy told Al, smoothing her pale
green uniform over her round hips.

He looked at her, those high round hips, and those
dimples, and for a moment he forgot Joe Stevens'
funeral and God's providence and punishment, and his
gimpy leg, too. She put him in mind of the very fine
nights a man might have.

But he caught a knowing gleam in the sideways
glance of her funny off-color gray eyes, and he reminded himself that Daisy Trunnel was a good girl, and
he was a long while away from those days when he
licked his lips over poontang.

"I'm an old man," he told her.

"You? Old?" she scoffed.

"Sixty-three," he said. "Widowed twice, five grandchildren. Retired from the police force eight years ago . . ."

"Is that a fact? Why, nobody would ever believe it. Sixty-three, you say?"

Dr. Harner appeared for a moment at the emergency doors, then yawned and went away.

Al drained his coffee, crushed the paper cup, and dropped it into the trash bin.

He had a lot more to tell her about Joe Stevens' funeral. The widow, leaning on Sam Upson's arm, surrounded by Gormans and Davises; all the society people of the city, come like him to pay their last respects to a man well loved. The great tons of flowers, flown in from God knows where. The mile-long cavalcade of black limousines. It was something to have seen, Joe Stevens' funeral.

But it was time for him to start on his rounds, and Daisy was already reaching for her book.

He sighed and told her, "Yep. Sixty-three. And I never, no, I never did see anything like what I saw last Sunday night."

If you have enjoyed this book and would like to receive details of other Piatkus publications please write to

Judy Piatkus (Publishers) Limited
5 Windmill Street
London W1P 1HS